Praise for the authors of
Once Upon a Regency Christmas

LOUISE ALLEN

"Allen deftly pulls fans into the glittering, dangerous world of England's elite."
—*RT Book Reviews* on *His Christmas Countess*

"Allen has written another spellbinding and adventurous Regency romance."
—*RT Book Reviews* on *Beguiled by Her Betrayer*

SOPHIA JAMES

"Readers will be thrilled with this triumphant tale."
—*RT Book Reviews* on *Marriage Made in Hope*

"Delightful and seductive."
—*RT Book Reviews* on *Marriage Made in Shame*

ANNIE BURROWS

"Burrows is a master at Regency romance."
—*RT Book Reviews* on *In Bed with the Duke*

"The poignancy and humor will make any reader a Burrows fan."
—*RT Book Reviews* on *The Captain's Christmas Bride*

Louise Allen loves immersing herself in history. She finds landscapes and places evoke the past powerfully. Venice, Burgundy and the Greek islands are favorite destinations. Louise lives on the Norfolk coast and spends her spare time gardening, researching family history or traveling in search of inspiration. Visit her at louiseallenregency.co.uk, @louiseregency and janeaustenslondon.com.

Sophia James lives in Chelsea Bay, on Auckland, New Zealand's North Shore, with her husband, who is an artist. She has a degree in English and history from Auckland University and believes her love of writing was formed by reading Georgette Heyer during holidays at her grandmother's house. Sophia enjoys getting feedback at sophiajames.co.

Annie Burrows has been writing Regency romances for Harlequin since 2007. Her books have charmed readers worldwide, having been translated into nineteen different languages, and some have gone on to win the coveted Reviewers' Choice Award from CataRomance. For more information, or to contact the author, please visit annie-burrows.co.uk, or you can find her on Facebook at Facebook.com/annieburrowsuk.

Louise Allen
Sophia James
Annie Burrows

—

Once Upon a Regency Christmas

HARLEQUIN® HISTORICAL

ISBN-13: 978-0-373-29903-4

Once Upon a Regency Christmas

Copyright © 2016 by Harlequin Books S.A.

The publisher acknowledges the copyright holders
of the individual works as follows:

On a Winter's Eve
Copyright © 2016 by Melanie Hilton

Marriage Made at Christmas
Copyright © 2016 by Sophia James

Cinderella's Perfect Christmas
Copyright © 2016 by Annie Burrows

Recycling programs
for this product may
not exist in your area.

Printed in U.S.A.

www.Harlequin.com

CONTENTS

On a Winter's Eve

Louise Allen

Dear Reader,

The idea for this story began with a Regency cartoon showing a frantic Norfolk turkey escaping from its Christmas doom in Leadenhall Market. I wondered what became of it and found the answer when my hero rescued the ungrateful bird from a snowdrift. From there the story just grew, set in a snowy Norfolk landscape not far from where I live.

We don't often get heavy snow, let alone a white Christmas, in this part of the world, so the idea of my lovers snowed in together was a Christmas fantasy for me, as well as for them.

I hope Giles and Julia's story gives you a warm glow this winter, wherever you are.

A happy Christmas,

Louise Allen

Chapter One

When had she last seen snow? It must have been at least nine years ago, before she had left England. Remembered in the heat of a Bengal summer, it had been pretty and fluffy. Not like this, heavy with a subtle, beautiful threat. The great billowing drifts, like ocean waves, were poised to swallow the coach whole. *Oh, this was such a bad idea.*

There was a convulsive movement beside her, a blurred reflection in the breath-misted glass, but when Julia turned her stepdaughter was smiling, even as she shivered.

'Miri, darling, I am sorry it is so cold. I didn't think, I just wanted to be away from that dreadful woman.'

'Aunt is strange, isn't she? I suppose she was angry that Father didn't leave her anything in his will.' Miri shrugged, slender shoulders struggling to lift the layers of rugs. 'And I didn't expect her to like me, but she did offer us a home while you arranged your affairs in England.'

Of course Grace—*parental optimism in the naming of her had been severely misplaced*—Watson did not like her niece. Miriam was illegitimate, half-Indian and beautiful. What was there not to hate for a bigoted woman with a plain daughter of her own to launch?

'Did you not realise? My sainted sister-in-law was sell-ing introductions to me, the indecently rich nabob's widow who must, of course, be in need of a man to relieve her of her wealth.'

'No! You mean those parties and receptions were to set you out like goods on a stall? No wonder you are so angry.'

'Too angry to explain properly to you. I am sorry, you must have thought I had lost my mind, dragging you out of there at five o'clock yesterday morning.' Julia did not often lose her temper, it was not a profitable thing to do, but when she did she was well aware that it was like wildfire over the grass plains of the Deccan, sweeping everything before it.

Miri had meekly held her tongue and left Julia to a fuming silence broken only by curt orders to servants, coachmen and innkeepers. 'I must have been a perfectly horrid companion yesterday, I should have explained. I overheard your aunt agreeing terms with Sir James Walcott on what he would pay her if I were to wed him.' She took a steadying breath. 'I lay awake all night brooding and the thought of seeing her sour face over breakfast was too much.'

'I rather liked Sir James.'

'So did I,' Julia agreed grimly.

'You *are* very rich.' Miri sounded as though her teeth were clenched to stop them chattering. There was only so much that fur rugs and pewter hot water bottles could do against the Norfolk weather on a late December day.

'Oh, indecently so.' Julia's own teeth were gritted, but not because of the cold. 'And it is a well-known fact of life that indecently rich widows are fair game for any impoverished gentleman who fancies lining his pockets. After all, marrying money is not the same as lowering oneself to engage in trade and actually *earn* it.'

There was silence as the coach lurched through another drift. It gave Julia ample time to rue allowing her temper to land them here.

'So what will you do now?'

'See what this house your father left me is like. I have no hopes of it, but, if it at least has a roof, then we shall stay there for Christmas and by the New Year I will have a plan.' She *always* had a plan and usually they were rather more successful than her bright idea of leaving India and returning to England with her stepdaughter and a fortune, expecting to find it easy to make a new life.

She had wanted to give Miri everything a restricted upbringing had denied her stepdaughter, find her a husband to love her. Now she suspected that Miri would have been much happier in India with a dowry, making her own choices. Had she dragged her along because of her own desire for companionship? She had been so lonely throughout her marriage that if it had not been for Miri's warm affection when her father brought home his young bride she would have gone mad, she thought.

Nothing is easy. Nothing. In England money seems to be a curse for an independent woman. Or perhaps expecting to be independent is the curse in itself.

'It will be very pleasant to have a real English country Christmas.' There was that at least to look forward to. 'Plum pudding, mulled wine, decorating the house with evergreens, sitting around roaring log fires. We will give the staff Christmas Day off and listen to them singing carols. You'll love it, Miri. I remember it all so well from my childhood. Christmas is wonderful for children.' She trod firmly on that image and imagined instead a fatherly old butler, a rosy-cheeked cook, cheerful, willing maids and footmen… 'But whatever else we do, remember that we are two ladies of modest means.'

'Very well.' Miri gave a determined nod. 'We will dress simply and warmly and leave our jewels in their cases.

After all, I am not looking for a husband and you do not want one who desires you only for your money.'

That ruled out all the gentlemen of England. Who would want a sallow-faced widow of twenty-five with no connections for any reason other than her money? It was a good thing that seven years of marriage had removed any romantic delusions she might ever have nurtured about the institution. As for Miri, if and when she found a man she wanted, Julia would do everything in her power to make her dreams come true. If this mythical lover deserved such a pearl. And if that meant losing her, seeing her go back to India, then of course she must go. She could not be selfish and hold on to her.

But meanwhile they were shivering in a wasteland. 'How much longer is this going to take?' Julia jerked on the check string and dropped the window glass, letting in a blast of dry, frigid air and a dusting of snowflakes. 'Thomas?'

'My lady?' The coachman leaned round and down to face her, his face red with cold.

'How much further?'

'A mile or so, I reckon. The snow makes it difficult to judge distance at this pace.'

'We will stop at the next inn. Miss Chalcott is becoming very cold.'

'There's nothing ahead of us now but Chalcott Manor, my lady. It's a dead end.'

'It most certainly is.' She sighed as he straightened up on to his seat, then leaned back down before she could raise the glass again.

'My lady, there's someone on the road in front of us. A man on foot.'

'In this weather? We had best take him up.'

The man turned as they approached, seeming larger and more monstrous the closer they got. Squinting against the snow, Julia could see that the thick white crust covering his head and shoulders added to his bulk, but he was also holding some large black object to his chest.

'You there!' Thomas hailed him. 'Are you in difficulties?'

'Difficulties? Not at all.' The response was sarcastic, the voice deep and confident. Julia felt her lips twitch. 'I am unhorsed and lost and have no feeling in my extremities, but otherwise I am enjoying a country stroll.'

'My lady bids me say that you had best get into the carriage, sir.'

She opened the door, then gasped as the man turned to face her. 'What on earth is that?'

'A turkey, ma'am.' He hitched his burden up further in his arms and a hideous red and blue head on a wrinkled, naked neck poked out from the front of his greatcoat and produced a raucous gobbling cry.

'It is alive!'

'Yes, ma'am. I had noticed. Might I enter? The snow is blowing over your rugs and my boots may freeze to the road if I stand still much longer.'

'If we wrap it in this, you can lift it in.' Miri, ever practical, held out a rug.

The man looked up from under his snow-laden hat and his jaw dropped, just a fraction.

Most males were rendered dumb for minutes at a time by their first sight of her stepdaughter. It was wearily predictable, but she supposed she could not blame them. 'Get on with it, please, before we are buried in snow.'

The turkey succumbed to the rug after a few seconds of frantic flapping and gobbling, the man heaved it on to the seat and climbed in, slamming the door behind him.

'Drive on, Thomas.' Julia yanked up the glass and flapped the snow off her skirts. 'There is no village ahead, sir.'

'I was coming to that conclusion. My horse went lame some way back. There was a byre with a herd of cows and fodder, so I left it there, hid the saddle in the rafters and walked in the hope of better shelter.'

'There is nothing along this road but my house, Chalcott Manor. You are welcome to shelter there until the weather lifts. I am Lady Julia Chalcott. My stepdaughter, Miss Chalcott.'

'Thank you, Lady Julia. Miss Chalcott.' He managed to look at Miri without actually panting, which raised him a notch in Julia's estimation. 'I am Giles Markham, late Captain in the Twelfth Light Dragoons. Is Lord Chalcott at home? He must be anxious with you travelling in this weather.'

'Sir Humphrey Chalcott is deceased, Captain Markham.' She saw the question he was too polite to ask. 'He was a baronet. I am the daughter of an earl and chose to retain my title.' It was the only thing she had managed to keep from her early life. 'Why do you have a live turkey, Captain?'

'I found it in a snowdrift. It's a very fine Norfolk Bronze, with a label on its leg reading *"Bulstrode, Leadenhall Market"*. I assume it escaped from captivity on top of a stage-coach bound for the City of London. Christmas is, after all, only six days away.' He took off hat and gloves and pushed his hand through his hair, which was brown, straight and in dire need of a crop.

Without his hat he should have looked smaller. He did not. Nor any less male and sure of himself. That would be the army, she supposed. A serving officer was unlikely to be a shrinking violet. Although one of those would certainly take up less room. Her skin felt…strange. Julia wanted to shiver even though, quite suddenly, she was not chilled. Odd. Perhaps she was sickening for a cold, which would just about put the crown on this disaster of a journey.

What were we talking about? Oh, yes. 'And the entire point of turkeys at Christmas, Captain, is to be dead. Dead, plucked and roasted. Not shedding feathers all over the interior of my coach.'

'I have some sympathy with his daring escape, Lady Julia. I have dodged the French often enough to have fellow feeling.' Judging by the thin scar on his left cheek he had not always dodged successfully. Captain Markham's voice was deep, amused and as smooth as warm honey.

Oh, pull yourself together, Julia. It is a man. A large, handsome, masculine creature who is cluttering up your carriage. They are two a penny and all equally mercenary.

'This is a fine coach, if I may say so.' Even in the gloom the interior with its mahogany, plush upholstery, brass fittings and heaped fur rugs murmured of luxury and the wealth to support it.

It was almost big enough for him, Julia thought, covertly watching his efforts to keep his long legs under control and his sodden boots away from their skirts and rugs. Men did fill the space up so. This one was a gentleman, the educated voice attested to that. But he was a rangy specimen with a straight nose, a stubborn chin and an excess of stubble. After the smooth, groomed males inhabiting the drawing rooms of Mayfair he was something of a shock to the system. That was all this flustered feeling was, reaction to such a virile creature at close quarters.

'We were lent it,' Miri said demurely, lying without a flicker of her long lashes. 'It is very different from the carriages we are used to in India.' At least she was keeping up with the conversation and not allowing a pair of long legs to turn her brain into mush. This was what came of indulging immodest and improbable fantasies: they climbed into your carriage at the least convenient moment.

'India?'

'We arrived in England three weeks ago, Captain.' That was better, cool and polite.

'And are returning to your family for Christmas.'

'No. We have no family in England, except for the most distant cousins.' To describe her sister-in-law as *family* stretched Julia's willingness to mangle the English language. 'And you, Captain? Are you on your way home?'

'Home.' He said the word as though it tasted of something entirely new and he was not certain that he liked the flavour. 'I suppose I am. It is a very long time since I set foot in England.'

'You have been in the Peninsula, sir?'

'For several years. I have just sold out.'

Why? The war is still going on and he doesn't appear to be suffering from some disabling wound. The coach turned sharply to the left and Julia caught a glimpse of gateposts. 'We have finally arrived, it seems.'

'You are not familiar with the house?'

'No. It is the only thing my husband left to me. As I met him in India I have never seen it.' From what Mr Filbert, her solicitor, could tell her, the possession of Chalcott Manor was not going to give anyone the impression that she was rolling in money.

They stopped and all looked out at the redbrick house that loomed through the snow. As a piece of architecture it appeared to be without merit, except for the possession of a roof with no visible holes in it and a number of chimney stacks, both features that were at the top of Julia's desiderata for a house, just at the moment. A light showed in one of the semi-basement windows, so at least some of the promised staff were present, but there was no rush to open the door. Perhaps the snow had muffled the sound of the carriage.

Paul, the groom, opened the door and let down the step. 'The snow's deep, my lady.'

'Let me.' Captain Markham jumped down beside him. 'We'll trample a path through. Put an arm around my shoulders.' The two of them moved forward, stamping in unison.

'What a good thing we found the Captain,' Miri observed, watching their progress.

'Thomas and Paul would have managed between them.' At least the man did not have expensive clothing to ruin. She had noticed the worn boots and the roughly mended cuff of his greatcoat. If he had sold his commission then he ought to have bought himself some respectable civilian clothes with the proceeds and not be traipsing around the countryside in that state.

He came back to them, leaving Paul pounding on the front door. 'It's as cold as Satan's ar—as cold as the devil, ma'am. I would wait there until someone answers.'

'I am not shivering in a coach on my own doorstep, Captain.' *Or being managed by a man.* She climbed down, ignored his outstretched hand and started up the trampled path. Behind her she heard him offering his arm to Miri, who murmured her gratitude. Then her right foot shot up, her left foot skidded to the side and she was falling backwards.

'Oh—' The very naughty word in Urdu clashed with a small scream from Miri, then an arm lashed round her waist and she was lifted off her feet and into Captain Markham's arms. Really, the man's reflexes were astonishing. So was the strength of his arm—Julia knew she was no lightweight, not with all five feet six inches of her bundled in layers of winter clothing. 'Thank you, Captain, you may put me down now.'

'Best not.' He adjusted his grip, raising her higher against his chest and getting one arm under the crook of her knees.

'Captain!'

'No call for alarm, I have you safe.'

That was an entirely new definition of safe. Certainly her heart rate had kicked up in alarm. 'I am not a turkey to be lugged about.'

'No,' he agreed, striding up to the door. 'You are much easier to get a grip on and you aren't shedding feathers.'

The door creaked open before she could think of a retort. The light etched a thin ribbon of gold on to the snow.

'Yes?' The voice wavered eerily.

She shivered and the arms holding her tightened in response. *Oh, for heaven's sake, this is not some Gothic novel!* 'I am Lady Julia Chalcott. This is my house. My solicitor wrote to say that I was coming to stay. Now kindly open this door properly and show us to the drawing room.'

'Maa…' It was a bleat. Which, as it issued from the mouth of a man who looked more like a sheep than anyone decently should, was appropriate. 'Ma'am? We never heard from no solicitor.'

She felt decidedly at a disadvantage and gave a wriggle. An amused *huff* of breath warmed her temple. 'You address me as *my lady*, and who are you?'

The man retreated into the depths of the dark hall as the Captain strode forward. 'Light some candles immediately, please.'

'Yes, maa… Sir. My lady. Smithers, my lady. The drawing room is there, but the fire isn't lit.'

Nor were the covers off the furniture or the curtains drawn. Captain Markham set her on her feet and waited while she released her grip on his sleeve before he removed the candle from Smithers's unsteady hand and walked round setting the flame to every candle in sight, then dropped to one knee and thrust a hand into the kindling laid in the hearth. 'Dry, although I'd not take a wager that the chimney will not smoke.'

'Er…'

That was an improvement on bleating, but there went her daydream about a cosy house and equally cosy staff. Efficient, cheerful, staff. 'Tell Cook that we need tea, Smithers. And sandwiches and cake. Then send the footmen to bring in the luggage. I require bedchambers for myself and Miss Chalcott, a maid to attend on us, a chamber for Captain Markham and accommodation for my coachman and groom. Hot water. We will dine at seven.'

'But there's only me and Mrs Smithers, my lady. And the Girl.' He somehow managed to give the word a capital letter. 'And I don't rightly know as how we've got any cake, nor anything much for dinner, my lady. Just the rabbit pie and the barley broth.' Smithers's face was a mixture of bafflement and deep apprehension.

The butterflies that had been flapping around ever since Captain Markham picked her up turned into a lead weight and sank in her very empty stomach. 'Oh. The beds are aired, are they not?' It was foolish optimism, she knew as soon as she spoke.

'Er…'

No, that was not, after all, an improvement on bleating. 'I had best speak to Mrs Smithers.' She waited until he shuffled out of the door and turned to the others. 'Captain, please will you light the fire? We must risk the smoke.'

'Me lady?' Julia turned, praying not to be confronted by another sheep, and was rewarded by the sight of Mrs Smithers, a birdlike woman in a vast apron, a ladle clutched in one hand. Over her shoulder could be glimpsed a freckle-faced child of about twelve. The Girl, presumably.

At least the ladle promised food of some kind. 'Mrs Smithers. Good afternoon. As I explained to your husband, we require beds—*aired* beds—made up in three chambers. Fires lit. Hot water. Dinner for seven o'clock and accommodation for the coachman and groom.'

The other woman stared, her mouth working, then she plumped herself down in the nearest chair, threw her apron over her head and burst into tears.

Julia took a deep breath and turned to Captain Markham, the shredded remains of her Christmas fantasy fluttering around her like so many falling leaves. 'Are you skilled at bed-making, Captain?' she enquired sweetly.

Chapter Two

'**B**ed-making?' Giles drawled. 'I have more experience *un*making them, I fear.'

He hadn't thought the remark that *risqué*, but Miss Chalcott smothered a giggle with her hand and a wash of colour came up over Lady Julia's cheekbones. She was tired and upset and he admired the fact that she hadn't followed the example of the cook and given way to tears.

'I will see that your coachman and groom have what they need, then I will return and light fires, fold dust sheets, chase spiders…whatever you require, ma'am.'

She regarded him, lips tight as she controlled her emotions, a tall woman with skin still glowing unfashionably from years in the sun. Her nose was straight, her eyes were blue and her hair, what he could see of it, was blonde. It was difficult under the brim of that bonnet and with the poor light in the room, but he assumed she was in her early thirties. Certainly her air of command and authority was striking.

'Thank you, Captain.' Her voice was still sweet, just as lemonade, imperfectly sugared, was sweet. Then she turned to the servants with a string of clear instructions that had Mrs Smithers mopping her eyes and hurrying from the room and Smithers tugging at the dustsheets as though his life depended on it.

Perhaps it did, Giles mused as he let himself out and walked round the house to find the stables. Perhaps she would produce some exotic Indian weapon and behead the lot of them if they disobeyed her orders.

He was becoming whimsical with weariness, but it had been a long day and his life was so upside down these past weeks that it was no wonder he found himself oddly stirred by this woman. Most likely it was the memory of the weight of her rounded body in his arms, the womanly scent of her.

The coachman and groom were manhandling the carriage into a barn and he lent his weight to the shafts until it was fully under cover. 'Have you all you need?'

'Aye, we'll do, thank you, sir.' The coachman straightened himself, recognising authority when he heard it. 'There's stabling aplenty with bedding and fodder, although it's a mite dusty and past its best. Shall we take that turkey to the kitchens?'

'No.' Giles looked into the stable block. Four brown rumps were all that could be seen of the carriage horses. 'There's an empty loose box, he can go in that. This is one turkey that is going to live though Christmas.' Ignoring their carefully bland expressions, Giles lugged the heaving bundle out of the carriage and into the stall. He scattered some straw, filled a bowl with water and dumped a few handfuls of grain in a corner. 'There you are, catch a few spiders while you are at it.'

The bird shook its wattles and emitted a furious gobbling, then proceeded to strut up and down, feathers puffed up.

'Stop carrying on and eat your dinner. There are no stag turkeys for you to scare off and no hens to impress.' There was a muffled snort behind him, but when Giles turned the two men were industriously hanging up harness. 'Have you found anywhere to sleep?'

'There's a room overhead here with beds and a stove with kindling. We'll be snug enough, sir.'

'Go over to the kitchen when you're ready to eat. There'll be something. This is not what Lady Julia is used to, I imagine.'

'Wouldn't know about that, sir. We've only been in her employ a few days.'

Nothing to be gleaned there. Giles retrieved his saddlebag and went into the house through the kitchen door to find Mrs Smithers scurrying between larder, table and range.

'What are the supplies of food like?' he asked, stopping the harassed cook by the simple expedient of standing in front of her. The first thing you learned in the army—after the discovery that it was no use ducking in the face of artillery—was to secure the provisions. 'The roads are deep in snow and more is falling. There'll be no marketing done this side of Christmas unless we get a sudden thaw, and there's eight mouths to feed for however long it takes.'

'Hadn't thought of that, sir.' The cook sat down in the nearest chair and managed to compose herself. 'I'd best take stock. There's the mutton stew for tonight. We can eke that out with potatoes—we've sacks of them in store. Root vegetables in the garden clamp. Then there's two full wheels of cheese. Dried apples and lots of flour. The butter will last a few days, then there's lard. I've eggs in isinglass and the cow in the byre will stay in milk awhile longer. And game outside for the shooting. It'll be plain fare, sir, but we won't starve for a month. Her ladyship won't like it, though. We never got no letter from the lawyer.' She sniffed, on the verge of tears again.

'Her ladyship can lump it,' Giles said, making her gasp

with laughter. 'Do your best, Mrs Smithers, I'll see what's going on upstairs.'

He followed the sound of voices, or rather the series of thumps and flaps and one very clear voice issuing from a bedchamber. The hapless Smithers struggled to turn over a mattress while the Girl gathered up dustsheets and Lady Julia and her stepdaughter sorted linens.

'Captain.' She turned as he entered, still brisk, but he could hear the weariness under it and perhaps the relief that there was someone else to help cope. 'The fire, if you please.'

He set a taper to it, then she had him tucking in sheets on one side of the bed before he could make his escape. 'Tighter, Captain. Get some tension in it.'

She was certainly making him tense, most inappropriately. Giles wrestled the coverlet straight, then gathered up pillows in a strategic attempt to disguise just how tense.

He was handed a pile of pillowcases. 'When you've done those we will be next door.'

'Yes, ma'am.' It was tempting to tease her with a salute. Instead he admired the way her hips swayed as she strode out of the door. Giles stuffed pillows and told himself this was not some bivouac in the Spanish mountains and Lady Julia was not a camp follower.

The next chamber was smaller. He lit the fire, then went to help Miss Chalcott drag a heavy curtain across a window, but even with that in place the draught still stirred the bedraggled bed-hangings. The fire smoked foully. Giles kicked it out with a muttered oath. 'I'll take this chamber, I'm used to the cold. I'll see if there's another room with a clear chimney, otherwise you ladies will be better together in the first chamber.'

The army had certainly been good training for this house. He'd been in more comfortable tents in the snow before now, he mused as he followed Miss Chalcott into the next room along. The chimney there obliged by drawing steadily. It was a small room, but that made it easier to heat, he pointed out as he helped her make the bed.

'Thank you, Captain.' Her smile was enchanting, he thought, discovering that he was admiring her as he might an exquisite artwork, not a living woman.

On the other hand there was certainly one of those next door, judging by the sounds penetrating the wall. 'Smithers, is there another mattress? Captain Markham cannot sleep on that—the mice have been in it.'

'Lady Julia is obviously used to dealing with servants,' he remarked as Miss Chalcott draped blankets over a chair in front of the fire.

She laughed. 'She has had a great deal of practice.'

'You had many servants?' he asked, puzzled. A borrowed carriage, plain, sensible gowns, this frightful house her only legacy from her husband… Something did not add up.

'Seventy, perhaps. Look at this fabric! Moths, I suppose, though by the size of the holes I would not like to meet one.'

'Seventy?'

'Oh, everyone in India has servants if they have any kind of a household at all. Inside servants, outside servants, the grooms, the gardeners, the sewing women and the laundry, my father's business… It all adds up and it costs a fraction of what it does in England.'

'Your father was a man of business, then?'

'My husband was a merchant, a trader in many things.' He had not heard Lady Julia's approach. 'But, despite the common misapprehension here, not every man who trades in India is a nabob, wealthy beyond compare. Or even wealthy at all.'

'I beg your pardon, ma'am. I allowed the informality of

our circumstances to lead me into curiosity.' He really had been in the army, and in the wilds, too long if he had forgotten not to discuss money or trade. As an earl's daughter Lady Julia's marriage might have been deemed acceptable if sweetened by vast wealth, but a mere merchant would put her firmly on the wrong side of the social dividing line. Why had her family allowed it?

'No matter. India makes everyone curious, I find.' Lady Julia came further into the room and he saw how weary she was, for all the firm voice and straight back. Then she smiled and he realised something else. He had been quite out in placing her in her thirties. Surely she could not be more than twenty-five or six, at the most. And Miss Chalcott was, what? Twenty, twenty-one? Which meant her husband, unless he had been sowing his wild oats in India at a precocious age, must have been in his late forties at the very least when he married her.

An earl's daughter marrying a not very successful India merchant twice her age. How had that come about? He felt the curiosity stir like the flick of a cat's tail at the back of his mind and bit down on the question he had nearly allowed to escape.

She ran one hand over the draped blankets and wrinkled her nose. 'This house had been in my husband's family for years. I had no idea it had been so neglected.'

Considering that she had travelled thousands of miles to discover her expected security was a ramshackle house miles from anywhere, Lady Julia was showing remarkable resilience. Perhaps she was planning to go back to her family.

'Mrs Smithers should have water heating, although I doubt it will run to a bath. I will have some sent up to your chamber, Captain. Until seven o'clock and dinner.'

'I'll see to the water myself.' Giles almost told her to

go and rest, then decided that telling any female that she looked weary was not tactful. 'Until dinner time, ladies.'

Captain Markham had shaved, donned a clean, if rumpled, shirt and neckcloth, and made some improvement to the state of his breeches and boots. He also looked as though he had managed to snatch some sleep, which was more than Julia had, she thought resentfully as she regarded him across a dinner table much in need of polishing.

She had lain on the bed in her dusty, draughty chamber and willed herself to sleep, but oblivion would not come. What had kept her awake was the sickening realisation that she had allowed a sentimental memory of childhood Christmases to blind her to reality. She had set out on this journey in a temper, clinging to the belief that at the end of it would be a charming country house, complete with its charming staff. It would all be modest but comfortable, warm and safe.

Instead she and Miri were stranded in a cold, neglected house, miles from anywhere, with three nervous servants. Plus a turkey they couldn't even eat. Plus one down-at-heel army captain who looked at her in a way she could not decipher, but which made her both irritated and...*aroused*, damn him. She had rescued him from a snowstorm. He should be as exhausted as she was and yet he just looked tough and competent and ready to lead a cavalry charge if necessary. Just as soon as he had finished reducing her to idiocy with one glance.

He didn't look at Miri that way. He treated *her* with perfect respect, as though she were no more than the average unmarried girl and, after the first shock, appeared utterly unmoved by her beauty.

'More potatoes, Lady Julia?' Not that he didn't treat her with respect also. His manner was perfectly correct, so correct that she kept telling herself that she was imagining the warmth in his regard, the occasional double meaning in what he said. It must be her imagination. She had felt an immediate attraction to him in the carriage so perhaps now she was reading an answering interest where there was none at all. How lowering.

'Thank you.' The food was adequate. Plain but hot, dull but filling. Miri ate with a delicacy that concealed any distaste for what was unfamiliar for both of them.

'After shipboard fare for months this has to be an improvement.' She reached for the pepper. 'But if we stay I must order some spices. I cannot endure such bland seasoning much longer.'

'You are in two minds about remaining?' Captain Markham twirled the stem of his wine glass slowly between fingers and thumb. The cellar had revealed a number of dusty bottles of dubious vintage and they were cautiously sampling one.

'This house is a disappointment,' Julia admitted. More than the house, if she was honest. After six years of brutal realism and clear thinking she had allowed freedom to go to her head. She had let herself dream and had followed that dream. She looked at Miri and acknowledged that she had been selfish as well. All for the very best of motives. 'I will sell it.'

'You will achieve a better price if you wait until the spring,' Markham suggested. 'Once it has been cleaned and had a lick of paint and the sun shines on it, it might be transformed.'

'And a maharaja on a white elephant might come down the driveway and offer me chests of gold for it,' she retorted and was rewarded with a laugh from Miri.

They ate the apple pie, the desire for cream politely unspoken. 'There was no port in the cellar, I gather,' Julia said as she and Miri stood up. 'We will leave you to your wine. If you will excuse us, we will retire now.'

'Of course.' The Captain got to his feet. 'Goodnight, ladies. And my thanks for rescuing me from the snow.'

Julia saw Miri to her door, then turned, restless, and walked back to the head of the stairs, back to her own door. Dithered. What was the matter with her? She never dithered. Perhaps fresh air would steady her. If nothing else it might drive her to her bed and then, surely, she would sleep.

She jammed her feet into her half-boots and swung her cloak around her shoulders. The front door opened with its sepulchral groan and then she was picking her way cautiously towards the stables, the only destination for a stroll in the freezing darkness.

It had stopped snowing and she could see the glow from candles in the room above the stables and the drift of smoke from the stove chimney. Below, the light of one lantern shone out across the trodden snow and she followed it to the door and went in.

The air was warmer here and smelt of dusty hay and horse. Four heads appeared over the half-doors of the boxes, but Julia did not approach them. She missed her mare, Moonstone, and these handsome beasts were no substitute for a brave little horse who was afraid of nothing, not even elephants. Another mistake, to have sold her, but Julia had thought she was being strong and decisive.

An irritable sound drew her to the door without a horse behind it. Scratching about in the straw was the turkey, his pompous dignity returned now he was free of the rug. He thrust out his chest and spread his tail at the sight of her.

'Ridiculous creature. You've no doubts, have you? You make an idiotic dash into a snowstorm and certain death, but of course you are rescued and looked after and now you will escape your proper fate.'

Whereas she had made an idiotic escape and ended up here. And if she wasn't careful and didn't make the right decisions she would find herself trapped, or lured, or simply cornered into marriage—the proper fate for a rich widow. 'Oh, what have I done?' She bent to rest her forehead on her arms, crossed on the top of the loose-box door.

'Well, what *have* you done?' a voice behind her asked. *Captain Markham.*

'Let my heart rule my head,' she said wearily without moving. 'I left India full of nostalgia for England, dragging Miri behind me. I hate it here.'

'What will you do?' He was so close she felt her skirts brush against the backs of her legs. For a moment she thought he would touch her, but he stayed still. It must be she who was shivering with reaction. Not with cold. Not with his heat at her back.

'Go back to India. I know where I am there.' *Who I am.*

'Do you love it so much?' Giles Markham asked softly, the deep voice intimate, as though he asked her about her feelings for a man.

Julia straightened, but she kept her gaze on the turkey cock. Was it her imagination or could she feel Markham's breath, warm on her neck?

'Most of the time I fought it as though it was a person, an enemy. But sometimes it was an exotic fairy tale. It can take your breath with beauty and magic so deep and rich it cannot be true. The people. The colours. Oh, and the mornings…just at sunrise, when it was cool and clear and the whole impossible place was coming to life and I would ride my mare and the world was mine.'

'That sounds like love to me. An attraction that goes soul-deep, but which you fought against even as it seduced you.'

'You are a romantic, Captain.'

She shivered and he moved closer, put his hands on the stable door either side of her, caging her against his heat, the muscled wall of his body. There were responses she should make to that. A sharp elbow in his ribs, the heel of her boot on his toes, a jerk backwards with her head into his face. She knew all the moves, had used them before now.

Julia turned within the tight space and stared at the top button of his waistcoat. Hitting this man was not what she wanted. 'A romantic,' she murmured.

He made no move to touch her, to crowd closer. 'Only a man who has ridden at dawn over wide plains before the battle started, who has seen the mist rise and heard the birds begin to sing and who has tried to hold the moment, hoping against hope that the sun will not burn away the mist and the guns will not begin to fire and that the earth will not be reddened with blood.'

'That seems strange for a soldier to say.'

'Soldiers are not immune to beauty. Only a few of us want to fight and kill for the sake of it. But when the mist vanishes and the guns begin, then we forget those moments of peace and plunge into hell.'

'Who do you fight for, Captain?'

Chapter Three

She had surprised him. 'It is my duty,' Giles said after a moment.

'Is that always what soldiers fight for? King and country? Or did you become a soldier to impress your lady-love?' She had meant to tease and he smiled when he shook his head. 'So you have been fancy-free while you break hearts across the Continent.'

Darkness swept through his gaze, his jaw hardened. Julia glanced away, shocked and guilty. In her own awkwardness she had stumbled into something private, something that hurt.

After a moment she felt the big body caging hers relax and she dared to look up and meet his eyes. Grey eyes with gold tracing out from the pupil like tiny flames in the lantern light. The moment was a fragile bubble—one wrong move and it would be gone again like that morning mist. She reached up her hands and pulled down his head, lifted her lips to his and the iridescent shimmer of the bubble enclosed them both.

There was a momentary pause, the faintest hitch in his breath, then the Captain's lips moved over hers, firm, slightly cold. His tongue touched the seam of her lips, shockingly hot against her own chilled mouth as she opened to him.

Could he tell that she had hardly ever been kissed? Julia made herself hold back, forced down her need to simply drown in his embrace, drag him to the heaped straw, discover, finally, what it was like to know a virile man in his prime.

Over-eagerness would betray her inexperience. She let him lead, followed the strokes of his tongue with her own daring movements, allowing him to angle her head for his taking. Giles Markham knew what he was doing, she thought hazily, striving to focus, to learn and not to lose herself in this assault on her senses. On the few occasions Humphrey had actually kissed her she had been frightened by his forcefulness, repelled by the taste of him—cheroots, heavily spiced meat, strong spirits.

The taste of this man was enticing, which was puzzling as it seemed to be made up of faint traces of tooth powder, wine and…masculinity, she supposed. There was the heat of his mouth and the cold of his skin, the scent of plain soap and the dusty hay of the stables, the comforting smell of horses. And there was his body under her hands. Muscled shoulders, short hairs on his nape, the strength of his arms as he held her.

When he released her she swayed back against the stable door, dizzy and enchanted, her hands still on his shoulders. *So this is what it is like. After all these years. At last.*

'Julia?'

Just her name. She found she liked it on his lips.

'Giles.' She liked that, too. A good, straightforward name. She let her fingertips stray to the bare skin of his neck above his collar and even in the dim light saw his gaze darken. *You want me. Tell me you want me.*

'You are upset, cold, tired,' Giles said as he stepped back

a pace, leaving her cold and alone, her hands still raised. 'This is not a good time to begin—'

'Begin what?' *Cold, tired and upset* was sweeping back to smother *dizzy and enchanted*.

'A dalliance, I was going to say.'

So that was what she desired. Julia realised that she did not have the words for this. Giles probably knew all about *dalliances* and he was tactfully making it clear that he did not want one. And he was not exactly tearing himself from her arms with deep reluctance. How humiliating.

Julia found the cool smile, the mask she wore when bargaining, whether it was with Rajput gem dealers or desert camel breeders. 'Goodness, how serious you are. Dalliances indeed! I had merely the impulse to kiss when I found us almost nose to nose.' She laughed, aiming for sophisticated amusement, fearing pathetic bravery. *Share the jest. Please.*

He smiled crookedly, almost as though he did not find any humour, but his eyes were warm, the gold flames intense. 'Of course. Forgive me. If you give me a moment to check on the livestock, I will walk you back to the house. It is treacherous underfoot.'

'Certainly.' How cool she sounded. Not at all like a woman who was quivering with desire, lapped by heat, almost speechless with embarrassment at her own recklessness. When Giles came back from checking water buckets and feed she was ready to slip her hand under his proffered arm, curl her fingers around his sleeve.

He was rock-steady as they negotiated the yard, lit by starlight reflecting off the snow. 'My goodness, I am chilly.' An exaggerated shudder would hide her shaking, surely?

Once inside she went directly to the stairs—walking, not breaking into a run, not fleeing to her room to bury her head under a pillow. 'Would you check the doors and windows are secure and the fire safely banked? I do not yet know how much reliance to place on Smithers.'

'Of course. Goodnight, Lady Julia.'

'Goodnight, Captain. Sleep well.' He would make sure all was safe, she was certain of that. Giles Markham made her feel protected, sheltered. Rejected.

Sleep well. Lady Julia, *Julia,* had a sense of humour hidden under that baffling exterior because she surely couldn't have been serious with that blessing. Giles hauled the blankets up over his ears and wondered why the arousal was not keeping him warm. Or why the cold was not killing the arousal, come to that. This was the worst of both. He was stone cold and hard as a hot icicle.

You shouldn't have kissed her, common sense pointed out. *She kissed me first,* came the answer from considerably south of his brain. *Yes, but you were going to kiss her, weren't you? Telling yourself she needed comforting, pretending that all you wanted was to offer a shoulder to cry on. Haven't you learned your lesson? You start out in a fit of gallantry, or of lust, then you get yourself tangled deep in whatever webs they are spinning and you end up as damaged as you would after a bayonet in the chest.*

He was a soldier—that was what he was, what he did. What he had been, he reminded himself, giving the pillow a thump. No more.

Yes, but... That was what was keeping him awake, almost more than his frozen feet and the throb of desire. *She kissed me and she had no idea what she was doing.*

Not that it had been any less delightful for that. Julia had tasted delicious, her lips under his had been sweet and generous, her body curving into his had promised an abundance of the femininity that her practical manner struggled to deny. Yet she was a widow and, from what had been said, had been married and in India for several years. So what was the truth? A marriage in name—or was the husband a complete fiction? In which case, was she even Lady Julia Chalcott and the daughter of an earl?

A blast of wind hit the window panes, sending a draught swirling around the room. Giles swore and got out of bed, still fully dressed save for his neckcloth and boots. He had slept like a log in far worse conditions than this, but not if there was an alternative. He bundled up the bedding and let himself out of the room, then went down to the drawing room, where at least there was a fire.

He made himself a nest in front of the hearth on top of the sofa cushions and set to work on the sullen coals. By the time he had a cheerful blaze going he felt warmer and his brain was beginning to focus. He climbed the stairs again, dug in his bag for the thick red book he had bought to study, that had cost too much to throw away as he'd ploughed through the snow.

Giles settled back into his makeshift bed before he began to investigate the *Peerage and Baronetage*.

Sir Humphrey Chalcott, second baronet, born London 12th May 1752.

He would be sixty now, if he had lived.

Only son...
Married 1804, in Calcutta to Julia Clarissa Anne, daughter of Frederick Falmore, Fourth Earl of Gresham.

No first wife, so Miss Chalcott must be the daughter of a mistress.

Giles looked for the Falmores. Julia had been born in

1787, the only child of the Fourth Earl, who had died in early 1803, five years after his wife. The title passed to the son of his youngest uncle. Giles did the calculation. She had married a man thirty-five years her senior when she had been barely seventeen years old.

Who would put a grieving, orphaned girl of sixteen on a ship to India? The 'fishing fleet' was for the desperate and the poor, the plain or the otherwise ineligible women seeking a husband eager to take any British wife of gentility as they struggled to make their way in India.

If Julia really was who she said she was, then perhaps her husband had been unable through illness or infirmity to consummate the marriage to his young bride. He had obviously once been virile, Miss Chalcott was proof of that.

Giles threw another log on the fire, blew out the candle and settled down to sleep, his curiosity now thoroughly aroused. Which was, he concluded as he finally began to drift off, rather more comfortable than what he had been suffering from earlier.

There were doubtless more embarrassing social situations than meeting over the breakfast cups the man you had inexpertly kissed the night before and who had then firmly but kindly rebuffed you. Just at the moment Julia couldn't think of any and she was applying her mind to it when Giles opened the dining room door.

Having all one's clothing drop off in the middle of a dinner party? Walking in on the Governor General in his Calcutta mansion while he was pleasuring his mistress on the billiards table?

'Good morning.'

She dropped the sugar bowl, sending lumps of sugar scattering across the table.

'Julia!' Miri was laughing at her. 'Whatever are you thinking about? Good morning, Captain Markham.'

'Billiards,' she managed.

'And what is there about billiards to make you blush?' Miri was intent on teasing.

'If you must know, I was thinking about the Marquess of Hastings. His billiard table. Government House.' She cast a harassed glance at Giles, who had seated himself at the end of the table. 'Good morning, Captain. There is bacon, eggs, bread and butter. You could ring for cheese. There are also some preserves. Damson, I think. Tea? There is no coffee or chocolate.'

And if I keep on talking long enough the floor may simply open up and swallow me.

'Thank you.' Giles accepted the tea cup. 'What is there about the Marquess of Hastings and billiards to bring the colour to your cheeks? Is he such a bad player?'

'No, I am.' The floor remained disappointingly intact and Giles's—*Captain Markham's*—faint smile remained provoking. 'It has stopped snowing. Perhaps the roads will be open soon.' *And you can leave. Please. Before I make more of a fool of myself than I have already.*

'I'll go out and see, although I doubt it. The temperature is as low as ever, so nothing will have thawed.' He buttered a slice of bread and addressed himself to his food while Julia sought for innocuous topics of conversation.

'I'll come with you,' Miri announced. 'Mrs Smithers has some stout boots that she said she would lend me.'

'Have you ever seen snow before?' Giles asked.

'No, not before yesterday. It is very beautiful, but rather frightening.'

'There is no danger if we stay near the house, which I suspect is all we will be able to do. It is best not to take liberties with snow, although I've moved troops in worse in an emergency. But it is a sneaky killer and it is best not to provoke it.'

He sounded utterly matter-of-fact and professional about what must have been a nightmare. Julia cast a covert glance at the firm jaw and the broad shoulders and found she could easily picture Giles leading men through any kind of danger and doing it well. He was still talking to Miri when she pulled herself out of her imagination.

'We can build a snowman if you like. Won't you join us, Lady Julia?'

'Thank you, no. Please do not let Miss Chalcott get cold. She is not used to low temperatures, let alone these conditions.'

Those unusual grey eyes were quizzical. 'Neither of you are, which is why it would be unwise to wander about outside alone at any time.'

'That all depends what one encounters, doesn't it?'

Giles's eyes narrowed and, to her confusion, he smiled, not at all embarrassed. Miri, apparently blissfully unaware of any cross-currents, beamed at her. 'Please come, too, Julia. It will be fun. There are sure to be more boots.'

Of course it will be fun. Miri would love the novelty of the snow and she was a miserable friend to grudge joining in, just because she had made a fool of herself last night. 'Very well. Let us have fun.'

The sun was shining when they emerged, swaddled in layers of coats and scarves. Giles followed the partly-filled wheel ruts to the gates. 'Not as bad as I feared,' he reported back.

'Thank heavens for that.' Julia stamped her feet in their layers of woollen stockings inside the clumsy boots. 'Is the road clear?'

'The hedges have stopped the snow drifting off the fields

for as far as I can see, although it may be bad further on. It is still too thick for the carriage and too soon to try on horseback. We may get out by Christmas if this weather holds. Now, snowmen.'

He showed Miri how roll a snowball across the lawn so that it grew. 'We need a big one for the body and a smaller one for the head.'

'Let me.' She pounced on the ball and began to push it, laughing with delight, her breath making white puffs in the air.

Giles left her to stand beside Julia. 'Shall we walk along the edge of the shrubbery, see if there are any evergreens for your Christmas garlands?'

'Is it worthwhile, decorating this place?' A nice safe topic.

'Walk, before your toes freeze.' He possessed himself of her hand and tucked it under his elbow before she could object, studying her from his superior height. She was not used to having to tip her head back to meet a man's eyes. 'You are determined to be miserable, aren't you?' he enquired.

'No!' She glared up at him, indignant. 'I am determined to get out of here, that is all. Poor Miri, dragged all this way from home. I was mad to even contemplate it.'

'Poor Miri?' He tipped his head towards the lawn where her stepdaughter was already working on a second snowman's body, every line of her bundled-up body radiating enjoyment.

'Snow is a novelty. So is being cold, being snubbed, feeling homesick. I wanted to do the right thing for her, I told myself. Now I wonder if I wasn't being selfish in demanding her company.'

'What was it like for you, arriving in India, being hot,

being homesick? Not snubbed, I imagine. Not an earl's daughter.'

He was curious, but she was not surprised. She would have found it strange if he was not. 'No, not snubbed.' The temptation to pour it all out into a sympathetic ear was almost overwhelming. Instead she said what she had been avoiding all morning. 'I must apologise for last night.'

'Whatever for?'

'If you had pounced on me in the stables, forced a kiss on me, *you* would be apologising.' She risked a sideways glance when he remained silent.

'You are very refreshing, Julia.' When she frowned up at him the corner of his mouth kicked up, emphasising the scar on his cheek. 'If I had done that then, yes, an apology would be in order unless it was obvious that a kiss was welcome. But I could have stepped away at any point, which might give you a clue that I enjoyed it. I assure you, I would have fled screaming if I had been unwilling—the door was right behind me.'

'How very gallant you are, Captain. You kiss the poor, needy widow, you refrain from taking advantage of her and then you protest that you enjoyed the experience.' She must stop talking *now* before she made any more of a pathetic spectacle of herself.

'If you are suffering from a lack of male attention, Julia, then I can only assume that the passengers on the ship and every man in London between the ages of sixteen and sixty had something seriously wrong with them.' There it was again, that narrow-eyed, very masculine assessment that had her pulse pounding.

Oh, yes, the men on the ship had looked. They had seen either a rich widow ripe for the plucking or her beautiful stepdaughter to be seduced. Or, in one or two cases, both. What none of them saw was a woman yearning for experience, for passion and for a virile man in his prime to deliver them.

Well, she had a virile, attractive man by her side at this moment. One who appeared to be discreet and considerate. She could be a coward or she could risk a monumental snub and tell him what she wanted. Julia took a steadying breath, but Giles was before her.

'Tell me how you came to be in India, married so young to a man who must have been much older than yourself.'

Why not? None of it was a secret and she had already abandoned any pretext of pride with this man. 'I was poor and unlucky in my relatives,' Julia began. 'My father died five years after my mother, when I was sixteen. He had married below him, his family said, and it was good that he had no son by such an unsuitable woman, a merchant's daughter. The title went to his cousin, who was horrified to discover the state of the family coffers. Papa was not the most provident of men and there was no money, not enough to maintain the estate as it should be.'

'One can understand the heir's feelings,' Giles observed.

'Cousin Richard said I was a further drain on his pocket and that he had no intention of funding a Season for me the following year. An acquaintance was going out to India, so I could make myself useful by accompanying her as a companion and then I was sure to pick up a husband for myself. The problem was solved.'

She glanced up at his face when he said something sharp under his breath. He looked appalled. 'You were sixteen, bereaved.'

'I was also exceedingly pretty and his daughters are rather plain. I can say it now because my looks did not survive long. I was blonde and curvaceous and I had a beautiful roses-and-cream English complexion. Enchanting, though I say it myself. I arrived in Calcutta just as the cholera did. It killed thousands, amongst them many of the eligible young men who had come down to meet the Fishing Fleet. I caught it, too. They shaved my head because of the fever and when I recovered I was as thin as a rake, the roses had fled and my hair grew back straight and much darker. My travelling companion was dead, my looks gone, my pockets empty. I was desperate.

'And so Sir Humphrey Chalcott won himself the daughter of an earl.'

Chapter Four

Giles tried to imagine what it would have been like for a girl scarcely out of the schoolroom to find herself in an alien land, weak, abandoned. Where had she found the strength to carry on?

Julia's voice was quite steady as she told her tale, almost as though she spoke of someone else entirely. 'Sir Humphrey thought he was acquiring status and influence. What he did not realise until too late was that the new earl had no intention of giving him anything, let alone the allowance he was hoping for.'

'He was much older than you were.'

Julia nodded. 'I suppose I hoped for a substitute father. I soon learned that he couldn't even be a decent parent to his own daughter, let alone comprehend the fears and needs of a young bride.'

They came to a gap in the planting. Julia waved at Miri, who now had a line of five snow bodies in descending order of size. 'I think Miri is building a snow family. She was the one bright spark at first. Her mother died when she was fifteen so she was shut away in the women's quarters. She is four years younger than me, the sister I never had.'

'And your husband was not a successful man?'

'He was self-indulgent, indolent and had made himself ill by surrendering to all the temptations of the east. The food, the drugs, the women. He did not have to lift a finger to live a comfortable life, so he did not. He never saw it was his fault that he did not achieve the wealth of other merchants, who did apply themselves.'

They reached the corner of the shrubbery and Giles ducked under a snow-laden branch and into the shelter of the plantings. With the evergreens arching overhead the winding path was almost clear of snow.

'It was not as bad as it might sound.' His silence had left a space that she seemed compelled to fill. Giles wondered whether she had bottled all this up for so long that she was confiding things that she never had to anyone else. 'You can live much better in India on little money than you can over here. I rapidly learned to be a housekeeper.'

'It must have been hard, even so. A strange and alien land, marriage to a man like that.' He felt caught up in her story. Here, for the first time in a long time, was a woman who told the truth without artifice, just as she had asked for his kiss with total simplicity.

'I learned to fill my time.' Julia made a business of adjusting her shawl. 'So that is my story. Now you must tell me yours, Captain Markham.'

'Is it not to be Giles, this morning?' He snapped off a sprig of holly, laden with berries, and tucked it in her bonnet.

'No. You know why not. I made an error of judgement last night.' She put up her free hand, touched the holly as though to pluck it out again, then left it where it was.

'The timing, perhaps, with us both tired, was not ideal.' She had kissed like a virgin and he had reacted instinctively to distance himself, he realised. Giles tried a little cautious fishing. 'You miss some aspects of marriage, no doubt.'

That provoked a sudden burst of laughter. He had never heard her laugh before and he grinned back, enjoying the way those blue eyes sparkled, the curve of that lush mouth. All the severity in her face vanished, just for a second. Then the laughter was gone.

'By the time he married me my husband's amorous days were long past. His health would not allow him to make a great deal of effort, especially as I think he found the whole exercise humiliating. I had none of the training of the Indian courtesans he was used to. They can pretend passion, feign an amorous attraction that it was completely beyond me to attempt.' She shrugged. 'These past four years I might as well have been a widow.'

'There were no children?' He regretted asking the moment he saw the way her face tightened and her shoulders braced.

'No.' Julia released his arm, reached out to pluck an ivy tendril and began to fashion it into a circle. 'I cannot think how I can speak so frankly to a man about this.'

'I am a stranger. You'll never see me again.' *And we are met by chance on this snow-covered island of ours, bound together for a few days.* He felt his body stir and harden as the temptation began to form into intention. *If she is willing...*

Giles picked more ivy and held the strands out one by one for her to add to her wreath, enjoying the concentration on her face as she wove the whippy lengths, struggling with the thickness of her gloves. Her brows were drawn together, her teeth were closed on the fullness of her lower lip and she looked sensual, intelligent and flustered, a heady combination. 'I imagine you found no shortage of gentlemen willing to offer you diversion.'

He surprised a short, bitter laugh from her. 'I had married the man and, whatever his faults, he gave me shelter when I was desperate. Besides, I made myself too busy to be tempted. There was a business to run.'

'You managed your husband's affairs?' That he could well imagine.

'Hardly. Humphrey would never have allowed a woman to make decisions. But I acted as his representative, travelled on his behalf, carried out his instructions. That gave me freedom, the chance to see more of India.'

Her face was vivid with remembered pleasure, the colour up in her cheeks. He had no idea how she could denigrate her appearance, mourn her lost beauty. Didn't the woman have a looking glass? 'You could travel safely?'

'I had two huge wrestlers as bodyguards. No one would have dared rob or attack me when they were there, I assure you!'

Julia held up the wreath, head on one side as she studied it. 'Not bad. It will make a base for some holly and fir cones and I will hang it on the door to greet our numerous callers.' She looped it over her wrist, then took his arm again. 'Now you tell me your story, Captain Giles Markham.'

What to tell her? The truth, he supposed. To a point. 'Only son of a country clergyman, destined for the church and determined on the army. I don't know where that came from, but I rode almost as soon as I could walk. I learned to shoot, enjoyed swordplay. Led my friends into trouble and, I suppose more helpfully, out of it. I knew I hadn't the faith to be a clergyman, but the army seemed to offer excitement with honour.

'My godfather bought me my first commission, saying I might as well have his legacy to me while he was alive and I needed it. Then last year I received a field commission to captain. Two months ago it became clear I needed to come home for family reasons.' Home to an inheritance of debts. He had more than a little in common with her cousin.

'You must have done something outstanding to merit a field commission, I know that. A Forlorn Hope? Is that what they call those appallingly dangerous attacks where everyone is a volunteer and if it succeeds against all the odds the survivors are almost guaranteed promotion?'

Giles shrugged. He was never comfortable talking about fighting. The battle was against fear and against bad luck and it sounded like cant to prate about courage and honour. Those were private things. 'I wasn't going to get promotion any other way, there was no more money to buy one and I had no intention of spending my career as the oldest lieutenant in the British army.'

That day he had felt that nothing else mattered beyond winning promotion because nothing else in his life was true. The softer things—a woman, love, a family—they were not for him because he could not trust his own heart, his own judgement. From then on, if he survived, the army would be his life. For life.

He had fought until he arrived filthy, tattered and bloody, on top of the breach, the standard in one hand, his sabre in the other, his feet on rubble and dead bodies and a French officer surrendering to him. Afterwards they had praised his courage, his leadership, his gallantry. He told himself that was all that mattered.

He had been silent too long, lost in his thoughts. 'An appalling experience, I imagine,' Julia murmured.

His face must have been betraying him as much as his still tongue. 'After a few days I realised I had lost whatever naïve ideas I still had about war. I'd been down into hell and survived. It made me a better officer.'

'And yet when we first met you said you were *late* of the dragoons. After going through hell to gain your promotion, you left it.'

The unasked questions struck at his pride. Did she think

he had lost his nerve, couldn't face fighting any more? He had led a forlorn hope to secure his career as an officer and within months another kind of duty had made all that meaningless.

'My family needs me,' he said. 'Things have changed. People depend on me.' He did not understand that duty yet. It had never been intended that he should. But now it was on his shoulders and he would have to learn to carry it.

'That is good to hear.' The hand tucked under his arm tightened for a moment. 'A man who will make a sacrifice for his family, put his own ambition aside for them. You must love them very much.'

I don't know them, he wanted to say. *They are strangers who will resent me.* He could tell her what he had inherited, tell her anything, he sensed. But then he would not be Captain Giles Markham any longer, he would be the stranger he must become, and he wanted to hold on to the man he was now, just for a few more days. *That isn't too much to ask, is it?*

They had reached the glade at the centre of the shrubbery. Giles turned and positioned Julia in front of him, toe to toe. He could forget the army, forget what lay ahead, in a brief *affaire* with this woman, if that was what she wanted, too.

'What do you think you are doing?' she demanded, the sharp question enchantingly at odds with the uncertainty in her eyes.

'Remember I told you I could have fled screaming when you kissed me?'

'Yes.' She looked at him warily, but she did not move. *Yes, she wants me at this moment just as much as I want her.*

'If you look behind you will see the path out of the clearing. A perfect escape route if this provokes the urge to scream.' He took off his hat, then, hands at his sides, he leant in, brushed his lips over hers, closed his eyes.

Julia gasped. The pressure of warm lips on hers increased, but his hands stayed still. Her decision then. Flee screaming as the provoking man suggested, or...not. She jerked at her bonnet ribbons, tipped the thing off her head and into the snow, flung her arms around his neck and returned the pressure. Giles took one staggering step backwards, then his arms were around her.

'Steady,' he murmured. 'There's all the time in the world.'

Oh, yes. Julia made herself relax, eased the stranglehold, as all her senses flooded back to her. She knew how to assess the quality of silks and cottons by touch, the variety of wood by its weight and strength. Under her hands his hair was silk, a rough, wild variety turning into velvet where it was cropped closer at the nape. His neck was teak, so were his shoulders, his chest. She did not dare think about his thighs, pressed against hers.

She had learned to grade perfumes, spices and essential oils by their scent, by the subtleties of taste. Her tongue stroked over his and discovered tea and that spicy, tantalising man-taste again. He smelt of man, too. Clean linen, slightly musky skin warming under her hands, an overtone of leather, a hint of pepper.

Giles held her, his hands unmoving, only his mouth caressing her, creating an infinite variety of subtle touches and provocations. She had thought a kiss would be an exchange of heat and desire, straightforward, blatant even. But this... She sighed into his mouth and he caught her lower lip between his teeth, gently worrying it as he sucked at the fullness.

She sighed again and he groaned, deep in his chest and finally, wonderfully, his hands moved, slid down. Cupped her behind through the layers of clothes and lifted her against him. Warmth and steady strength and something very like trust. And excitement. She needed to tear his clothes off. She wanted him to tear hers off.

'The weather is an excellent chaperon.' Giles released her. 'There is no danger of things getting out of control when every flat surface is under snow.'

He was making light of this, treating that kiss as though it had been a fleeting moment of flirtation. Nothing to be embarrassed about, simply something that two adults might exchange when they found a mutual attraction. Julia found she could smile. 'We would sink without trace.'

'Or start a thaw.' There was more heat in his regard than she had expected. Perhaps she was being naïve to imagine that this was mere flirtation. Did he want the dalliance he had spoken of last night? Did she?

'Julia! Do come and help!'

'Miri is calling. I expect she needs instructions on snowmen.'

Giles picked up her bonnet, shook the snow off and handed it to her. 'Soggy ribbons, I'm afraid.'

She left them dangling as she took his arm and they retraced their steps through the shrubbery and on to the lawn. Miri had the parts for her family of five snow people and Giles helped her lift the heads into place.

What had happened just then was what she had wanted, surely? The experience of an attractive man's kiss. She should treat it as a test, to establish whether her secret yearning for a lover was a foolish daydream or something that she truly desired. Because a lover would be so much better than a husband. You could dismiss a lover when you tired of him or he proved not to be the man you had hoped. A lover would not control her money, have no claim on her beyond what she granted him in her bed. A lover would give her pleasure, but would not take her power.

'We are just going to get some things,' Miri called. 'We won't be long.'

But have I power? How does a woman wield it in this cold country? In India she bought and sold, bargained, traded. Humphrey had believed that all she was doing was carrying out his orders, and, as far as his business was concerned, that was just what she did. No more, no less.

But she had learned how to run a business, had created her own and it had flourished. She had absorbed everything a seventeen-year-old youth might be sent to India to learn in order to return home to England a nabob, rich enough to buy a county. Once she had saved enough money from her housekeeping allowance it had been easy to trade on her own account, to invest in gemstones and gold for herself until she had believed that having such wealth was all she needed to be free, to control her own life. But in London it seemed that she must be a man to play by their rules, to wield the power that money gave.

Perhaps, she mused, as she gathered twigs to make the snow family's arms, a woman could make her own rules. *But I never learned to be a woman.* Julia looked down at what she was holding and found her cold lips were curving into a smile. *But I can play again, just for a while.*

Giles and Miri returned, his arms full of straw and battered old hats, her hands heaped with small lumps of coal and a bunch of wizened carrots. They laughed and joked as they began to dress the snow figures, Miri measuring carrots against Giles's nose to get the length right for the male figure, him teasing her by sticking handfuls of straw for hair under the female's hat just when she had adjusted it to her satisfaction.

How long had it been since she had been able to play with as little inhibition, with almost childlike joy? Julia began to break off lengths of fir needles, just long enough to make bristly eyebrows for the snowman, then used more pieces to create ludicrous eyelashes for the snowwoman, stepped back to admire the effect and found she was laughing, too.

Giles came to her side. 'We have done a fine job with our snow family. Just one more adjustment.' He took hold of the twiggy arms, tipped some up, some down and there they stood, Mama and Papa Snow holding hands and, on either side, their arms sloped down to take the little twigs the snow children held up. 'There. A happy family.'

A robin flew down, perched for a moment on the snowman's old beaver hat, then flew off, its breast a flash of fire in the air. Julia scrubbed at her eyes with the back of her gloved hand. That had been the last time she had played and laughed uninhibitedly, as a child. That Christmas when she had been eleven. The December before Mama died. Papa had never been the same after that.

I want children. I want to share this with them. Simple pleasures, joy that money cannot buy, pleasure without calculation.

But society was hateful to children who were different and she could not deliberately set out to give a child an extra burden to carry. Life could be hard enough. Which meant she needed a husband. It was almost a relief to have her mind made up for her, to have a fixed purpose for returning to England and not just the desire to get away, to be in control of her own destiny at last—even when she'd had no idea what she wanted that destiny to be. But this husband, the father of her children, must be a man with money, who would not care whether she had ten pounds or ten thousand, because otherwise how would she know why he wanted her? For her wealth or herself? But now, if this, whatever *this* was, happened with Giles—who was clearly not a wealthy man—then she would embrace it for the happiness it might bring them, just for a day or two.

Chapter Five

That had been a pleasant evening. Giles stretched out his legs in front of the cold hearth in his bedchamber, waiting for Julia and Miri to settle in their own rooms before he moved down to the warmth of the drawing room again.

He could hear their voices because the fireplaces were back to back and shared a flue. What they were saying was unintelligible, otherwise he would have moved, but the murmur of feminine voices, the occasional soft laugh, was pleasant after years spent in male company where any women were more inclined to be raucous than sweetly spoken. Even when the regiment was back in camp and there was time for short-lived relationships, the Iberian women had been vivid, vibrant and not much given to whispers.

Claire, of course, being the colonel's daughter, had been different. Sweet, refined, enchanting to her father's officers when they withdrew back behind the lines. He had fallen for her, inevitably, it seemed. And she had returned his interest, flirted and then, as his feelings deepened, so had hers. So she had said. A pity that all his not inconsiderable experience with women had been with those who were not ladies, who had not learned the polite art of deceit.

Miri laughed and Giles came back from the dark vortex

of his thought. She had been bubbling over with good spirits that even vegetable stew with dumplings, followed by another dried apple pie, had done nothing to repress. The snow was beautiful, she declared. Building snowmen was wonderful and tomorrow they must plan Christmas decorations for the house. She was charming, unspoiled, beautiful, sophisticated in many ways and in others, almost a girl. A product of her upbringing, he supposed.

But she did not attract him, not as a man. Perhaps because of her youth, perhaps because he could not forget the taste of the woman who sat on the other side of the fireplace all evening, quiet, almost abstracted.

Had that second kiss been a mistake? Was he wrong in thinking she would welcome a fleeting *affaire*? He was attracted, intrigued and confused by Julia Chalcott, which was an arousing and uncomfortable combination when one thing was uppermost in his mind: he needed a rich wife and he needed one soon.

To be exact, what he required was a rich, well-bred, fertile, exceedingly practical wife because what had brought him home, forced the sale of that hard-won commission, had been the news that he was now Earl of Welbourn.

When the news reached him that his cousin Henry had died of blood poisoning he hadn't thought anything of it, beyond the regret for any man's death. It had been the culminating tragedy in a series of premature deaths that had brought him close to the title, but Henry had left a pregnant wife to mourn him, and, the family solicitor had delicately hinted, she was expected to be brought to bed of twins. No daughter had been born to the Markhams of Welbourn for almost one hundred years.

When the letter announcing the birth of twin girls had reached him he had been stunned, although not quite as shell-shocked as he was a moment after reading the second page. Mr Prettiman regretted to inform the new earl that the family finances were still in the dire state that they had been in when Henry had inherited. His lordship must hasten to Welbourn Hall without delay. Decisions on the sale of assets could not be postponed much longer.

So here he was, snowbound with two hundred guineas, a horse, his sword and a turkey to his name and a grieving widow with two infants to support from an estate that, somehow, with no experience whatsoever, he must drag out of the mire.

So, a rich wife to fund the recovery. An intelligent, fertile wife who could learn how to be a countess, while he, a clergyman's son, an army officer, learned to be an earl. A practical wife who would stand at his side while he tackled whatever needed to be done.

And the snow had given him a few days' respite between his old life and his new, a pause before the distasteful business of finding himself that rich wife, mingling with the *nouveau riche* who would be delighted to bail out a bankrupt earldom for the sake of a titled daughter and grandchildren.

'I do like him, although I don't think him *very* good looking.' Miri's voice brought Giles out of his chilly half-doze with a start before he realised that she must be right by the fire. 'What do you think?' There was a thump as a log was tossed into the grate.

Julia's answer was, mercifully, inaudible.

'He's not a rich man, is he? Such a—' Miri's voice faded as she moved away.

Hell's teeth. I've been sitting here weighing up Lady Julia's attractions and it seems what is sauce for the goose is sauce for the gander. Serves me right. Giles bent down and tugged off his boots, gathered up his bedding and let himself quietly out of the bedchamber before he heard any more home truths.

'Have you decided what to do with the house yet?' Giles leaned on the banister rail of the top-floor landing and Julia looked up from where she sat on the step beside him. They had spent the morning going from room to room, assessing the state of each and listing what work needed doing. As she was used to Indian houses and Giles maintained that his only architectural knowledge related to how to stop bivouacs leaking and how to estimate the strength of French fortifications, she did not have much confidence in their calculations. But at least calculations kept her from thinking about his kisses, even if it did not help when he stretched up to measure a window with the span of his arms and the muscles shifted deliciously in his back, or their fingers touched accidentally—she was almost certain it was accidental—when they both reached for the same object and her breath caught for a second.

'Sell it.' She was quite clear about that. 'But this hasn't been wasted time. I wanted to be certain that there is nothing here that draws me to the house.'

'What about the staff?' Giles asked. 'I thought they were intimidated by you, but they aren't, are they?'

'They know they are needed, that their work, done properly, is valued. They haven't had any clear direction for an age, since the last tenant left, and they have become purposeless and lacking in confidence.' She shrugged. 'Everyone needs purpose and reward. I can give them good references and I hope the buyer will keep them on.'

'I misjudged you at first.' Giles shifted his rangy body, getting his elbows comfortable on the rail. 'I thought you bossy.'

Julia set her hands behind her and leaned back to look up at him more comfortably. It was very easy to look at Giles, unless he met her gaze and put her to the blush. He wasn't handsome, but he was so *male*. She wanted his hands on her, not just his eyes. 'I *am* bossy,' she admitted with a laugh, hoping she was not turning pink, that he could not read her thoughts, which were concerned with anything but what the servants needed. 'No, actually I am decisive and sometimes impatient. Decision and clarity are considered admirable qualities for a man. In a woman they are bossiness.'

'I like it.'

'You do?' she enquired, dubious.

'I like women who know what they want and aren't afraid to say so. Not everyone finds that attractive but you will be a breath of fresh air when you return to London. No doubt you'll do the Season.'

'It may take more than one Season to become accepted.' She shrugged. 'I have no friends in London, no sponsor, so I must ease into society. If I decide to make the investment.'

She meant the emotional investment, but Giles took it, as she intended, to mean the financial cost and shifted the conversation again, away from the sensitive issue of money. 'You have the freedom to choose anywhere in the country to live.' He straightened up and went to look at a print hanging crookedly on the wall.

He was right. If only she knew what she really wanted. Other than Giles. Wanting him was becoming an ache.

'Julia.' He had moved back and was kneeling right behind her while she had been fantasising about him. Only this wasn't a fantasy. Could he read her mind? His arms came round her and she leaned back against his chest, eyes closed, lips parted for his kiss. She felt his breath on her lips. 'Julia, do you want this?'

'Yes.' His arms tightened and she felt a stab of panic. *Do I? Am I ready for an* affaire? Too late, his mouth was brushing over hers, his hands held her as he moved to sit with his back against the wall with Julia sideways on his thighs.

This time she was prepared for the taste and the feel of him, for the thrust of his tongue and nips of his teeth. The warmth of his palm cupping one breast was new and she leaned into the caress, gasped into his mouth as his thumb fretted slowly across her nipple.

'Julia! Giles! Where are you?'

Julia sat up with a jerk, banging her forehead against Giles's nose. 'I must—'

'In a moment.' He pulled her back and kissed her again, long and languorous, ignoring her wriggling. After a moment she realised she didn't know whether she was wriggling to be free or to be closer. He let her go and watched her from his position on the floor, all delicious long sprawled limbs and tight breeches and very evident arousal. 'You are all dusty, Lady Julia.'

'And you, Captain Markham, are a rogue!' She started down the stairs, shaking out her plain woollen skirts. 'Coming, Miri!' Three steps down she stopped, turned back and knelt to stretch out to catch his hand. 'A rogue.' Then she was running down the stairs, listening for the tread of booted feet behind her.

'There you are.' Miri was in the hallway. 'I was speaking to Paul, the groom, who is something of a weather-wise man,' she reported. 'He says this dry spell will hold and predicts a thaw in a few days.'

'If so, I will see if I can get to my horse tomorrow.' Giles came up behind Julia, his hand resting unseen at the small of her back. 'I'll take one of the carriage team, if one of them is willing to be backed. When the thaw comes I want to be ready to leave here before the rivers swell with melted snow and we start losing bridges or the fords flood.'

'By all means.' That was prudent. *I don't want to be prudent.* The hand at her back was trailing lines of ice and fire up and down her spine. 'Is it far to where you left it?' If the carriage horses could be ridden, then she was going, too. It was so long since she had been on a horse, too long since she had been outside beyond the bounds of walls and roads.

'I'd walked about four miles when you picked me up, I estimate. So six or seven. I'll set out after breakfast to make the most of the light.'

'You had better find out whether there is a rideable beast in the team. Could you check all four? It would be useful to know in case we need to ride them later on.' She wouldn't tell him she would go, too, not yet. He would be sure to object that it was too cold, too dangerous, too *something* and she was bursting with a restless energy that chasing spiders and organising servants was doing nothing to dissipate. In fact, it was getting worse and the remedy was Giles.

Hell, but he was frustrated, aching with the need for Julia. And she wanted him in return, he knew that. The cold of the stable yard was some help as he stamped through the snow to the barn. There was light in the window above the stable door and, when Giles entered, the sound of footsteps from above. He made for the ladder to the loft space, but stopped when a voice behind him said caressingly, 'Oh, you are a handsome fellow, aren't you?'

It was Miri. He couldn't see her, but as she was answered by a series of gobbling noises she was not hard to locate. Giles found her sitting on the hay with the turkey cock leaning heavily against her knee, eyes closed, while she scratched the feathers at the base of his bald neck. 'You're a very clever turkey,' she praised him. 'Fancy finding that nice Captain Markham to save you. Any other bird would have flown right into trouble.'

'He's such a weight I can't imagine him doing anything but flopping off the stagecoach.' Giles grinned at her when she looked up with her charming smile. 'What are you doing in there?'

'I came to see the horses and he was worrying at the label on his leg so I took it off. It must be his name, don't you think? Bulstrode sounds so fat and self-important.'

'Unfortunately I suspect the Family Bulstrode is lamenting the disappearance of its Christmas dinner.' He opened the half-door for her as she got to her feet with one last caress for the besotted turkey. 'I assume the men are upstairs?'

'You will be glad to be on your way.'

He was getting to know Miss Chalcott and the sweet smile and calm façade hid a more complex character than met the eye. One with bite. 'And you'll be glad to see the back of me, no doubt.'

She coloured a little at that, but she met his gaze frankly. 'Yes. I have enjoyed meeting you, Captain. I had fun with the snowmen and I'm grateful for your help with the house. But Julia deserves peace and time to recover herself, decide what it is she wants.'

'To complete her mourning?'

'To recover from everything that has happened to her since she was sixteen, Captain. Don't hurt her.'

'Well, that's frank.' His sense of humour was faltering in the face of the attack.

'It was meant to be.'

'I have no intention of hurting her.'

'Good. I hope you are not offended.' She smiled again

and left the stables, her cloak swinging around her heels, leaving him torn between amusement and irritation.

'Offended? Certainly not. Why should I be offended by having my amorous intentions questioned by a pretty chit?' he muttered, climbing the ladder.

'Captain?' Thomas, the coachman, looked round the door of the snug room he and the groom occupied. 'Thought I heard someone talking. Anything amiss?'

'Nothing at all. Can any of the coach horses take a rider? I must retrieve my own mount and you'll not want to send out the carriage and team.'

'They can all be ridden, no problem. Come into the warm, sir.' He closed the door behind Giles and put down the harness he had been mending. Beside the stove Paul, the groom, got to his feet and nodded respectfully. 'We train them so they can be ridden to the farrier. Not the smoothest ride you'll ever have, but any of them will do you for a few miles. I'll get some short reins on a bridle for you this evening. You'll be bareback, though.'

'I'm a cavalryman, Thomas. I'll ride most things with or without a saddle.' The room was warm and smelled not unpleasantly of horse, leather, tobacco and hard-working men. It was simple and reassuringly familiar from years spent in billets, in tumbledown cottages, in tents, all made into homes for professional soldiers.

'Have you far to go, Captain? If you don't mind me asking.' Thomas nudged a chair forward and Paul produced a stone bottle that sloshed cheerfully.

'Under a day, unless any bridges are down or roads blocked. Thanks.' Giles took the bottle and tipped his head back to take a swallow, then lost the power to breathe. 'Hell's teeth,' he managed after several seconds. 'What is this?'

'My old mother's winter tonic.' Thomas accepted the

jug and took a hefty swig. 'Secret recipe handed down for generations. Here you are, Paul, keep it moving, lad.'

Ah, well, there are worse ways to spend a snowbound afternoon than blind drunk, that time-honoured way to deal with the pain of a woman on your mind.

Chapter Six

'Oh! Are you sickening for something?'

Giles came through the door into the dining room and stared at the food on the table as though he were not quite certain what it was for.

Julia stood up, took his arm and pushed him into the nearest chair. 'You are the most ghastly colour. Let me feel your forehead. Have you a fever?' No, his skin was cool. 'I'll see if Mrs Smithers has any tonics or medicines in stock.' Under her hand she felt him shudder.

'The last thing I need is a tonic. Thank you. Coffee. Please.'

'No coffee, remember? It will have to be strong tea.' Miri, smiling wickedly, lifted the pot.

'Very strong. Sugar.' He took the first cup, appeared to inhale it and took the second, which she had already pushed across to him. 'More.'

Light dawned. 'You are drunk.'

He finished the third cup. 'Hungover.'

'So that is where you were yesterday afternoon! Have you drunk the cellar dry?'

'Some sort of tonic your coachman swears by. Proba-bly one needs several years' training to get the full benefit.' Giles regarded the bacon with a jaundiced eye, carved two thick slices of bread off the loaf, buttered it liberally, slapped four rashers between them and began to demolish the resulting sandwich. 'That's better. I think,' he remarked when all that was left were crumbs.

'You should go back to bed and sleep it off.'

'Bed is *very* tempting.' The slightly bloodshot grey eyes crinkled at the corners with amusement and she felt herself blushing. 'My dear Lady Julia, if every officer who woke up after a night spent with a bottle of dubious liqueur was unfit to function we would have been rolled up by Bonaparte within weeks.'

That wicked almost-smile convened layers of meaning about *bed* and his ability to *function* and the wretched man knew it. Julia pursed her lips rather than run her tongue along them. 'I am delighted to hear it. I had been looking forward to the ride.'

'You?' The smile vanished. 'There are no saddles. I don't know how bad the roads will be or how long it will take. You should stay safely here.'

'Captain Markham, I have ridden over Indian deserts, through jungles, across plains on just about everything there is to ride in the country—horses, mules, elephants and camels. I can assure you I did not do so side-saddle wearing a fashionable riding habit and only venturing out when it was entirely safe to do so.' The look on Giles's face as she stood and walked to the door, the divided skirt swishing against her tall leather boots, was worth braving any depths of snowdrift for.

'And your husband permitted this?'

'In India such travel is a matter of routine. If my husband wanted me to be about his business, he had no choice. I hope for your future wife's sake that you will not be the kind of husband who keeps an English version of a *zenana*.

I will be over at the stables when you have finished your breakfast and calmed your poor, aching head.'

'You would say *harem*, I imagine, Captain.' Miri's earnest explanation followed Julia into the hall as she shrugged into a heavy greatcoat borrowed from Smithers. Her riding skirt had been made to withstand thorns and blown sand, but not an English winter, and beneath her outer clothes she was layered like an onion with silk undergarments.

Thomas was walking one of the carriage horses up and down, a rug over its back. 'Morning, my lady.'

'Good morning. I am riding, too, if you can shorten another set of reins for me.' He stared at her, looking remarkably like Giles for a second. *Man confused by woman*, she thought with an inward grin and took the reins, led the horse to the mounting block and pushed back the rug over its rump before she swung a leg over the broad back. It was a stretch after her own little mare, but it was no more uncomfortable than a camel.

Thomas was muttering under his breath as she shook out her skirts on either side. Perfectly decent and perfectly practical whether one was on an elephant or a large carriage horse. 'The Captain will be out directly.' *Once he has his head on the right way round.*

Giles emerged a few moments later, buttoning his greatcoat as he stood on the threshold and looked at her. For a moment she wondered if he was going to be difficult, then he shook his head and walked across to Thomas, who was leading out another horse. He might not approve, but the Captain had the tact not to lecture her in front of her servants.

He vaulted on to the back of the big bay. *Oh, my goodness. Yes, well, don't stare. Just because he moves like a god, just because he looks like one sitting there as though he is part of the animal...* She fussed with the reins, brought her own horse up alongside his and had her mouth firmly shut before she looked at him again.

He was a cavalry officer. Of course he can ride. There had been fine horsemen everywhere she travelled in India, but she had never seen a rider who took her breath as this man did, sitting relaxed bareback. She was aware of his body now, aware of what they both wanted, and that was decidedly uncomfortable.

Miri came out carrying saddlebags. 'Food and drink,' she said as she handed them up to Giles who slung them over his horse's withers. 'Don't get lost.'

'We won't. Ready, Lady Julia?' At her nod he moved his horse forward and she followed on a loose rein, letting the animal find its own footing in the snow.

They rode silently in single file, their breath forming clouds in front of them, their track stark and lonely in the white perfection. The sky was an exquisite pale blue, the sunlight sparkled on the snow-fringed branches, every twig encased in crystal.

After perhaps a mile Giles turned, one hand on his horse's rump, and looked back. 'All right? Come alongside if you want, the hedges are far apart, so there must be wide verges. We should be safe from ditches.'

He waited until she was almost knee to knee with him. 'I offended you this morning, I apologise.'

'And I was rude in return. I am sure you will make a most amiable husband and not be over-protective at all.' She had her tongue in her cheek, just a little, and Giles's sharp glance told her he knew it.

'A man's instinct is to protect a woman. You must forgive me if that becomes patronising.'

'And you must forgive me for attempting to mollycoddle your hangover. A woman's instinct is to wrap sufferers up in blankets and administer beef tea,' Julia said sweetly.

That provoked the snort of amusement it deserved. 'I find it difficult to imagine you doing any such thing.'

'Certainly not the beef tea. The cow is a sacred animal in India. I found it a shock when I was served it in England again.'

'One gets accustomed to anything.' Giles shaded his eyes to scan the surrounding fields. 'I ate rook and squirrel stew once, in the mountains. There might have been the odd rat added for extra body.'

'Was it delicious?'

'Anything is if you are starving. Although if you boiled a brick and a rook together, I suspect the brick might be the more tender.'

'I had thought battles must be the worst part of soldiering. It sounds as though simply surviving day to day was horrible.'

'The battles are merely the punctuation.' Giles rode on in silence until she thought that was all he had to say. 'I have never tried to explain it to someone before. Or to myself, come to that. The tactics, the organisation, the detail and the wider picture are all fascinating. Learning to lead men, learning the craft of warfare or how to light a fire when everything is wet and the enemy are so close you can almost hear them breathing or how to communicate with a Spanish partisan who is half-inclined to cut your throat are all interesting. The camaraderie is…important.'

The most important thing, she guessed. 'And you gave it all up.'

'I inherited land, and debts and people who relied on that land. And a woman with twin baby daughters into the bargain.'

'So, duty?' Giles nodded. 'And are you expected to marry the woman with the daughters?'

'I hope not!' He glanced at her sharply. 'I have no intention of doing so. I've never met her.'

'Do you know about land?'

'I'll learn.'

'And the debts?' He shrugged, but the horse, on its loose rein, sidled sharply as though his thigh muscles had clamped tight on its sides. 'You need a rich wife,' she suggested, her tone careful, somewhere between teasing and helpful.

'Yes,' he agreed. The horse tossed its head at the sudden jerk on the bit. 'And what are your plans?'

'Oh, to find a rich, titled husband and enjoy the cream of London society, or take a lover and settle for a life on my own terms on the fringes of that society. Or perhaps go back to India and be a disreputable widow. So much choice.'

Giles laughed, not knowing her well enough to hear the truth when she spoke it.

'Money is a very depressing subject. If one has it, one no doubt worries about it. If one doesn't have it, then one thinks about it all the time.' Which was how she ended up married to Humphrey Chalcott. Sheer panic at being destitute when she was too weak, too disorientated, to realise that she had another choice, that of being poor. But she hadn't realised her own potential then, hadn't seen anything but the terror of ending up earning her living on her back in some Calcutta brothel. Once she discovered what she was capable of she had sworn never to be in a man's power, under his control, again.

'This is where you picked me up,' Giles said. 'See that dead oak tree?'

She was becoming stiff now, the inside muscles of her thighs aching with the unaccustomed breadth of the horse under her, her shoulders tight as she concentrated on balancing. Giles seemed to have no problem, she thought, torn between resentment and admiration of the relaxed back, the strength of the supple spine.

I want him. Not just his kisses. I want to take my courage in both hands and make love with him. I need his strength and his gentleness and the raw masculine power that lurks beneath. This isn't sensible, it isn't rational...but for once in my life I don't care. When Giles was gone she could go back to planning, to listening to her head and not her heart, to finding a husband who would not need her money. The thought of seeing calculation come into *this* man's eyes was hateful.

If they did not find the barn in another half-hour he was turning back. The sky was still clear, but the temperature would drop once the sun began its shallow winter slide towards the horizon and Julia had been out far too long for someone used to the heat of India. He should have refused to let her come. *Good luck with that, Markham. Try reasoning with her then,* he suggested to the mocking inner voice. But she went her own way, did Julia Chalcott. *Stimulating,* the insidious little whisper suggested. That independence was not the only stimulating thing about Julia, he thought, grimly attempting to ignore the one warm part of his anatomy which wanted to join in the conversation.

She was intelligent, capable, had a sense of humour, loyalty. *And, yes,* he snarled silently at the other parties in the discussion, *I want her.* In his bed, under him, around him. He knew how she tasted, how she felt between his hands. He knew her skin carried traces of jasmine and bergamot and some spice new to him. He knew she was as full of passion and curiosity as a champagne bottle was of bubbles. And he wanted to shake that bottle and be damned to the consequences. It was a few days, that was all. This wasn't like before, he wasn't losing his heart, or his head, over a scheming little minx who was using him to make his best friend jealous.

'Is this it?' Her call jerked him out of his introspection. How long had he been riding blind, brooding? They were almost level with the cluster of sheds and the small barn. A row of brown heads poked out and stared and a thin line of footprints snaked away up the lane ahead of them. Giles whistled and the cows parted as Trojan came out, dwarfing them. He neighed piercingly and trotted through the snow, throwing it up from his great hooves like spray on the bow wave of a frigate.

Giles talked to him as he dealt with the carriage horse who wasn't used to helping open gates. 'Missed me, did you? Have you learned to speak cow? Sideways, you stupid lummox, and push. Someone's brought you all hay, I see. No, back off, damn you. What?' he demanded.

Julia was bent double over her horse's neck, breathless with laughter. 'You. Give me the reins otherwise we'll be here all week before that dim animal works out what he's supposed to do.' She rode up alongside him as he slid down, then got the giggles again when he landed thigh-deep in the snow. 'Your horse is enormous and very handsome. What is his name?'

'Trojan. Yes, we're talking about you.' He managed to drag the gate open while the big chestnut butted him with his nose, slobbered into his ear and generally checked that he was in one piece.

'Why?'

'Because he's a horse.'

'Trojan Horse. That's dreadful.' She urged the two carriage horses through and rode on to the barn while he shut the gate and led Trojan, now investigating his pockets, back into the shelter.

Someone had definitely been there. The thin ice had been cleared from the water troughs and the hay was more or less in heaps. The note he had left on a nail beside the door had been opened and something added in shaky capital letters. *Ten shillings livery. F. Hoskins.*

'Cheap at the price,' Giles observed. He dug through his clothing to an inner pocket, took out a banknote and rolled it up in the paper, then spiked that on the nail. 'Come inside where it's warmer and I'll get my gear from where I stowed it.'

She looked at him, then dropped her lashes so that he could not read her eyes. But the colour on her cheeks was due to more than the cold and the hard pulse in his throat was not exertion.

The hayloft was shadowed and gloomy, but there was just enough light filtering in to guide him as he reached up and lifted down his sabre from the high beam, then dug the saddle and bridle out from behind a feed bin.

'It is positively snug in here.' Julia had climbed up behind him.

'The cattle below are as good as a stove.' *And we are alone.*

She moved closer and he could smell the rinse she used on her hair, herbs and something sweet and fresh. He could smell the cold on her skin and the scent of the hay and she met his gaze as the sabre dropped from his fingers. He was vaguely aware of setting down the saddle. 'Julia?'

'Giles.' And she was in his arms.

Chapter Seven

A question had been asked and answered in the chilly, dusty gloom. Giles's arms around her were familiar now. His taste, the scent of his skin, the plain soap he used, the warm male muskiness, stirred her senses and steadied the trembling in her limbs. Between their bodies their hands tangled as they struggled with buttons, as she pushed the greatcoat from his shoulders. He spread it over the piled hay before taking hers.

'I am not going to make love to you with my boots on.'

'Nor am I.'

Giles caught her as she tottered, balancing on one foot, and they laughed, collapsing on to the hay. The last of her nerves fled with the laughter as he said, 'We'll take it in turns. Give me your foot.'

Bootless, they turned to each other, dragging her great-coat over them. 'How does this garment undo?' Giles demanded, wrestling with tapes and hooks.

'Let me. You worry about your own breeches.' Then she was in his arms, their naked legs touching, both of them fully clothed above the waist. 'We're wearing woollen stockings, it doesn't seem very romantic.'

'Neither is frostbite.' Giles was intent on the buttons of

her bodice. 'I would rather romance your breasts than your toes, although given a warm bed…' What he was going to say was lost as his hands, big and calloused, slid between the layers of silk and cotton and cupped her, his thumbs stroking nipples that were hard and aching before he had even touched them.

Lightning flickered across her skin, down to her belly, between her legs, and Julia cried out, her fingers clenched in his shirt front. 'Let me. Let me touch you.'

She pushed impatiently at linen and wool, burrowing towards his heat, then stopped, her cheek against the hard, flat planes of his chest, her nose tickled by curls of hair, her hand caressing slowly down as his skin tightened under her fingertips and his heart thudded under her ear. *Is this right? Will I please him? Will I hate it with him as I did with Humphrey? Please, not that.*

'I want to be slow, to take all day learning your body, listening to the way your breathing changes when I touch you…here.' His own breath hitched as she arched into his palm. 'I want to discover the landscape of your skin.' Giles kissed her, rolling her so he was over her, sheltering them both under the coat in hay-scented darkness. 'But I can't risk you in this cold, can't risk losing the light. *Julia.*' He gasped as she found him, curled her fingers around the hard length and stroked, awestruck by his reaction to her.

'Giles, please. I just want you. Need you.' Her thighs embraced his hips, welcoming him home. A moment of fear flickered through her as he lodged himself, nudging at admittance where she ached, for him, wet and yearning. It had been so long and he was so very…

'Julia.' His voice was a hoarse whisper against her throat. 'We'll take all the time you need.'

He had felt that tightening, her tiny jolt of apprehension, even though she could feel the tension in him, the fight he was having to stay in control. That awareness of her was all she needed. 'Now, Giles. Now.'

She had expected discomfort, been prepared for it, but it did not come. There was only the sensation of being filled, of being joined. She tightened around him, felt the shudder that ran through him, felt their blood beating together, his breath harsh and hot on her cold skin, the delicious weight of his muscled body surrounding her as he moved in and out, teasing the tension higher and higher. Giles shifted his weight, slid one hand between them, touched her so that she cried out, arching into him, and then the strain broke and the world behind her closed lids was full of lights and all that stopped her flying into fragments was Giles's anchoring embrace.

When she opened her eyes he was cradling her, the coats swathed around them, the hay prickling through the tiny, draughty gaps. 'Giles.'

'I'm here.' His arms tightened. 'We didn't talk about it before, but I was careful.'

It took her a moment to realise what he meant. It had never occurred to her for a moment that he would not have taken care of both that vital detail and of her, she realised.

'Come. I want to linger, but we must be going before the light fails.'

So soon. Now he was getting up, adjusting his clothing, his face unreadable in the gloom. So cold. The temperature was dropping and with it her mood. Julia scrambled into her riding skirt, pulled on her boots. That had given Giles pleasure, too, hadn't it? He hadn't made love to her out of pity for the poor, frustrated widow after she had confided so much, so unwisely, had he?

He stretched out gloved hands and pulled her to her feet so fast and smoothly that she ended up tight against his chest. His mouth found hers again. 'That was a delicious, unexpected, Christmas present. Thank you.'

Either Giles was a loss to the London stage or he had found pleasure in the act, however inexperienced she had been. She had been braced for indifference now he had lain with her, but Giles handed her down the ladder with care, kept her close with fleeting touches, a passing kiss or two as he saddled Trojan, checked the horse's leg. *Cherishing me.* Despite the cold something blossomed, warm and tender inside her. *I like this man so much.*

'He's not at all lame. Come and I'll give you a leg up.'

'You want me to ride your horse?'

'I do not think it was very comfortable for you coming out and I am certain it will be even less so going back.' There was a wicked smile in his eyes and she felt herself blushing. Yes, she was a little sore. It was not an entirely unpleasant sensation, she realised as she busied herself gathering up the reins and talking to the horse. Even so, it was easier to fiddle with stirrup leathers than it was to meet Giles's gaze.

'That is the way I must take when I leave.' Giles nodded towards the tracks the farmer had left. 'Smithers says there is a turning to the right along there leading to the Norwich turnpike.'

'So you'll leave soon?' Strangely, her voice was steady.

'The day after tomorrow, unless it snows again.'

'But that is Christmas Eve. Won't you stay for Christmas Day at least?'

'I must be back as soon as possible.' After a moment he said, without turning, 'I would prefer to stay. Much prefer it.'

Duty, of course. His reluctance to leave the army, to come and take up this family burden, had been obvious every time he spoke of it, but he would not shirk it. *An honourable man.*

'Yes, I understand. Miri will be disappointed, but your family will be so longing to see you.'

His silence spoke volumes.

Under that tart exterior, Julia is as sweet as honey. There was a murmur behind him and he turned to see that she was talking to Trojan, who swivelled one ear back to listen. He was not used to a female rider, but the big chestnut was behaving with exemplary manners and she was a good horsewoman.

Camels, she said. And elephants. His imagination conjured up Julia in exotic silken garments, the breeze fluttering the fragile tissue against those long legs, the sweet bounty of her breasts decked with golden chains and glittering gems as she was carried on an elephant towards some fantasy palace rising from the sun-baked plains.

Fantasy indeed. He could not even afford to deck her in one length of precious Indian silk, even if he could justify spending a penny on frivolity, let alone sensual indulgencies. Giles reminded himself that this was simply a liaison for a day or two, an isolated incident in their lives. A touch of fleeting magic.

The journey back was easier than he feared it might be and they were home as the last of the light leached from the sky. The lanterns were lit in the stable yard and in the downstairs rooms, painting the snow with sharp rectangles and squares of gold.

Giles lifted Julia down, indulging himself by letting her body slide down his, enjoying her blush. The men led the horses away to hot mash and hay nets and Bulstrode created a fuss until they leaned over his half-door for a word.

'That is the smuggest turkey in Norfolk, I'll wager.' He

took Julia's arm as they picked their way across to the front steps.

'With some reason,' she said with a chuckle. 'If I were him I would suspect an elaborate charade and would be expecting a cook with a cleaver at any moment, but he has no imagination, the lucky bird.'

The image was amusing, but Giles found he had lost the inclination to laugh. 'Are you all right?'

She turned as his hand tightened on her arm, just as they reached the front steps. 'Of course.' Her lips on his cheek were cold until they pressed the kiss harder and the heat of her mouth made his breath catch. 'That was lovely. I am so glad we...'

'Made love?'

'Yes.' She would not meet his eyes. Was she simply shy? Years in the army were not the best preparation for understanding emotions, his or anyone else's.

'Miri has made a wreath.'

He followed her pointing finger and saw, as the door opened, a circlet of holly and ivy with crimson ribbons floating from a great bow at the bottom.

'Come in, you must be frozen.' Miri pulled them in to the warm hallway. 'Is your horse all right, Captain? Are you starving? Paul snared rabbits, so we have a pie for dinner. Doesn't it smell good? Come and see my decorations.' Talking nineteen to the dozen, she towed them after her into the sitting room, then the dining room. Everywhere holly and ivy edged shelves with swathes of glorious silk woven in and out to create the oriental richness of his fantasy.

'Those silks.' He was enchanted by the effect. 'Amazing. But surely you should not risk such expensive fabric amongst the holly?'

'Oh.' Miri seemed flustered. 'They are just some saris. They pack down to nothing and they are dagger cheap.

They look finer than they are. Listen, Smithers is taking the hot water cans up. I'll come and help you, Julia.'

She bustled her stepmother out, leaving Giles to stroke his hand along the nearest swag of vermilion and gold. It felt like Julia's skin under his palm—warm, soft, sleek. He felt himself harden into arousal and closed his hand around a sprig of holly until the sharp stabbing pain over-rode the heavy ache.

He'd leave the day after tomorrow even if it snowed again. He was certain he could reach that turn and the farmer had come to tend his beasts on foot, so the farm-house could not be far. It would offer shelter if things got really bad. They had two nights, one day to be happy, to find a magic together.

Giles was very quiet, Julia thought, as he set out a chess-board and proceeded to play against himself. He had asked them to play, but Miri was deep in a tattered Gothic novel and Julia knew she could no more concentrate on chess moves than she could fly.

Was he regretting their passion in the hayloft? She knew convention said that she should, but she could not. Words like *immoral* and *unwise* flitted into her head and promptly flitted out again. Giles reached out, touched the white queen, stroked it with his fingertip while he thought and the heat pooled in her belly, fuelling the insistent little pulse between her legs, making her shift uneasily, embar-rassed by her own wantonness.

Tomorrow they would decorate the house, she decided. She'd had enough of being angry, disappointed, missing the remembered Christmases of her childhood. Miri had made a start and she would throw herself into it, give all three of them memories that would glow like the heart of the yule log.

Giles picked up the queen, playing with it one-handed while he frowned at the board. Those hands, so strong and gentle on her body, so knowing, so skilful as they wove magic across her skin. As she watched, he glanced up, caught her gaze, held it with such heat in his eyes that she could have sworn that it burned her. *He wants me still, this decent man, this brave soldier who has given up the life he had built for duty.*

The hall clock struck ten. This was torture. 'I am for my bed. Miri?'

'Mmm? Oh, yes. Provided I have a lamp to finish this. The faceless monk is haunting the ruins of the abbey, just as Philomena is hurrying to her moonlight tryst with Frederick. I cannot imagine why I never found any novels as good as this in India. Goodnight, Captain.'

Julia took her arm. 'Goodnight.'

'Goodnight, Lady Julia. Sleep well.'

How he expected her to sleep at all, let alone well, when he looked at her like that and spoke in that soft, deep voice that vibrated through her to the base of her spine, she had no idea. 'And you.'

Did she imagine the muttered, *I doubt it*, as she closed the door?

'I expect he'll bed down in front of the fire again.' Miri removed her nose from her book to climb the stairs.

'What do you mean?'

'Didn't you realise? I noticed the first night when I came down in the night for a glass of water. He makes a bed with the sofa cushions and curls up in front of the fire. I heard this rumble, like a tiger, and peeped round the door and there he was in the middle of a mound of blankets, snoring very softly.'

'Sensible of him,' Julia observed briskly. 'The bedchamber he took must be like an icehouse. Don't sit up to all hours with that horrid novel or you'll be fit for nothing tomorrow.'

'Just until I discover whether the monk is a faceless spectre or the wicked Count Alfonso in disguise,' Miri promised, kissing Julia's cheek and vanishing into her bedchamber, nose in book again.

Giles asleep before the hearth. The picture would not leave her. Julia scrambled out of her clothes and into her nightgown, then into bed, her feet searching for the hot brick.

Giles sounding like a great sleeping tiger. Giles naked in the glow of the fire, those long limbs bathed in red and gold. Giles looking up as she came into the room, shedding her robe, walking into the firelight as naked as he was.

She would wait until the house slept and then… Of course he would not be naked and uncovered, she scolded herself as she pummelled her pillow into some kind of comfort. It was far too cold for that. But it was an image to keep her warmer than the hot brick.

What was the life he was going to when he left here, left her? She would find her place in society, amongst the rich and fashionable, and he would be somewhere in Norfolk, doing his duty, creating a new life for himself. Would he think about her sometimes, recall their brief snowbound interlude? They would never meet again and that, suddenly, was intolerable.

The house settled for the night in creaks and groans, the tick of clocks, the scamper of mice in the walls. The pad of feet along the landing past her door, the creak of a door opening, the return of the footsteps. Giles had gone downstairs.

Chapter Eight

Sleep should have come easier, now he had made love to Julia. The desire that had been burning him up was assuaged. Surely now he could relax.

Giles tossed. Turned. Burrowed into the blankets. Got up and shook the whole lot out, built up the fire and tried again. Now he was too hot, which, in this house, was ridiculous. The fire was blazing, his mind was on fire and his body was joining in with incendiary enthusiasm.

He threw off the blankets, dragged off his shirt and lay there, scorched by the fire on one side, getting cold from the draughts on the other, focusing on the discomfort. A handful of snow, strategically applied, might help.

A soft gasp brought his head round with a jerk. 'Julia.'

She stood just inside the door, her robe clutched to her throat by one hand. With the other she pushed the door closed, then simply shrugged off the robe and stood in the flickering firelight. Naked.

Before he could move she was beside him in the tangle of bedding. 'I imagined you here like this, golden, barred with flame shadows. A tiger.'

A tiger? He knew what he felt like—a ravening wolf confronted by such beauty that it was incapable of movement. She was all pale skin and soft shadows, the triangle of curls that hid her secrets a tantalising mystery. All her shyness had fled, leaving a woman confident of her power to bring him to his knees.

With the exercise of more willpower than he knew he possessed he rose until he knelt facing her, not touching, simply breathing in the warmth of her skin, the perfume of aroused femininity. 'This is a dream, this isn't real.'

She reached for his hand, lifted it to her breast. 'I am real, this is real.'

His fingers curled until she was cupped in his palm, living, trembling, real woman. 'Two nights. I must leave the day after tomorrow.'

'I know. This is all that exists. Just us and now. Here.' She began to touch him, her fingers tracing trails of inquisitive fire over his skin. Everything seemed to fascinate her, the definition of muscles, the curve of his ear, the lump of his Adam's apple, the way his nipples responded to the scratch of her fingernails.

Giles clenched his hands by his sides, his muscles aching with the strain of not touching her. When he did he wouldn't be able to be slow, be gentle, all the things he wanted to be for her. He would consume her.

Julia edged round him, stroking his shoulders, running one finger down the length of his spine. 'So elegant and so strong. I love these.' She began to caress his buttocks and he felt her breath on his nape as she gave a little huff of laughter when he groaned. 'So hard.' Her fingernails dug in a little, then she was against his back, her hands sliding round, over his stomach, her fingertips exploring down into the coarse hair until she could grip the length of him. *'Oh.'*

'If…you want this to end now, just…keep doing that.'
Julia felt Giles's body shivering with the effort to control

himself and the knowledge of power, that she could reduce a strong, experienced man to this, swept through her. She tightened her fingers on the velvet-smooth iron in her grip, bit gently on the rigid tendon in his neck and found herself flat on her back on the cushions.

'Are you in haste?' Giles was above her, supported on straight arms so he could look down at her, so that his pelvis pressed down on hers as she lay with her thighs cradling him. In one thrust he would be inside her.

Julia writhed, helpless, gasped as her sensitive flesh rubbed against him. 'Yes. Yes, I am in haste.'

'Pity.' His grin was wicked, the smile of a man who was back in control of the situation. 'I want to go *very* slowly. I want to look at you as I pleasure you, watch your face, enjoy your beauty.'

'I am not beautiful.' If she could just wriggle a little more she would be in the perfect position.

'If you say things like that I will take even more time. I don't lie to you, Julia. You are lovely and I—' He closed his eyes. 'I want you very much. Now, where was I?'

'Torturing me.'

'Oh, yes. How cruel. Is this what you wanted me to do?' He slid into her, just an inch.

'*Yes*. More. Please. *Yes*.'

So slow, so agonisingly, blissfully slow. So big, so deep, so…much. Julia looked up, deep into his eyes as Giles made love to her with all the gentle strength of his body, saw the man stripped bare to his soul. Honest, honourable, loaded with obligations he would fight to fulfil, whatever he wanted for himself.

'Giles!'

He took her cries into his kiss as he surged once, twice, hard and deep, beyond control now, then, at the last moment, tore himself from her body and spilled his hot seed on her stomach.

Julia thought she would faint. Perhaps she did. When she came to herself she was tangled in a tight, sticky embrace under the covers. Giles had shifted his weight off her, but he still sprawled, possessive, against her, his arms holding her to him, his head on her shoulder. He was asleep, already snoring softly, a big cat's rumbling purr.

She had heard of Christmas miracles and this was hers, this man. And now she had received this gift she was going to toss it aside because that was the sensible thing to do. Julia buried her face in the thick brown hair and slept.

'Julia, time to get up.'

'Mmpf?' She blinked and found Miri, wide awake, a steaming cup of tea in her hand. 'Where am I?'

'In your cold and lumpy bed at Chalcott Manor.' Miri put the cup down on the bedside table. 'It is eight o'clock and Captain Markham is complaining that he is starving and the bacon is congealing.'

'Yes, of course.' Julia gulped the tea. 'I'll be right down. Tell him to start without me.' Giles must have carried her back to bed.

And she remembered as she saw the sunlight lying in bars across the floor. It was thawing. This was the last day before Giles left. She closed her eyes on the tears that threatened, fighting the despair. How had he come to mean so much in such a short time?

A short time was all they had, one day, one night. Julia opened dry eyes and flung back the covers. Time to create a Christmas to remember, the Christmas of her dreams.

Giles and Miri blinked at her when she swept into the dining room. 'I am starving.' She ignored the wicked twinkle in his eye, the unspoken suggestion that making love all night was enough to give anyone an appetite. 'There is so much to do today. Miri made a wonderful start on the decorations, but we need a yule log and mistletoe and table decorations and presents.'

Giles was openly grinning when she ran out of words. 'I haven't experienced a Christmas like that since I was a child.' He didn't point out that he would not be there on Christmas Day, and she was grateful for that. *One day at a time.*

'I haven't either and Miri never has. Where should we begin?'

'Outside while the sun shines.' Giles was on his feet. 'I saw some mistletoe yesterday.'

They followed him out, bacon crammed into slices of bread to eat as they struggled into heavy coats and boots, found scarves to wrap each other in. Giles tramped across the snowy waste behind the house and pointed up into an ancient apple tree. 'See?'

'It is a very big tree,' Miri said doubtfully. 'Won't it be dangerous?'

'Just the thing to say to a man if you want him to risk his neck,' Julia teased as Giles began to strip off coat and gloves.

He shook his head at her and began to climb in a shower of dislodged snow and broken branches. 'Stay back.'

Julia edged away, holding Miri's arm. He was making steady progress, long legs stretching to solid footholds, his hands testing and tugging as he climbed higher. She saw him hold on one-handed while he pulled something from his boot, then he was tossing down mistletoe to land bright green on the sparkling snow.

'The berries are poisonous,' she warned Miri as they collected it up. 'That's enough!' she called up and Giles began to climb down, faster than he had gone up, swinging from branch to branch. 'Show-off,' Julia called as he turned a somersault around the biggest bottom branch and landed at their feet.

Giles stumbled against her and they fell into the snow, laughing, as Miri, doubled up with laughter, waved the mistletoe over their heads and called, 'Kiss her...kiss him.'

'That was my first kiss under the mistletoe ever,' Giles said as he got to his feet and pulled her up in a shower of snow. 'Now for a yule log.'

'We could try the shrubbery. I saw some dead trees.' *The first mistletoe kiss. He will remember it, years hence*, Julia told herself as they trooped past the snow family, stopping for Miri to put sprigs of mistletoe in their hats. *And so will I.*

The log they found was so large that Giles had to fetch one of the carriage horses and rig up long traces. He lifted Miri on to its back where she clung, waving to the staff who all came out to see what the noise was about as they towed it back to the front door. It took all the men to heave it into the front room and wedge it into the hearth, but eventually they managed to set a fire under it and it began to smoulder.

'It burns until Twelfth Night,' Julia explained to Miri, on her way out to pick sprigs of evergreen for table decorations.

Giles hung the bunch of mistletoe from the hall lantern and kissed her again, this time without an audience and without laughter and she clung to him for a moment before breaking free to let in Paul with an armful of fragrant pine branches.

The men went off to find a saw to cut up pieces to fit over the doors, leaving Julia standing in the hallway, the cold breeze from the open door stirring her hair, her fingers to her lips. *I love him.* That was what this was, this hollow feeling when he wasn't there, this warm glow when he was. It wasn't simply desire, it was something far, far more.

But he was a poor man, a man with debts, a man who made no bones about needing a rich wife. The sort of man she had resolved to avoid at all costs. *It is the lovemaking,* she told herself. *That, and the isolation and the magic of the snow and of Christmas. I am letting my emotions rule my head and I vowed not to do that again. And yet I trust him more than I have ever trusted before.*

'Julia?' Miri shut the front door with a bang that made her jump. 'Stop daydreaming and tell me what we must do next.'

'Christmas presents,' Julia said, her smile so bright it hurt the muscles. 'We surely have enough things in our luggage from India to find something novel for everyone. Let's go and see.'

She already had some gloves and a muff for Miri, bought in Bond Street, but she had given no thought to having a houseful of servants and no way to reach the shops.

They unearthed a cache of silk scarves and chose several each for Mrs Smithers and the Girl, whose real name they had discovered was Jennet. Miri suggested the carved sandalwood boxes that were so useful for everything from buttons to cufflinks, so they chose one each for Smithers, Paul and Thomas and then wrapped up the gifts in silver paper tied with silk threads.

'What about the Captain?' Miri asked.

'Oh, I'll find something,' Julia said. 'You take these down and arrange them on the sideboard. There was another box, smaller than the others, just the size of the palm of her hand. From her jewellery box she took an ivory heart deeply carved with exquisite twining vines and flowers. It was too large to be worn as a pendant, but she had been entranced by the carving and had bought it anyway. Now it nestled in a bed of silk in the little box as though it had been made for it and she wrapped it carefully, then went downstairs and slipped it into the breast pocket of Giles's cavalry greatcoat where it would lie over his heart for him to find when he was miles away.

'Julia?' he called. 'We need a decision on holly in the dining room.'

'Coming,' she called back and found her smile again.

The morning came with a sickening inevitability on the heels of a night of lovemaking, of sleepy embraces in front of the fire, of murmured words, none of which had been, *I love you.*

Julia sat up in her own bed in the cold light of dawn to the sound of voices from the stable yard. She looked down from her window to see Giles talking to the men. Paul was carrying a saddle. This was the end, then.

She began to dress, blindly, and then stopped, one shoe still in her hand. It didn't need to be the end. She knew this man, she trusted him as well as loved him. He needed a rich wife and she could be that woman. He would not feign liking or passion for her because she knew he already felt them. And surely he might learn to love her, too? She only had to have courage and believe in him, in herself.

She must talk to him, now. There was no need for such haste, no need for him to ride off into the freezing wilds of Norfolk. She would tell him he had the rich wife he needed and she could watch his face break into that wonderful smile, see the anxiety of those debts fall away. This would be the perfect Christmas Eve.

When she ran downstairs Giles came into the hall from the kitchen, hat and whip in hand, his greatcoat already fastened. 'I am glad you are down, I did not want to scandalise Miri by going up to you.'

'Giles, I must speak with you.' She caught his arm and tugged him towards the drawing room. 'Please, close the door.'

He was sombre as he closed it, leaned against it. 'Goodbye isn't easy to say, Julia. I will never forget you. I hope you will find what you want in this life.'

'Giles, don't go.'

'Last night…' He shook his head as though there were no words. 'Last night was…extraordinary. This is abrupt, but it must be, Julia. We were trapped here, trapped into an intimacy that otherwise would have taken weeks, perhaps months to achieve. We must put it behind us now.'

'You need a rich wife, I know.' He made an abrupt gesture with his hand, but she pressed on. 'I should have told you before, I suppose… Giles, I am a rich woman. A very rich woman. Marry me.'

She saw the shock strike, then his expression became blank. 'Explain. You said your husband was a failed merchant.'

'He was. But I began to trade in secret on my own behalf. At first just with what I could save from my allowance, from the housekeeping. I found I was good at it. When I carried out Humphrey's orders for his company I was trading for myself as well. It is easier in India for a woman to find places to invest, to keep her savings safe. By the time Humphrey died I was a very rich woman.'

'So you came back to England to be a female nabob, did you? And what else—to buy a big house, of course, that's what nabobs do—and to find yourself a husband, perhaps? You weren't joking when you told me that was what you were looking for, was it?' His voice was cold, mouth hard.

'If I found the right person. But—'

'So you tried me out. On approval, as it were.' He pushed away from the door and stalked across the room to the window, over six foot of darkly furious masculinity. 'You know, I really do have the worst judgement when it comes to women. I really hoped that one day I would find an honest one.'

'No! It isn't like that. Giles—'

'You lied to me. The carriage is borrowed, is it? You don't wear these plain gowns without a single piece of jewellery as a matter of course, I'll wager. All part of the disguise while you survey the goods. After all, you don't want the studs you are choosing from to get too excited about the money, do you?'

'That is so right,' she flared. 'Men become mesmerised by money far more than they do by the sight of a naked bosom. They'll do anything to get their hands on it. So, yes, I would like a rich husband, because I know he would want me for myself, not my bank balance. But you, you were different, I felt *different* with you.'

'Charitable, presumably?'

She slapped his face then. He made no move to avoid her. 'You said you needed a rich wife.' *What have I done?* She had never used violence against another person in her life—and this was the man she *loved*.

'I *need* a rich wife, yes. I *want* someone who is honest with me. I was prepared for open negotiation, for contracts and settlements, a business transaction. What I was not prepared for, madam, was an emotional entanglement where I am lied to, used for sex and then insulted with offers of money. I have a secret to share, too. I am the Earl of Welbourn. Good day to you, Lady Julia.'

She was still shaking when Miri came running into the room. 'He has gone—and his *face*. Julia, did you slap Giles? Why?'

'Because I love him.' She collapsed into the nearest

chair. 'I hurt his pride and insulted him and he said hateful things and I hit him and…and I will never see him again.'

Miri came and huddled into the chair next to Julia, held her tight. 'Perhaps he loves you, too. If he does, he will realise when he calms down.'

'No. He doesn't.' But Giles had said *an emotional entanglement.* That, surely, meant he had *some* feelings for her? Feelings she had turned to disgust and dislike. Best not to hope. Somehow plan, to survive, to endure.

'I was an idiot, Miri. But this is Christmas and we have made this dreadful old house look festive and Mrs Smithers promises Christmas pudding for tomorrow. We will celebrate all that we have and make plans for the New Year.' Plans that did not involve men. She had not wept when she had woken after that dreadful fever to discover that she had nothing and no hope of happiness. She would not weep now. 'I will be fine soon, just give me a little time.'

The rest of my life.

It was almost dark when Giles turned a weary Trojan between pillars topped with griffins. There were no lights in the lodge houses flanking the entrance. Gatekeepers were a luxury that could be dispensed with. He wondered where the dispossessed family had gone.

Trojan fidgeted, perhaps scenting a stable, but Giles kept him at a walk. He had been valiant today and he would not risk him on this last stretch home. *Home.* That was an interesting word for a ball and chain on his ankle, but he must start thinking of it like that. This was his home and his duty. Behind him an indignant gobbling emerged from the basket tied to the crupper. Bulstrode was furious at his imprisonment and had complained ceaselessly.

'Be quiet. If I'd left you she'd have eaten you. She does that to males.'

The stables contained only half a dozen horses and fewer grooms. The men hurried out, their faces lighting up when they realised who had come. 'We've been expecting you, my lord,' Fraser, the head groom, explained as an underling led Trojan to a warm rug and a bran mash. 'But not this side of Christmas, not with the weather so bad.'

'The last fifteen miles weren't a problem, once I'd got round the broken bridge.' Giles stretched the stiffness out of his back and looked round for his saddlebags, but the footmen who had appeared as if by magic had taken them, leaving only a rush basket full of furious stag turkey. 'The bird needs putting into a stall and feeding. It is not, under any circumstances, to be harmed.'

'Certainly, my lord.' A groom picked up the basket. At least an earl, even an impoverished one, could get first-class service for his livestock.

'Her ladyship has been apprised of your arrival, my lord.' One of the footmen was back.

'I'll get cleaned up first.' Giles walked beside the man to the front steps. 'I can't come to her in all my dirt.'

'Certainly, my lord. I will show you to your suite.'

It was a beautiful house, he realised as he followed the man through the great doors. Classical, elegant, exquisitely furnished. And…cold. Strangely it felt chillier than Chalcott Manor had, although it was not a matter of temperature.

It was a house in mourning, of course. There was none of Miri's exuberant greenery and swags of silk. Perhaps it was the knowledge that he would soon be forced to sell much of the furniture to mend the roof that was letting in water like a sieve.

Or perhaps it was the absence of a warm heart at its core. Julia, organising, chivvying, giving the staff purpose and direction, praise and confidence. *Do not think about Julia. She is a merchant and she tried you out like a customer taking home a painting to see if it looked well on the drawing room wall before deciding to purchase.*

'The Earl's suite, my lord.' The footman threw open the door to a large bedchamber with a fire burning in the grate.

Firelight on her skin, her hair tossed and tangled on the cushions...

'Your dressing and bathing rooms, my lord. There will be hot water there.'

'I will be causing the Countess inconvenience if I take this suite.'

'Her ladyship moved to guest rooms several weeks ago, my lord.'

Poor woman. A guest in her own home. 'Not the Dower House?'

'It is not habitable, my lord. One of the chimneys fell in last month's gales. If your lordship's valet is not with you, I can assist.'

'Thank you, no. I can manage. Please tell the Countess I will be down directly.'

Giles washed and put on his uniform with the speed most officers acquired early in their careers. It was not strictly correct to wear uniform now, but he had no mourning beyond a few black neckcloths and his breeches and boots were in a dire state.

A butler—*his* butler—waited at the foot of the stairs. 'I am Greaves, my lord.' He opened the nearest pair of doors in silence. Of course, an earl was not announced in his own home.

The woman seated by the fireplace rose to her feet and curtsied in a flutter of black veiling. 'My lord.'

He bowed. 'My lady.' He came forward, took her hand and urged her to sit again. 'I must apologise for not arriving sooner. The exigencies of foreign service and then the weather.'

'Of course.' The widow was a fragile brunette with wide brown eyes and a rosebud mouth. Very pretty, very feminine, he thought as she began to prattle nervously about how glad she was that he was there…not that she did not completely understand the delay…only it was so necessary to have a *man* to manage everything…dear Mr Temple had explained things so patiently, several times. But now dear Lord Welbourn was here everything would be all right…

Oh, Lord, a fluffy bunny rabbit. 'Call me Giles,' he said. 'Do not worry, I will take care of everything.'

She managed a tremulous smile. 'Oh, thank you, Giles. I feel so much more *comfortable* now.'

Of course you do. Your future is in the hands of a man so masculine, so masterful, that his pride rules his heart. And his head.

'Now, do tell me all about this house and the staff. What do you think needs doing first?'

'Oh. I do not know. I leave everything to Greaves and the housekeeper. Darling Henry said I was not to worry my head about anything practical.'

'Of course, how foolish of me. Tell me about your daughters instead.'

You used to like feminine, fluffy little brunettes, didn't you? jeered an inner voice. *Yes,* he snapped back. *At least they haven't the wit to deceive me, the calculation to weigh me up like a pound of peppercorns.*

Chapter Nine

He should be able to sleep. The bed was comfortable, the room was warm, he was bone-weary. Giles had tossed and turned until faint light showed between the curtains, then gave up, dressed and went exploring.

A footman materialised at the head of the stairs. 'My lord?'

'Coffee. I'll be somewhere along here.' He waved a hand vaguely at the expanse of corridor running off along the front of the house.

'Of course, my lord. That is the way to the Long Gallery.'

The Long Gallery was magnificent with the dawn light flooding across the polished boards. Opposite the windows were two fireplaces with portraits lining the walls between them. The fires were both blazing. How much longer before he had to ration the wood and coal? Giles began to pace, reading the names on the bottoms of the gilded frames, studying his ancestors.

Fragments of his face looked back at him from portrait after portrait. His nose here, his chin there, his eyes from most of them. It occurred to him for the first time that he actually belonged here. This was his family, these genera-tions of Markhams who had built this house. At the far end he stopped and gazed out over the gardens, across the park to the just visible village rooftops, the spire of the church. His family, his blood, had cared for this land and its people since the fifteenth century. This place was his by rights, his responsibility. Being Earl of Welbourn *meant* something. It had value.

An idea was stirring in his sleep-deprived brain, loose ends were trying to tie themselves together.

'Your coffee, my lord.' Two footmen with trays of coffee and cream, pastries, rolls and preserves. They arranged a table by one of the fires, set a chair in place, shook out a napkin for him.

'Thank you. Excellent. I can manage now.' They looked ready to put jam on his rolls for him if he asked. A wave of longing for a bivouac with a few fellow officers and a rabbit stew came over him, followed by an even sharper craving for vegetable hotpot in a draughty dining room with Julia.

He drank the coffee and brooded. He needed to plan the day, but there was a pain under his breastbone and he couldn't seem to focus on whether he should go to church, or stay in and make lists, write letters. Or perhaps the widow expected his company.

He tossed back a third cup of coffee, got to his feet and strode downstairs and out before the startled footman could reach the door. The stables were quiet, with a couple of grooms mucking out stalls and voices coming from the tack room.

Giles found Trojan and let the big horse slobber into his ear, which was disgusting, but vaguely comforting. An irritable *gobble* reminded him about his other livestock.

'I suppose you think you've fallen on your scaly feet here.' He leaned on the half-door and eyed Bulstrode. The turkey glared at him with boot-button-black eyes and scolded some more. That, too, was comforting. Giles thought of Julia leaning on that other stable door in an attitude of despair. She had kissed him then. Looking back on it, he realised now that she had only done so because she trusted him, because she thought he was a romantic, someone with imagination who could follow her thoughts and her longings.

'Have I been a stiff-necked idiot?' Bulstrode gobbled, then unfurled his tail and stalked off. 'I suppose that's *yes*. She's not had much luck with men, has she? Her father squanders the family fortunes, her cousin throws her out, her potential suitors die on her, her husband is an ageing, lazy lump and now men see her bank balance and not the woman. She took a risk, telling me she was wealthy. I could have pretended feelings that were false to get her or I could have done what I did and acted like some starched-up aristocrat whose pride has been mortally wounded.

'I think I love her.' From across the fields church bells rang out Christmas peals into the crisp air. In the yard one of the lads began to sing 'God Rest You Merry Gentlemen', and other voices joined him, some lusty, some flat, all joyous. 'She didn't tell me because she wasn't certain she could trust me and then when she did I threw it in her face.'

And all for pride. All because once a selfish woman had used him for her own ends and he had been braced for betrayal ever since. Apparently he was able to face negotiating with some cit for his daughter's hand and vast dowry in exchange for giving her a title and ensuring the man had aristocratic grandchildren, but he couldn't accept being bailed out by the woman he loved.

Giles strolled out into the yard, gestured to the grooms to keep singing and stood looking at the house. He had thought he had nothing to offer Julia, but he had. He should write, apologise. But those harsh, bitter words needed a face-to-face apology and she deserved another chance to slap his face.

'Saddle my horse.'

'Now, my lord?'

'Now.'

In the house the clock struck nine o'clock. 'Festive greetings, my lord. My lady is taking breakfast before morning service.' Greaves gestured towards doors opposite the drawing room and he went in.

'Good morning, my lady. I hope you will excuse me, I must leave. I may be back tonight, possibly tomorrow. Or next week.'

'But aren't you coming to church?'

'No. Forgive me.'

Trojan looked fresh, despite the long ride the previous day, and now he was sure of the route it would take less time, Giles told himself as they crunched down the village street, past the church. The bells were still ringing and on impulse Giles dismounted, tied the reins to the lychgate and went in.

He had given up on prayer during the long years of war. It had seemed like hypocrisy to be praying to be saved while dealing death himself. Now he sat on a hard pew just inside the door and tried to assemble some sort of plea, for forgiveness, if nothing else. Someone had set up a nativity scene with a thatched stable and figures carved from wood. There was an example of travelling hopefully and with faith and finding what you wished for at the end, he thought, smiling at the rather lumpen figures of the shepherds grouped around the crib, each clutching a woolly sheep.

He stood and buttoned his greatcoat and noticed a bulge in the breast pocket. The small package was wrapped in silver and when he opened it the scent of sandalwood rose in the cold air. Inside, nestled in blood-red silk, was a heart.

Perhaps there was hope for an ungracious, prideful, desperate soldier.

They all sat around the dining room table with its candles and evergreens in brass pots down the centre and shining glasses and flatware.

There had been a brace of pheasants—she was not going to enquire where they came from—and after experimenting with spices and honey, even a very potent wine punch to drink, which helped ease any awkwardness amongst the staff.

'It's dark outside now.' Mrs Smithers carried in the steamed pudding and set it in the centre and Thomas poured over something from his flask that burned blue and sharp when he lit it.

'The days'll be lengthening soon,' Paul observed, passing bowls of pudding down the table. 'But I'm glad we're in here and not out on the road, that's for sure.'

'I think we should drink a toast,' Miri declared, her nose decidedly pink from the punch. She lifted her glass. 'Here's to Mrs Smithers for a wonderful Christmas dinner, and to a merry Christmas for all of us!'

Julia raised her glass, forced her aching face into another cheerful smile, and echoed, 'Merry Christmas!' She wanted to go out into the snow and walk and walk until she vanished into a deep drift and oblivion. She wanted to weep. She would do neither because some instinct told her that there was always hope unless she despaired. But hope of what, even at Christmas? The little inner voice was silent on that.

'Is that the kitchen door?' Mrs Smithers stopped, spoon raised.

'It must be the wind in a shutter. I'll go and see. I want to fetch the Christmas presents in any case.' Julia got up and took a lamp, leaving an excited buzz behind her as she went out into the dark hall. There was a thin line of light under the kitchen door, which was strange because Mrs Smithers was careful with lamp oil and candles. Best to check first, perhaps.

The kitchen was warm and lit by a lantern on the table and there, stripping off his greatcoat, was Giles. 'May I come in?'

'What are you… Why are you here?' The punch had gone to her head, she was seeing things.

'I have come to apologise. What I said was unforgivable, but I cling to the hope you can forgive.' He was white with cold and, she realised, tension. 'That was hurt pride talking. Stupid pride and the memory of an old hurt. It had not meant anything to me to plan marrying a woman I did not know, had no feelings for, so long as there was a mutual exchange of benefits. A City merchant's daughter would like the status of a title, the big house in the country.

'I had no idea how it would be if my feelings were engaged.' He looked at her, his heart in his eyes. 'But I love you.'

'You love me?' Julia groped for a chair and sat down.

'Yes. And because I love you I should be able to give you everything. I should be able to lay the world at your feet, see that you want for nothing. But I couldn't be the man I wanted to be for you. I was angry and something seemed to break. I said those unforgivable things.'

'But you came back.' He was here, there was hope. She clung to it like a lantern in the darkness. Clung on and prayed.

'A letter is a coward's way of apologising and I am foolish enough to hope that perhaps I can offer you something in exchange. I can restore you to your rightful place as an earl's daughter. I can share a great estate and the life you were born to live.'

'It isn't enough,' she whispered. 'That isn't what I need.'

Giles smiled, just a faint, rueful curve of his lips. 'I know. Those are the material things. Julia, I can protect you to the death. I can cherish you with every fibre of my being. I can love you with all my heart. Is that enough? Can that be enough? Am I so wrong to believe that you would never have lain with me, told me about your money, if you did not feel *something* for me? You sent me on my way with your heart, after all.'

She was on her feet and in his arms before she was aware of moving. 'I love you, Giles. I don't care about titles or land or money. I love you and I want to be with you and raise a family with you and never feel cold again because I am yours.'

'My darling Julia.' Giles's voice was husky, his hands as he held her, not quite steady. 'All my love, everything I am, always, for ever.'

His kiss was a claiming and so was hers in return. This would be a partnership, she thought as she held him, felt his heat through his cold clothes, the strength of his hands on her back, the beat of his heart against hers, the pressure of his mouth as he found her again. They would build a kingdom together, she and Giles. They would restore the estate, raise a brood of children who would never want for love, discover each other, deeper and deeper, every day for the rest of their lives.

A burst of cheering shocked her back to where they stood on the rag rug in front of the range. Miri and the entire household were pushing through the kitchen door, laughing and clapping.

'Captain Markham! You came back!' Miri hugged him, hugged them both.

'Actually, I am the Earl of Welbourn,' Giles said, with a most un-aristocratic grin. 'And this is my future Countess. Wish us happy?'

Mrs Smithers burst into tears, the men cheered, Miri ran out and returned with a sprig of pale greenery in her hand. 'It was the mistletoe that did it. You kissed her and realised how much she meant to you.'

Julia caught Giles's wicked look and shook her head. They had managed to do a lot more than kissing before the mistletoe appeared. She took the sprig and held it above their heads. 'Once more for luck then, my love.'

'Once more, for now,' he agreed. 'And then I am going to come in and drink a glass of whatever it is that makes you taste of wine and cinnamon and honey. But it wasn't luck that brought us together and gave us love. It was a Christmas miracle and we can find it every year.'

'For the next seventy at the very least,' she vowed as she went into his arms and the church bells rang out into the night.

* * * * *

Marriage
Made at Christmas

Sophia James

Dear Reader,

Christmas.

Christmas in New Zealand is a summer celebration and for me it's a time of family. We have long tables set up on our veranda overlooking Chelsea Bay and usually at least twenty-five people for lunch.

All the girls make the meal, the boys concoct the punch, my husband finds chairs and tables, and my mother keeps us all on track. This year we are joined by two small grandchildren, so that will add a whole new and wonderful dimension to our day.

I love the joy and the hope of Christmas, the end of the old year and the beginning of a new one. We always say a prayer for those loved ones missing and then the eating and drinking begins...

Christine Howard in *Marriage Made at Christmas* has forgotten the meaning of love until she meets a man who makes her remember everything wonderful about the season. The weeks of Advent mark the growing admiration between Christine and the mysterious American William Miller, emotions that blossom into forever as the last candles are lit.

Sophia James

Chapter One

London—late November 1816

'Is that gentleman bothering you, ma'am?'

The voice came close, gravelly and raw as Lady Christine Howard turned. A man stood there very still, his eyes a dark bruised green and his hair a lot longer than that worn by most of the men of the *ton*. A big man dressed in the clothes of trade.

Amazingly she was not in any way afraid of him and made her decision instantly. 'Yes. I've no idea who he is, but he has been following me and I can't seem to shake him off.'

'I can easily deal with him if that is what you would wish?'

'Deal with him?'

'A quick jab to the face followed by a harder one to the groin is best. It always makes them think twice next time.'

'A fight, you mean?' She suddenly felt sick.

'Well, hardly,' he drawled and smiled.

The breath simply left her body in one single and shocking realisation. He was beautiful in the way an ancient warrior might once have been, hewn by violence, a man who knew his own worth and would never let others define him;

a man unused to the sedate gossip of London society and more at home in places she would never go.

'You look pale. Here, let me help you to a seat. If it's only a talking-to you'd like him to have, I can do that instead.'

'No.' Christine did not wish for him to touch her and she moved back. She didn't want to feel his hand against her own because she couldn't trust herself to know what might happen next. 'I am quite, quite all right, sir. Do I know you?'

'Me?' Now puzzlement lined his face. 'I do not think so.'

He gave no name. He did not remember his manners and introduce himself. No, in fact all he did was remove his slouchy ill-fitting hat and slap it against his thigh. A cloud of thick dust motes blossomed and he laughed even as the late winter sun reflected in the browns of his hair.

'Horses, ma'am, I've been seeing to them. They tend to be on the dirty side, you see.'

The lilt in his words alluded to another place and one far from here. The Americas, if she could name the accent, the vowels pulled long and slow.

'You are a groom?'

'Sometimes, indeed I am.' Again that smile that made her want to reach out just to see if he could be real.

She blinked then, hard, because sense seemed to have escaped from her. Already they were back on the foot path near Stanhope Gate, a minute from the safety of the crowd. The early snow from last week lay in dirty mounds on each side of them, melting into thick mud.

'Well. Thank you for your help.' Extracting a coin from her purse, Christine went to pay him, but he merely looked at the money before taking a step back.

'I imagine England is not so different from the land that I hail from and it is a poor place that would insist on payment for the helping of a lady. It was my pleasure.'

Then he was gone, through the weeping bare branches of the willows, his long stride taking him away from her. She felt a loss that was startling even as her brother and the group she had walked with came into sight.

'Are you quite well, Christine?' Adelaide Hughes, Lady Wesley, came across to stand next to her and looked around. 'I could not find you for a good few minutes. Where on earth did you go?'

'I walked towards the Serpentine behind some trees and lost my direction. Then I felt as though a man was following me.'

'What man?' Adelaide swivelled about. 'Where?'

All about them was the quiet of the park and further afield the ruffled grey surface of wind on the water. 'Perhaps I was mistaken. Perhaps no one was there at all.'

'You do seem rather distracted, Christine. Shall I find your brother? He is talking with Gabriel just over there.'

'No. It was probably all in my imagination and I certainly do not wish for a scene.' She made a point to peruse other pathways as she spoke. Was the unusual groom still about? She almost dared not look in case she caught his eyes again. A servant on an errand for his master would be most unnerved by the particular notice of a high-born woman like her.

But still she could not quite help herself, her eyes finding him standing on a slight rise, a horse behind him now and the cheap homespun jacket he wore straining through the thickness of muscle. He watched her, caught in stillness against the tableau of a wide blue winter sky.

As her world tilted she had the distinct impression of herself beneath him, naked and writhing in the last throes of some passion she had never felt.

Was she going mad? She hadn't enjoyed the intimate with Joseph Burnley, her betrothed, all those years ago as they had snatched at opportunity and lain with each other in the barn at Linden Park. He had been rough and they had been young and the stories of lovers, clandestinely read in her room at night, had not matched in any way or form his inexperienced and fumbling promises.

Her fingers reached for the ruby and diamond brooch Adelaide had given her once as a present. *'All losses are restored,'* she had said, *'and sorrows end.'* The quote from Shakespeare had been meant to soften her grief over Joseph's death on the icy passes of the Cantabrians.

'There is only so much sadness a person is able to sustain,' she'd added, 'and you have certainly had your share.' Rubbing the ruby, Christine breathed out. Marriage might be something she could no longer contemplate, but her love of family and friends, fine cloth and good design more than made up for it.

When she glanced back again the groom was gone.

Her brother Lucien joined her a moment later, her sister-in-law Alejandra at his side. 'You look cold, Christine, so we should make our way back to the town house. Linden Park is gearing up for an unforgettable Christmas this year and I hope you'll make plans to come down to celebrate it with us?'

'Perhaps.' She tried not to make any promises that caught her within a timeframe or an occasion these days. Her business took up many hours, but it was the series of small seamstress shops that she had founded that was taking a lot more.

Almost a hundred women depended on her now, a hundred families who needed the work and the money to feed their little ones and their old people. It was as if she was the pebble dropped into a still deepness of water, all the spreading rings about her demanding attention and care, any falter or wrong decision on her behalf bringing other problems, wider worries.

She had forgotten how to laugh, she thought, remembering the lines around the eyes of the American in the park when he had smiled. Most of the eligible men in London town slathered potions of all manner upon their baby-smooth faces and fashioned ruffles of lace at their necks. The man who had frightened her and followed her had been dressed as a gentleman, too. She tried to recall his features, but failed. All she had known was a sense of menace and she wondered what might have happened had he caught her alone.

A note had been delivered last week to one of the shops in St Giles. It had warned her to desist with her charitable causes and to leave the business of manufacturing garments to men who knew what they were about. She had shown the letter to no one because Lucien was not happy with her many night-time outings and her mother was making herself ill with worry over her daughter's business endeavours.

'Your father would turn in his grave, Christine, if he knew what you were doing. Besides, any suitor who might have been interested in pursuing you would hardly be pleased with discovering your shops in the slums with the riff-raff.'

Christine breathed out firmly. Her mother was a woman from another time when independence had not been possible for a female and all happiness hinged on a good marriage. Further away the sun caught on the limed boughs of a run of deciduous trees, reflecting their paleness on the greying surface of the Serpentine. Like a silk watercolour. She wished she might have been able to go home this instant to try to render such a painterly effect on fabric. A gown of that shade would be magnificent and she had just the client for it.

Instead she was here caught in the park with layers of emotion breaking inside her: fear, lust and wonderment. Her body was becoming like one of the marionettes on strings she'd seen last month in the Haymarket, pulled this way and that from above and below. Little wonder that she was exhausted.

He'd worn a ring, she suddenly thought, the groom with the dusty hat, a ring of engraved wrought gold on the fourth finger of his right hand, and it had looked valuable.

An oddity, that, given the small sum most grooms would earn for their toil. A year's worth of labour at least and easily lost in the day-to-day workings of a busy city stable. Why would he risk such a treasure?

She wished they could have spoken for longer or that he might reappear. She wished she'd known his name or the place that he worked, if only to send a thank-you note for the aid he had given her. But perhaps he could not read? Perhaps he was married? Perhaps he had in truth forgotten her, another wealthy London lady with all the time in the world to fritter away, her sights set on the grand and titled lords of the *ton*.

A ruction sounded through the town house later that afternoon, shouting and banging, the quick run of servants and the closure of doors.

Christine sat near the window in her room with a tapestry circle in hand, embroidering the last of a series of wildflowers on to a fragile silken bodice. The quiet pastime allowed the commotion downstairs to easily travel upwards. Placing her sewing on the table, she stood. 'What on earth is happening down there, Anne?' Her maid sat with her, stitching her own cloth, though she, too, had stopped.

'Sounds like a visitor, my lady, though I don't think the master is pleased at all.'

He wasn't. She could hear her brother Lucien's voice, loud and plainly angry.

'What the hell is the meaning of this?'

'This man was following your sister, my lord, in Hyde Park and she was frightened. I thought you ought to know of it.'

Shock tore through Christine's body as she listened. The foreign tones of the American groom here in her house, here downstairs, and he was talking with her brother. Plucking her thick woollen shawl from the chair, she caught her reflection in the mirror. Her hair was untidy and the deep flush of some high emotion was staining her cheeks, but she could not tarry. If he left…

She saw that a servant had been posted at the library door as she came from the stairwell down the short corridor. 'His lordship is busy, my lady, and is not to be disturbed.'

'I know he is, Whitby.' With just a smile she moved past him and unlatched the door, closing it behind her.

Inside the scene was one straight from the pages of a dreadful novel. Lucien was furious. The American was waiting patiently as he held the scruff of the neck of the same man she had seen following her in the park, his nose now bleeding profusely. My God, why had he brought the man here? As a trophy?

'You cannot just haul anyone off the street and hurt them like this,' she found herself saying. 'There are proper channels of law to follow in England and I hardly think—'

She got no further.

'He had a note for you in his pocket, my lady. I have given the missive to the Earl.'

'Do you know him?' Lucien spoke to her now and he was livid.

'I do. This man kindly helped me in the park to find my way back to the proper pathway when—'

'Not him. The other one. The miscreant? Is he known to you?'

She shook her head in a daze, the events of her day moving almost beyond comprehension as the shifty dark eyes of her stalker slid across her. He was dressed as a gentleman, but she doubted he was one. His first two front teeth were blackened by dental decay and his face was lined with hardship.

The blood flow from his nose at least seemed to have stopped though she could see large smears on the homespun of the American's jacket. He was holding the man up off the ground, but his stance held the look of one who was not even vaguely strained by the weight.

'What did the letter say?' She asked this of her brother.

'That you were to desist from your industry in the poorer parts of London.'

Stepping forward, she faced the battered man directly. 'Why?'

It was the American who answered her. 'I have already asked him that question, my lady, and even a considerable sweetener has not jolted his tongue. I think, by all accounts, he intends to remain silent. Perhaps someone else is paying him for such confidence, Lord Ross? It might be wise for you to find out just exactly who he associates with and why.'

At that Lucien rang a bell and the servant at the door opened it.

'Get Maxwell and Smith to take this man to the cellar and lock the door so that he has no chance of escape, for I shall wish to question him in a little while.'

Another moment and that order was obeyed leaving the American groom, Lucien and her in the library, an unsettled silence all around them.

'Who are you?' Her brother sounded as if he was at the very edge of his patience.

'Mr William Miller, my lord, newly come to London.'
Mr Miller used the exact same tone as Lucien. Irritated.
Wanting to get on. The arrogance was startling.

'Who do you work for?'

'The Earl of Hampton, my lord.'

'Would he vouch for you or give you reference?'

The green eyes narrowed. 'I imagine that he would,
my lord.'

'Good. Hellaby is a friend of mine. Have you been working there long?'

'No. Only a few weeks.'

'But he knows your character?' Her brother was noticeably sizing the stranger up.

'He does, my lord.'

'I want to offer you a job as my sister's keeper, Mr
Miller. She is a stubborn woman and refuses to think her
personage might not be safe and that others should try to
harm her.'

Christine had heard enough. 'I am neither blind, mute
nor deaf, Lucien. Should I even wish to have a keeper, as
you name it—'

Astonishingly, the American groom cut her off.

'When should I start, my lord?'

'Tomorrow. At nine. You will accompany Lady Christine to any appointment she may need to keep and make
certain that whilst away from the house, she is safe.'

'I shall be here, my lord. Tomorrow at nine.' Unrolling
the dirty felt hat from his pocket, he bowed to them both
and was gone. He'd removed his ring, Christine saw and
wondered. Each knuckle on the back of his left hand was
grazed.

'I do not think...' But Lucien was in little mind for argument.

'Read this,' he said quietly and handed her the note.

It was a missive cut from newspaper, each word torn carefully to make a sentence.

Close your workshops...or else.

'Or else...what?' She didn't like the quiver in her question.

'I think it's plain enough, Christine, that you have been made into a target.'

She swallowed at his words, the fright from this morning coming back as a thickening in her throat.

'Mr Miller is strong, direct and dangerous. As such he is a godsend. He also does not stand back and allow blackmailers the space to cause mayhem. He can protect you.'

'He is a man who takes the law into his own hands.' Her words were not given as a compliment, although Lucien threw back his head and laughed.

'The law of honour and protection has its own tenets and they are ones that all good men should believe in. Unless you accept Mr Miller as your bodyguard at all times when you are away from this house you shall not be leaving it.'

'And if I refuse?'

He stooped to ring the bell and his man came in quickly.

'You won't. Bring a carriage around, Whitby, I shall be going out.'

'And the man in the cellar, my lord?'

'Will be coming with me.'

A second later he was gone.

Chapter Two

Will lay down in the space he'd chosen and watched a spider crawl across the ceiling in the glare of a single candle. The webs on each side of the wooden rafters were thick, attesting to many other inhabitants of the same ilk across the years and when the specimen above faltered, a fragile strand of silk was caught in the light as he used it to return to safety.

It was cold here and the blankets provided as shelter were thin. Heaping straw on top of the matted wool, he tried to create more warmth with the weight of it as he burrowed into the prickly horsehair mattress.

He was tired and bone-weary. From the journey, from the worry, from the unexpected encounter today with Lady Christine Howard.

She was beautiful. He'd never seen another woman like her with her sky-blue eyes and pale golden hair. She had dimples etched into her cheeks and a body that looked like it had been drawn by one of the old Italian masters—Sandro Botticelli, perhaps, or Agnolo di Cosimo.

He smiled at such grand imaginings here in the stables of Stephen Hellaby. At least there were horses around him and good ones, too. He could hear them quietly whickering below as the moon waned towards the morning. His knuckles hurt. He had sucked the dirt from the grazes, winding the broken skin in a bandage he had made from the hem of his old shirt and fastening it with a knot of frayed ends, pulling it tight with his teeth.

The noises of London were loud to ears that had known the silence and grandness of nature for so very long. The trees. The land. The white rapids of the Fall Line at Richmond where the river crossed from hard bedrock to soft sediment and then fell down towards the sea.

He missed it. Missed it all. He swallowed and breathed in deeply, reaching into a pocket for his lucky coin. The Flowing Hair dollar was struck in silver with the bust of Liberty on one face and the American eagle on the other. It had been part of the bounty of his first sale of timber brought to the coast in sweat and courage and he'd kept it safe ever since. His payment for all the backbreaking hours, the bruising and the sheer danger of it. He traced the design in the metal before carefully wrapping it and returning it to his pocket.

Christine Howard had noticed the ring he'd worn, he was sure of it. He'd have to be more careful. The anger in him made his heart beat faster and he pushed it away for it was no good to think too much. He'd learned that lesson long ago.

A dog was barking plaintively in the distance and the noise was spooking the horses. With a shove at the straw he pulled himself free from the warmth and went out into the shadowed night to make sure that all was well, his breath caught in icy whiteness as he went.

Christine watched for the American in the morning, part of her hoping he would not come after a long restless night of wondrous dreams.

Wondrous. The word made her smile and she enunci-
ated it out loud so that it fell in all of its two silky syllables,
precisely spoken. She couldn't remember once before ever
using the word, so impossibly theatrical and so pointedly
inhabituel.

Inhabituel. There was another one. In French this time,
but no less a companion for the first. She barely recognised herself as she lifted her teacup and looked again at
the clock. He was late, the American. And if he did not
come...?

She saw him then, marking out the steps from the road-
way to the front door and then to the garden at one edge of
the town house. Her brother was beside him and they were
talking. She caught their quick laughter as she turned away,
the day falling to a new low in her observation of this masculine predilection for control.

She would soon be twenty-seven and all the good years
of her life were running down to her thirties. Not old, she
knew that, but older. She had not imagined as a young girl
to be this age and left on the shelf so to speak, uninterested
in the lords of the *ton* and unable to simper and flirt.

She breathed out heavily, noting that even indoors she
could see the shadow of it. A frost sat on the windows, fingers of ice across the glass. Four weeks until Christmas,
only a few days before the start of Advent. Thirty-five days
to the New Year. She frowned at her musing, for it seemed
she had been counting down her life for years now in some
form or another. She vowed to stop it.

He was there inside before she thought he would be,
her dangerous American, his eyes today shadowed and
distant. He was wearing the homespun navy jacket again
and although the bloodstains had been washed from it, it
still looked damp. He tried to smile as he saw her watch-

ing him, but even that was wary, a labouring man brought into the parlour of an earl and feeling ill at ease.

'Would you like a cup of tea?'

'No. Thank you, my lady.'

She saw he swallowed, the skin under his neckcloth moving up and down. The serving maid who stood to one side of the room was watching him closely. In avarice or in caution? Christine wondered. He looked like a man who might slip the family silver up his sleeve if left unattended.

She liked to think these things of him this morning given the unease he had allowed her last night. If she could have, she would have dismissed him on the instant and gone to her room, but she wouldn't give her brother the satisfaction of further argument or angry outburst.

She was as stuck with the man as he was with her.

Mr William Miller looked big in the dainty over-filled dining room, his head almost skimming the door as he had come within the chamber, but he was not clumsy. He had easily stepped about the pile of books Lucien had left near the head of the table, the same felt hat he had worn yesterday in his hand.

'Your knuckles look a little recovered.'

The green eyes glanced down and he smiled. This time it was more real. 'The stable master at Hampton gave me some ointment, my lady. Camphor, I think, with lemon balm and honey.'

'You know your medicinal herbs, then, Mr Miller.'

'That I do, Lady Christine.' This time she gained the distinct impression that he was goading her, leading her on into saying something she might regret. She swallowed and finished her tea.

'I need to be in town this morning. One of my ladies is ill. What is it you would recommend as a remedy for catarrh?'

'Whisky, and a good measure of it, too.'

This time she did laugh and the sound startled her.

'She is recently turned to the church after a chequered past. I doubt such a prescription would suit her.'

'In America we sometimes used peppermint and the oil of Cyprus for the lungs.'

'We?'

'My mother.' Anger flared to be chased by grief. She doubted the American had wished to show her either emotion as he looked away, the muscles to each side of his jaw grinding together, a loss kept in check, but only just.

'How old are you?'

'Twenty-five, my lady. Just turned.'

Younger than her, then. She was pleased by it. A small triumph to lessen his hold on her 'wondrousness'.

'Is the Earl of Hampton a kind employer?'

The question on his brow deepened. 'He is.'

'Do you have another jacket?'

'No, ma'am.' Now he looked neither comfortable nor indifferent. If Christine could have named his emotion, she might even have chanced *irritated*. His left hand was jammed deeply into a fraying pocket.

'I am a woman in charge of a great team of seamstresses, Mr Miller. It would be no task at all to make you a jacket that was warmer, one that was more suited to the cold winds of London.'

'Thank you.' This was inflected at the end as if in question.

Not a man to hold a grudge, then. Not a man to stew in the juices of his own ire. She breathed out and forced a smile, hating this person she had become here in the dining room, a mistress in charge of a man's thoughts and favours. A man who did not look as if he belonged in servility at all.

Usually she was kinder. Much, much kinder. She seldom annoyed people. She was always the peacemaker, the one to calm temper and to douse argument. But the groom Mr William Miller made her different because she wanted him to fight her back, as he had done yesterday in the park before this job had been foisted upon him with all of its attendant service.

He didn't suit the role. She'd seen him look over the Howard paintings around the wall, an art collection of note as he had come into the room. He observed the pictures with a quiet eye, but the passing of his glance had been both slow and careful. As if the subject meant something to him.

'Do you enjoy art, Mr Miller?' She gestured to the paintings around them.

'I do.' No explanation or qualification of his enjoyment.

'My brother has the eye of a connoisseur in his choices. Which is your particular favourite?'

He immediately pointed to a small painting near the doorway. 'That one. Is it of you?'

She blushed, horribly. She felt the wash of red rise from her throat like fire and stain her cheeks, but she did not look away from him as she answered.

'I was six when that was done. An artist came from London to Linden Park. It was just before my father and brother drowned.'

Why had she said that? She never talked of that time to anyone. She was glad when he didn't pursue the topic, but stood there his arms tucked behind him and legs slightly apart. Watching her. A man who did not feel the need to probe and question and find out all of the disappointments inside her that festered.

She was seldom still, always busy, always moving on to the next challenge and another creative project. Often she wondered if it was her frantic energy that made her pull away from men. But William Miller was strong and sure in his own right, a man who did not need the good opinion of others to boost his confidence. He was like her brother in that way, certain and steadfast and quietly in control of everything around him.

An idea that he was laughing at her, however, crossed her disassembled mind and she stood and pushed her chair back, giving her thanks as he came to help her. She'd always appreciated good manners even under duress.

'Well, we need to be off. If you could give me a moment whilst I find my hat and coat, we will go into the city proper first and then to the East End. I have shops to see in both places. My brother said that he would also be talking with the Earl of Hampton today and asking him if you could relocate here whilst you are helping us out. I hope that will not be a problem. Someone can be sent for your things.'

'No.'

She looked up.

'I would rather collect my belongings myself, my lady. This evening. When you no longer require me for the day.'

It wasn't a request. 'Very well. I will tell the Earl.'

'Tell me what?' Lucien had come into the dining room and, helping himself to a piece of fruit bread, he slathered it with the housekeeper's last summer's strawberry jam.

'Mr Miller will retrieve his own things from the Hampton stables, Lucien.'

'Then my sister has spoken to you about living here. I hope it will only be a short-term thing until we can find the group threatening us. Hampton was sad to lose you, though he asked me to tell you that your position will be there when you have finished with us. He also said you were the best man he had ever seen handle horses.'

'I have had practice, my lord. In Richmond. It's a town near my home in Virginia.'

'Hampton said you held references from the Melton family. Is that who you worked for in the Americas?'

He nodded.

'I wonder if they are any relation to the Duchess here. Elizabeth Maythorne. She is still alive at the grand old age of eighty-seven and runs the dynasty with an iron glove. Rumour has it she has come to London just recently and this is an odd thing indeed because she has seldom ventured out of the family lands in the north for decades. But I digress,' he said suddenly. 'A room has been set aside for you in the garden wing of the town house. I think you will like it there.'

'I am sure I will.'

Lucien chuckled. 'That is what I like about you, Mr Miller. Your certainty. Too many people these days have lost their confidence, I find.' Then he was gone.

The fleeting dash of humour on the American's face both surprised and worried her. He'd almost found the measure of Lucien and that was something few people ever did. The complexity of that thought confused her further. If he was not quite the man he appeared, this Mr William Miller, then who on earth was he?

Perhaps her brother had employed a fox to watch over the henhouse, was her next thought as she brushed past him and felt a tingling awareness inside her even at the tiny contact.

London was full of noise and movement and bustle, Will thought darkly, and Christine Howard seemed to hold no sense of the danger whatsoever. Anyone could have hidden a weapon in the copious layers of clothing, anyone could have turned on her amidst the distractions of traffic and colour and noise on the busy throughway as they walked from the carriage.

Death came in a second, unexpected and brutal. One

moment this and the next one that. How could she not know this? It was as if she moved through a different world from the one he did, softer, trusting and kind.

He felt the heavy shaft of steel in the sleeve of his right arm and another lighter blade tucked into his left boot. He could hit a moving target at fifty yards easily, more if the winds were light and the sun was up. His father had taught him the trick of it and he had honed his skills in all the days since his death.

He held his breath as a man approached them just before the doorway of the second shop, letting it go only as he passed by and was gone.

'If you want to wait outside…' She watched him as she held open the door. Without answering he came within.

She had that way with her that all beautiful women seemed to innately know. It was in her smile and humour, he thought, and in a confidence that was both beguiling and irritating at the same time. For the whole morning he had wanted to take her by the arms and shake her, make her listen, make her understand that this was not a game being played and the note held by the man in the park expressly for her was no boyish prank, but a serious threat of intent.

Or else…

Her stalker had been armed, too, but Will had not told them of this. He'd easily taken the knife from the man and disposed of any resistance, but not before understanding that there were others who wanted Lady Christine Howard's shops closed down and that they were gathering to deal with her.

Life could be split between the takers and the givers. His father had told him that again and again as he had grown up. Like a mantra that his father had based his life on after leaving England, running from his demons on a ship bent for the Americas and the freedom to be whoever he wanted to become.

Will leaned against a wall and watched Christine Howard do business. She listened and she was most practised at making decisions. She smiled a lot with everybody else except him, he thought, and closed his eyes for a second. With him she was wary and prickly and distant and he wanted back the trust he'd felt in the first few moments of meeting her in Hyde Park.

The blister on his right foot hurt when he moved, the new boots stiff and unyielding, like this place, this town, this country, these people.

The Duchess of Melton was in London just as she had said she would be, then? The ring with the crest of the family felt as if it was burning a hole in his pocket but he did not dare to leave it anywhere else save for on his person. The letter that had arrived in Richmond, Virginia, last February was addressed to Mr Rupert Melton, stating the Duchess would be in London for the coming Christmas season and could be contacted at the family town house in Portman Square. It gave the address and the directions and was signed personally by the Duchess, a signature both formal and carefully penned.

Christine Howard was speaking to him now and his interest snapped back into focus.

'This fabric would suit your colouring, Mr Miller. Is it a shade you would consider?'

The thick tawny wool looked a lot warmer than the homespun cotton jacket he had on and he nodded.

She turned back to the man beside her. 'And a shirt and trousers to match, too, I think, Mr Beaton. Perhaps you might measure our client now so that we could get started.'

The elderly man nodded, a box of pins in one hand and a

tape in the other. Depositing a notebook on the table, Beaton asked him to remove his jacket and shirt.

Swallowing with the damned unexpectedness of the request, Will turned for the door, settling himself once outside in the cool of the wind, the smell of snow in the air, and finding the balance of it all.

Lady Christine was there instantly.

'Are you all right?' Her hand touched his arm as she said it, the kindness in her words nearly undoing him and the feel of her shooting want into every single part of his body. Still reeling from his panic, he faced her.

'Yes, I'm fine.' He heard a tone in his voice that was strained and awkward as plainly as she probably did but a sound from behind had them both turning as a man hailed her. A lord by all appearances and most finely turned out.

'Lady Christine.' His hand came out to take one of hers and he was looking at her fondly.

'Warrington. I thought you were up in Scotland hunting.'

'Well, I was indeed, but family matters have brought me back here and a trying day of comedy and error has just got better. Could I walk you to your carriage? Your man here may go.'

She glanced around and William caught her eyes, the faint anger in them surprising. She did not like this newcomer.

'I am sorry, my lady,' he said quietly, 'but your brother the Earl asked me to escort you home personally, so…'

He let the inference hang in the air.

'Who is this?' The question came sharply.

'A safekeeper. I have had a letter threatening my person and my brother is taking the danger most seriously. Mr Miller here is accompanying me on my business to make certain of my well-being.'

'Then as I cannot waylay you I shall bid you farewell,

though I do hope I might see you at the Canning-Browne ball on Saturday night.'

In the carriage she was quiet, though Will could see she was trying to determine exactly what to tell him. Finally she spoke.

'Each of us has our secrets, it seems, ready to pounce at the smallest of warnings, you with your reticence to have new clothing fashioned and me with my dislike of Rodney Warrington. Shall we retire to our respective corners today and call it a truce?'

Will dipped his head, hoping to hide the shock of the name, but she went on unabated.

'Warrington is the second son of a viscount. He asked me to marry him once and I refused for he is a man of strong opinion and a great deal of arrogance.'

'Sounds difficult to live with.'

'And impossible to love,' she returned, smiling now so that her dimples caught the light as deep shadows. 'He does, however, have great tracts of valuable land and much in the way of money in his family coffers should he inherit. He also has the hopes to hold a lofty title very soon so someone undoubtedly will take him as a husband and happily. Just not me.'

'Money speaks here with a very loud voice.' He had not meant to say that, but he did and she frowned. There was a certain protection in servility that he had not felt before. In Virginia it was not what you wore but who you were and he wondered at the Melton acreage. His own land covered twenty thousand square miles, reaching from the fault line on the James River back into the Shenandoah Valley. As far as a man could see and further. If he closed his eyes he could smell the clean scent of the Virginian pines and the red cedar and hear the birdsong of the striking bright cardinals in the trees at dawn.

Shaking his head, he fought for breath. He'd had to come to England. He needed to know all the things his father had not told him. He needed to bury old demons and find the truth burnt in the ashes of lies. He did not expect the promise of the phoenix, but he hoped for peace at least. Only that. A peace to lay on the grave of his father so that his spirit might find a place in the afterlife allowing him some respite from anger, some understanding that he had not found in his troubled lifetime.

'You are quiet, Mr Miller. I hope I have not exhausted you? I shall not need your services for the rest of the afternoon as I am spending the day at home, designing a gown for a woman who is hard to please. It will take a while.'

'You enjoy it, though? The sewing, I mean?'

She nodded. 'It saved me once when I was so sad I thought I could not live.'

Such a truth brought the equal measure from him. 'Horses did the same for me.'

'Then we understand each other. It is why I cannot just close the shops, you see, even though my brother would wish me to.'

She could not believe she was talking to him like this and telling him things that she had let no other person know. She was usually so very private.

'Is that what you did in the Americas? Worked with the horses?'

He shook his head and the beauty of him hit her anew with his strong jaw and his dark green eyes and his hair the colour of every brown under the sun, from gold light to shadow dark.

'I am a farmer.'

He used the present tense as though the work he did here in England was only temporary.

'Where is your land?'

'On the upper reaches of the James in Virginia, a river that flows from the headwaters of the Appalachian Mountains to the ocean at Chesapeake Bay.'

'You were born there?'

His eyes flared and shuttered. *He does not like to answer questions*, she thought. His hands were bare again today, the ring gone, the grazes on the knuckles of the left one healing. They lay unmoving in his lap and she could see in the lines of them competence, labour and strength. The nail on the fourth finger of his left hand was missing completely. An old accident, she imagined, the opaque scars running down the skin aged and indistinct.

She wondered if anyone had ever simply held him in softness and in love, that thought so shocking she turned away to look out of the window.

The street was busy, for the start of Advent was less than four days away and there were people scurrying here and there with parcels and shopping and urgency. She'd never liked the Yuletide, Joseph's death in the December campaign under Moore ruining it for her. She reached for her brooch, the strange mixture of old sorrow and Christmas joy unsettling.

'Did you celebrate the festive season in America, Mr Miller? Is it a custom there?'

He smiled and shook his head. 'Indeed it is, though my own family did not hold much time for it.'

'Well, as you will no doubt soon see the Howards love the traditions.'

'But you do not?'

His question unleashed an anger that she seldom felt. 'Is it written on my face, such distaste, or is that just a lucky guess?'

'Sorrow is a universal emotion. No guesswork in it at all, my lady.'

He did not speak like a farmer or a groom. He spoke like a man who was well educated and well read, the hidden secrets in his voice as discernible as her quiet sadness. Such a tone laid her bare.

'I lost my betrothed, Joseph Burnley, in the Christmas of 1808. In the first Peninsular campaign in Spain.'

'And he was your beloved?'

'Yes.'

There, she had said it aloud after years of inward silence and after almost a decade of trying to forget. Sometimes she could barely remember what he had actually looked like, her intended husband, but her grief seemed locked up in a heart that had never opened again. The beat of it now was heavy and fast in her chest, as though the words had hurt her flesh and loosened the channels of blood, a confession trying its hardest to thaw the hard-held kernel of deceit. A love no longer true, but still hurting.

For so very long now she had not understood herself. Even the thought of that was frightening.

The green eyes on her were soft, though, and burnished at their edges in gold. There was no criticism in them whatsoever, only acceptance. She felt a relief that was so overpowering her hands clutched at the seat beneath her so that she did not lose her balance. Why would she feel like this with a stranger she hardly knew? What was it that drew her into discarding so carelessly her more usual and secure masks?

'Once I killed a doe on the high hills behind Churchville.' His voice was quiet and measured, the burr of a strange land pleasant and unfamiliar. 'It was December and the first snows were upon us. When I slit its throat for the meat I looked up and its fawn was watching me from the shadows of pine. It was new and born far too late, or too early.' He was looking right at her, but he was a long way from London in memory. 'When I made for home the next morning I saw it following me and my mother said it was my Christmas gift from the natural world and bedded it in the stables. She died three days later of the measles alongside my father.'

He stopped and took a breath. 'I escaped the illness by sleeping with the unsettled fawn and in doing so was taught a lesson that life is entwined in death in a way that few of us can fathom. Everything has good and bad mixed within it. Their death and my salvation.'

'I am sorry.'

'Don't be for it was a long time ago. 1808. The same year as your betrothed died.' His mouth twisted into a smile that didn't come anywhere near to touching his eyes.

This man was like no other she had ever met, Christine thought, a warrior but vulnerable with it. She hoped she would not cry, not in front of him at least, and was glad to see the Howard town house when it came into view, releasing her from the confined space of the carriage.

Wishing him good afternoon, she walked up the steps and into the house, leaving him there with the footman and driver to see to the horses.

Chapter Three

She danced and chatted, dressed in a fine silver gown. Her hair had been caught in a simple chignon with ringlets framing her face and the gold of it was reflected sometimes as she swirled in the light of many chandeliers on the ornate plaster ceiling of the Canning-Browne ballroom.

Around her others gathered, many wearing all the most splendid gowns of her creation, the silks and the organza and the fine Brussels lace.

'You look beautiful tonight, Christine,' Amethyst Wylde, Lady Montcliffe, said from her place beside her. 'You look as if the cares of the world have suddenly flown from you, and the most interesting thing is that you are not wearing your brooch tonight. The one Adelaide gifted you on the loss of your betrothed.'

'I took it off this evening. I decided I had grieved enough for Joseph Burnley and I did not wish to any more.'

'Then that is the difference—you are no longer gazing back but looking forward and it suits you. I thought you might be distracted tonight, too, for Daniel said your brother has employed a man to watch over you, a guard so to speak, because there has been some trouble at your shops?'

'Indeed he has, but Mr William Miller is dangerous, quiet and troublesome himself.'

Amethyst began to laugh. 'He sounds intriguing.'

'He is a working man.'

'As I was a working woman when Daniel met me, so that fact makes him even more beguiling. Is he beautiful as well?'

Christine could hear the interest under her friend's words and only smiled. 'When you meet him I will let you decide. I know if I tell you anything at all you will twist my meaning into knots with that particular way you have of trying to find out things.'

'Well, I can see that Freddy Smythe has been hanging around you all night. Is he still trying to inveigle you into marrying him?'

'Oh, I barely listen to his words any more. I did tell him the oldest Grayson daughter was more than keen on him, though, and pointed him in her direction.'

'And Lord Greenwood?'

'I swear you must have been watching me closely, Amethyst, and if so you should know he is far too young for me.'

'He is twenty-five.'

'Well, then that is that, for I am all of twenty-six.'

'I don't think love holds such exact boundaries, Christine. In my experience of it love more…just is.'

Love more…just is.

The odd words cut across her gaiety like a hot knife through butter, slicing into truth. She wished William Miller were here. She wished she might dress him in her best velvets and silks and show him off to all the other ladies of the *ton*. She wished he might hold her in a dance close and then closer so that his breath would mingle with her own and she would be able to see again the gold chips around the edge of his dark green eyes.

The ridiculousness of such thoughts made her smile. She could not even imagine Mr Miller enjoying the narrow set of rules the *ton* made such an art form of. She, after all, was less and less inclined to enjoy them herself and she'd had years of it.

Her age tonight seemed to bear her over a threshold into a landscape that was more and more empty. She was not a young debutante, rosy cheeked and starry eyed, any more, willing to be offered on to the marriage mart like a prize to be won. She was also not a virgin.

This lack of innocence was a far greater stumbling block than she would have once imagined it could be and the wild years of her youth with Joseph Burnley now reverberated into the fact that she was ruined for marriage for ever. Spoilt and sullied.

She shook away the thought and resolved to enjoy her night. She was so adept at allowing men to reach only a certain point of familiarity before she swatted them away it had become like second nature. Mr William Miller had far exceeded that point a number of times, though, and she wondered about her tolerance with him.

William Miller. William Miller. William Miller.

What was wrong with her tonight? She needed to enjoy the spectacle and the adoration and the compliments of the lords of the *ton* without complicating it with all the things that would never be.

Love more...just is.

The strange way Amethyst had put such a sentiment worried Christine because she could see a certain undeniable truth within it.

A hush to one end of the room had her turning, though, and she watched as Rodney Warrington squired a very old lady into the room. Her clothes were of an age long past the fashion of today, but were extremely elegant and her hair was piled in a great mass of snow-white curls on the top of her head.

'It's the Duchess of Melton,' Daniel Wylde said, his tone shocked. 'She has not set foot in society for nigh on thirty years so why on earth would she be doing so now?'

'Melton?' The name was familiar. Lucien had mentioned the woman was back in town the other day and Christine fought to place the significance of the title.

'Her only son tried to kill her husband years ago. No one knows what happened to him after that, though there were rumours.'

'Rumours?'

Daniel Wylde did not sound happy as he explained. 'When the Duke died last year the Duchess refused to hand the title to Warrington as the next heir in line and sent runners to all corners of the globe to try to trace the lost son. Perhaps she has had word of him. Warrington will not be well pleased if she is successful, but what can he do?'

'Squire her as he is, I expect.' Lucien had joined the group, Alejandra on his arm. 'And inveigle himself into being irreplaceable.'

'I never liked him,' Daniel said and her brother smiled.

'I should imagine the Countess does not, either, for he is pompous and arrogant and quick to rise to anger. It is said his fabric business is not as profitable as it used to be either and that he is looking into new avenues of revenue.'

Rodney had seen their group now and brought the old woman over to them for an introduction. He looked puffed up with the importance of being the centre of attention as he gave them her name.

'My aunt, the Duchess of Melton.'

He picked Christine out first to give a personal introduction and the embarrassing attention had her grinding her teeth together in chagrin.

'May I present Lady Christine Howard, Aunt. Her brother is the Earl of Ross.'

'How do you do.' The Duchess's voice was unexpected in such a tall woman, for it was almost high in tone and unsure. Falling into a curtsy Christine was pleased to see the Duchess nod her head.

'Rodney has told me much about you, for it seems you have a dressmaking business of some note. I suppose you must think I need help in that department, but I confess I am not much interested in fashion these days.'

Christine shook her head. 'I was thinking the exact opposite in truth, Your Grace. These years could certainly do with some of your style.'

Dark green eyes twinkled and for a moment Christine was reminded so forcibly of William Miller's orbs she blinked, for his were of the exact same unusual shade right down to the gold chips on the edges.

What was wrong with her? Why would she imagine the American everywhere? Her hand reached in habit for the ruby brooch and only emptiness greeted her. Joseph was gone, dead, buried in the snowy passes between Lugo and Betanzos on the high reaches of the Cantabrian Mountains.

And her heart had stopped then. Still and dead and had never beaten again with the same certainty of precision. She was like a well-dressed ghost who flitted in and out of the lives of her family and friends, never tarrying, never sticking, always moving to the next social occasion or the newest bolt of fabric.

Her hands ran across the embossed silver lace that lay across the blue silk in her gown and she spread them over the intricacy. A touchstone. Her life. She smiled then at Rodney Warrington and allowed him to partner her in a dance that was just being struck up. He was everything she did not like about a man and as such was the very perfect choice.

He would require no careful handling, no investment. And just by dancing with him she kept all the others at bay.

Will leaned back against the stone wall in the shadows of Portman Square, melded into darkness, indistinct and formless. Always he had lost shape when he hunted and here in London on a busy street the trick was as easy as it had been in the endless forests above Harrisonburg.

The stillness claimed him inside and out, only the whisper of breath to say he lived and even that was hard to discern.

The carriage came at last, the lamps burning low and the moon as high as it would climb in the sky that night. The call of the driver, the clap of hooves on a fine set of four, the shout from inside the gates and a final stop.

She was very old, he could see that by the way the woman beside her helped her find her footing on the step-ladder and another guided her from below. Her coat was thick and her hat ornate. When she turned suddenly he saw her face there in the street light, the whitened hair, the drawn cheeks, his father's nose. The shock of it made him move, breaking cover, something he seldom did, the night's quiet letting him go, exposing him, allowing the space he inhabited to be questioned, to be watched.

He was sure she had not seen him, though, as he relaxed back into invisibility, the dappled shade, the quiet moving shadows of a small many-branched deciduous shrub. His hand shook, however, as he clutched his thigh because his grandmother was a tall woman and her bones were as strong as his father's had been.

Betrayal was an amorphous thing, he supposed. It did not always live in the skin of the wicked and bend them to its shape. The stick she clutched was black and carved. Topped with the face of a snow hawk, his father had said, and he should know for it was his hands which had fashioned it.

It was a puzzle that she still kept the thing after all the years of treachery. If it had been him, he would have thrown it far into a river where it would sink into the mud and never be found again. He'd almost done that with the crested ring, but something had stopped him. He felt the gold and its engraving in the palm of his hand; crouching with warmth, a homing pigeon close to the roost. Perhaps it was the same with her. Simply the hope of it.

History here had a way of reeling you in, bringing you back, yearning for a place and a name and a family even if you had sworn a thousand times to the heavens above that you did not want it; sworn until your eyes ran with the tears of anguish and fury.

The small party was at the door now and other Melton servants had come out to help—he recognised servility when he saw it. William smiled to himself at such a foreign familiarity and then bit down on the humour.

Here was the woman who had ruined them all, who had followed the tenets of societal pressure to protect her husband and her assets even at the expense of her only son. He should hate her, but he found he did not.

Another carriage had drawn up now and he recognised the man who alighted from it. Rodney Warrington. The arrogant second son of a viscount. His cousin.

His father had told him about those who might covet the title and he had been right in his summation about Warrington, a man whom Christine Howard had so blatantly disliked. He would need to be careful. He would need to tread with caution and sureness if he were to discover the truth about a family he had never met.

* * *

Christine walked down to the small room in the garden wing the next day to speak with Mr Miller. She knew she should not be here finding him, but after last night's ball she felt a burning need to see him, talk to him and to understand what it was about him that made her...foolish.

Knocking on the door, she waited and waited before trying again. He was not there? She cupped her hands against the window glass and peered in. The bed was made tidily, the blankets pulled into order and the two pillows stacked. A frugal room, she thought, a wooden chair by the bed, a small desk next to that and a mat on the bare floor. No frills. No luxury. A single chipped cup sat on the table, but there was nothing else anywhere that she could see.

His meagre belongings could fit into the smallest of bags, she thought, and then footfalls behind her made her turn.

'Did you want me, my lady?'

This morning Mr Miller was dressed in the same jacket, but a different shirt. The tie at his neck was changed, too. Cleaner. Whiter. Washed. He looked tired, though, the shadows beneath his eyes darker this morning, giving the impression that he had not slept well, if at all.

She shook her head. 'I was wondering how you had settled in and if there was anything you need?'

'I am fine.'

Three words that cut off further discussion and she stepped back nonplussed. Today he seemed distant and distracted, his eyes flat and wary. He added a 'thank you' as though he thought he should and opened the door.

A haversack that she had not seen from the other angle was on the floor and there was a harmonica on the chair seat.

'You play this?' she could not help but ask.

'I do.'

A book lay next to it. *The Nicomachean Ethics* by Aristotle. She'd seen the same title in her brother's library, but it was here now, crouched on the wicker seat, a bookmark made of newspaper signifying he had read a great deal of what was inside.

Everything she found out about Mr William Miller was surprising.

Seeing where it was she looked, he crossed the room and lifted the tome. 'It's the study of personal morality and an insight into human needs and conduct. The Earl lent it to me.'

'Unusual reading for a groom, I should imagine?'

At that he laughed. '*"The good for man is an activity of the soul."* I do not imagine Aristotle thought reading was an activity only for the rich.'

She was astonished. He had not only read the book, but he could quote from it?

'Who are you, Mr Miller? Really?'

The words came from nowhere, forming a space between them of uncertainty and question. She wished she might have taken back such a blunt outburst, but she couldn't. He made her cross lines and blur manners. He made her desperate in a way she hated.

His hand came up to push a length of hair from his face, the grazes on his knuckles still evident. 'I wish to God that I knew.'

Just that. Words that led to more questions for them both, no promise at all of the truth.

'No one truly knows who they are, I suppose. I certainly have trouble with understanding myself.' It was the look in his eyes, she thought later, that made her give this answer. Gratitude had a certain soft ring to it and she needed him

to know that she did not care who he was or what he was.
He was enough. For her.

Moving forward, she reached out and heard him take
in a deep breath as she did so. His hand was big and warm
and safe. She could feel the roughness of the skin and the
slight curl of his fingers around her own. A small connec-
tion and rigidly controlled, but her heart beat as fast as she
had ever known it to. She wished she could have simply
draped herself about him to never let go, but the sound of
footsteps further off had them apart before Lucien came
around the corner of the house.

'Glad to find you here, Christine. I wanted to go down
to Linden Park tomorrow for a few days and thought it a
good chance for you to get out of London.'

She knew the subtext of her brother's words. To get her
out of London long enough to find out exactly who had
threatened his family.

'Mr Miller, I hold a fine stable down in Kent and Daniel Wylde, Earl of Montcliffe, has an even finer one that
is not far. You might enjoy the chance of an outing, too.'

Lucien spoke to William Miller as if he was an equal, a
friend. He did not in any way relegate the man to the status of a servant or an employee. She was astonished at such
an easy camaraderie between the two. Perhaps it was the
books. Lucien had always been an avid reader and could
discuss the ideas within them for all the hours of the day.
She knew Aristotle and Plato to be some of his favourite
philosophers and he was probably delighted to find another
who liked them as much as he did.

William Miller nodded at her brother before looking
back at her. There was a spark of some vivid shock in the
green, desire if she might name it, and hope, the two emotions intermingled strangely. He covered them quickly.

And even though she had no true wish to travel down

to Kent she found herself assenting. She had seldom gone home in the past years, her work demanding and the thought of old memories daunting.

'Very well. I shall go and pack.'

With that she was gone and she did not look back at all as she went inside and up the stairs. Once there she sat on her bed and put her hands to her face, the tears that fell worrying and numerous as she thought of where her life had come to and what she had lost on the way.

The trip down to Linden Park was begun early the next morning, the three-hour journey broken at the posting house they always stopped at.

Christine was glad to stretch her legs, though as she followed her brother into the establishment she looked back to see Mr Miller standing with the driver and several others. He was at least six inches taller than any man around him and he was laughing, his head thrown back in the thin December sun that was catching the lights in his hair.

He had been travelling on the box and she had had no chance at all to converse with him and now she did not either. The horses needed to be watered and fed so that they might make the next part of the journey without mishap and Lucien would expect her to come with him inside to freshen up.

'Alejandra has high hopes of a Howard family Christmas this year,' her brother said beside her, 'so I do hope you can bring Mama and the boys down with you, too, when you come.'

Christine laughed. The boys were her brothers and they were eighteen and twenty-one now, hardly children any longer.

'Did you find out anything else from the man who followed me in the park when you questioned him, Luce? Do you know who it is sending the notes?'

'I have a vague idea, but it's something I need to work on. Those who blackmail others are not so easy to flush out themselves and the whole situation requires careful handling.'

'You'll tell me when you know, though. For certain?'

When he nodded she took his arm and they went into the private dining room they always used, the publican having set out food and drink for them and most pleased to find himself in the company of an earl and his family.

An hour later Christine re-joined William Miller, who stood waiting by the carriage, a bread roll in hand that he was taking generous bites of. She was glad to see he had had some sustenance at least.

'Are you enjoying the scenery Mr Miller?'

He smiled and looked at her. 'It is a soft place, England, and full of green.'

'Linden Park is the same. My brother has his stables there, but he has other animals on the property, too, sheep and cattle mostly. Did you run livestock on your farm in Virginia?'

'No. It was timber mostly.' He finished the roll and tossed the crumbs to a small flock of birds gathering at their feet. 'But my father was from England.'

Now this was new. He had not offered anything remotely personal before without question. She caught his glance and he went on.

'From the north, I think. He did not talk of his time here much.'

'Because he did not enjoy it?' she countered.

'No, because he had to leave.'

As if he had said enough he walked over to one of the

horses and checked its harness, though as the homespun
cotton on the sleeve of his left arm fell back she could see
the scars on his hand running up the skin to his wrist and
further. More questions. Other unanswered mysteries. Why
had his father had to leave? she wondered. Had he hurt
someone or worse? 'Had to leave' implied little choice and
maybe even a skirmish with the law.

She wished she could have asked him of it, found out
more about his life in the wilds of the Americas, but her
brother had joined them now and the day was passing.

'If you would like to ride inside the coach with us you
would be more than welcome, Mr Miller.' The tone Lucien
used was surprising, almost humour in it.

Mr Miller tipped his head though and politely refused
the offer, then they were on their way south to the Howard
country seat of Linden Park.

Chapter Four

The horses were some of the finest Will had ever seen. In the stall nearest him was a chiselled pair of grey and white Arabians with their arched necks and high-carried tails. Next to them a powerful Friesian stood and further down was a Lipizzan of a rare solid bay.

At home he had sold on most of his livestock before he had taken ship to England because he did not know when he would return and he wanted his horses in homes where they would be cared for. His stables had never looked like this one, though, where the best of the most elegant breeds stood side by side. Lucien Howard next to him was full of a rightful pride.

'The Ross coffers were empty for years and I could not afford even a foal offered to me by the Montcliffe stables at a reduced rate. Now with my manufacturing businesses in the north paying handsome dividends, I can.'

Will nodded. 'Why did you really bring me down to the stables, my lord?'

'I needed to talk to you alone. The man you apprehended in Hyde Park is in the pay of the Melton heir, Rodney Warrington. I can't pin anything on him, though, and when I went to see him he fobbed me off with all sorts of excuses.

I thought you might wish to have a talk with him when we return to London, to scare him off so to speak, and to make certain he knows not to bother us again.'

'More than a quiet chat, then?'

'Sometimes being a lord has its drawbacks. I used to be a lot more dangerous than I am now, Mr Miller.'

Will laughed. From what he had heard of Lucien Howard he still was as dangerous. No, there were other forces at play here, other things that were not being said.

'I have made an appointment for you to see Warrington the day after tomorrow. He is staying with the Duchess of Melton at the moment in her town house at Portman Square. Perhaps you know of it?'

William now knew exactly why he had been brought down to Linden Park.

'You had me followed the night before last?'

'By the best there is in the business and he made certain to tell me that you were good. Rumour has it that the old Duchess is looking for her lost son?'

'I, too, have heard that story.' Will gave nothing away as their glances met.

'A mystery, they say, and almost a murder? There must be lots of secrets in the house of the Meltons.'

God. Lucien Howard understood too many things to just be ignored. 'Give me a week before you say anything to your sister and then I will leave.'

The Earl of Ross put out his hand and he gave over his, the shake between them firm.

'If Christine is in any way hurt—'

Will did not let him finish.

'She won't be.'

The house was full of the joy of the season, pine boughs decorated with silver balls on the windowsills and a life-sized manger to one side of the main dining room.

Alejandra's influence, Christine supposed, for her sister-in-law held strong beliefs in the religious meaning of Christmas.

William Miller had come into the house to find her as she was planning a ride around the estate and he was to accompany her. Her hands gestured to the room as he stopped to look around, astonished by the quantity of decorations.

'The first day of Advent was on Sunday. It's a spiritual preparation for the coming of our Lord.'

Clearly nonplussed, he looked away.

'Are you a religious man, Mr Miller?'

'Not particularly, Lady Christine.'

'Surely the book on Aristotle's ethics embraces the spiritual, though, in its treatise on the ideal of happiness?'

He looked surprised. 'You have read Aristotle?'

She smiled. 'Only the title,' she gave back, 'and the first few pages. I have now probably reached the outer limits of my personal understanding of such philosophy.' When he laughed she carried on. 'The primary colour of Advent is purple, the colour of royalty some say as in the coming of the King.'

She pointed to the table. 'The wreath there represents eternity and at the end of each of the four weeks a new candle is added. The first has already been lit.'

'In anticipation of the coming?' he queried and she laughed.

'It is exactly that, Mr Miller. Remembrance. Love. Joy. Peace. A white candle in the centre will be lit last. It stands for purity.'

Purity.

The word slid from her tongue like a snake and she knew why she'd never enjoyed the traditions of Advent.

'In order that one's sins might be made whiter than snow?' His query was soft and for a moment the room simply stopped still, caught in light, and Christine was blinded by a feeling she had never known before.

Goodness, if she might name it, or hope. The very crux of the Advent teachings, she supposed, and was slightly breathless as she carried on.

'The Jesse Tree on the mantel is something Alejandra has introduced across the past few years. She is Spanish, you see, though she is more of a mix now of the English church and the Catholic one, I suppose.'

'It's from the Bible, then? From Isaiah?'

'Pardon?'

'A shoot will spring from the stump of Jesse, and a branch out of his roots.'

'I thought you said you were not religious?'

'Well, my mother had a Bible she used to read to us.'

'Us?'

'My father and me. The winters are cold in the high mountains of Virginia and I remember passages from it.'

'How big was your farm, Mr Miller? What sort of acreage did it hold?'

'Enough to live on.'

'You seldom answer direct questions when I ask them.'

'My life before England is gone,' he said softly. 'There is no point in dwelling on what is past.'

'Especially if, like your father, you did not want it so.'

He shook his head. 'No, especially then.'

They rode into the sun to the west along the river for a while and then up into the hills greened from rain and wide. Linden Park was so much more beautiful than she remembered it and she felt immeasurably free for it had been a long time since she had sat upon a horse and galloped. But although she rode well William Miller rode a lot better, a man at home on a horse and out in the open air and nature.

When they rested their horses atop the peak of a hillock looking down across the estate she remembered stopping here with Joseph Burnley. Still, even the sad memories today did not put a dent in her utter happiness.

'If you could name one thing in your life that you would want to make different, what would it be?'

'Only one?'

'It's a game, Mr Miller. I am not asking for enormous secrets.'

'I'd have liked a larger family.'

She looked at him. 'Ah, you don't have any idea as to how difficult a whole swarm of brothers can be. Be thankful you were the only fêted and spoiled child.'

He laughed. 'Is that what you think I was?'

'I don't know. You rarely tell me anything of yourself and what you do…' She stopped and felt a joy inside that was growing. 'I wish that I had met you earlier. To talk with. To laugh with. To ride with. Usually I am far more circumspect and far less chatty. At court they call me The Frozen One. I have had a flurry of marriage proposals, you see, and turned every one of them down.'

She spread her fingers as though to underline the fleeting transience of her suitors. 'I gave them no thought and so they have named me such. I rather like the title actually. It allows me some breathing space when the newest lot of hopeful swains comes a-courting.'

'You sound ruthless. A heartbreaker. Perhaps it is because your own was broken.'

He got off his horse now, easily dismounting, and came across to help her down. When he let her go she turned her face into the wind and was honest.

'It did not so much break, I think, as shut down.'

'Because the sudden loss of your betrothed was more brutal than the love you held for him?'

'You speak like Lucien, did you know that? He uses words like you, too, carefully and to great effect. Most people would offer condolences if I were to bare my heart to them, not questions.'

He moved closer. 'And is that what you want?'

She shook her head. 'I just want to be…me again. To not be frozen.'

He took her then, simply covered her mouth with his own and kissed her. Hard, rough and urgent and she dug her nails into his arms and kissed him back because this was what she needed out here in the wind and the high hills with the cold around them and the warmth inside. She kissed him until her heart sung as though all the candles of Advent were alight in her breast.

Finally he broke away, her head resting against his chest. She could hear his heart beating in the same fast rhythm of her own and was pleased for it.

'God.' He sounded stunned and she looked up. 'I would never hurt you, Christine.'

'I know.'

'But you can't want me either. Not like this.'

'I know that, too.'

'So where does it leave us?'

'Here,' she said simply and held on to him as they listened to the wind rising across the fields of clover and drifting up against them, her skirts flapping in the strengthening breeze. 'I know there are things between us that haven't been said, but for the moment let this be enough.'

She thought of Joseph Burnley and her wild unhappy days. She thought of her father and brother drowned in the river and her mother, Alice, failing to cope with life after it, shutting herself off and falling into a depression that had never left her. Not even now all these years later. She thought of boarding school and the loneliness and of

Lucien struggling to bring Linden Park into some sort of order. She thought of the dark days after Corunna when her brother was lost to them, too, and then found again with a sickness that had taken a long time to heal.

She thought of the days since William Miller had come into her life, suddenly, unexpectedly, with his beautiful eyes and his strength and cleverness.

She did not want to ever let him go. She wanted to run away with him, this moment, this second, to some far-off place where they would be alone and unknown, where convention and society did not matter and where they could be who they were together with no other interfering force.

Tightening her grip upon him, she pushed back the tears.

Hell, he should not have kissed her. He should not have pulled her into his arms and taken all that he had thought of every night since meeting her. Even now when sense and responsibility had returned he was still hard pressed not to lift her skirts and discover her, all of her, to make her his.

He had promised her brother that he would never hurt her. He had promised himself the same until some resolution of his problem with the Meltons was made clear. At home he had land, a house and some money. Here he was invisible and he had wanted it such, made it such so that he might see the lie of the land before he needed to show his hand. His mother had always pressed it upon him that his father's family was neither safe nor trustworthy, and although she had never been to England to meet them, Rupert's stories of disharmony and violence had been many.

A mistake to arrive in disguise, perhaps, but one he was stuck in now. Besides, he could hardly walk into Linden

Park and proclaim his ancestry when he did not know it himself.

He liked the pale in her hair as it blew around his face in the wind, all the colours of gold and wheat dipped in honey. In America people were tough and sunburned and danger wary. Christine Howard was nothing like that. She was kind and fragile and gentle. Virginia would make her wilt and die, the strangeness of it, the harsh differences in the seasons. No one around the mountains owned a gown that was especially made for a ball or a soirée or an afternoon tea. Nobody he had ever met wore silk.

'I should take you back for it is getting cold.' And it was, her teeth chattering against each other and her cheeks pale. Stripping off his jacket, he brought it about her, lifting the collar on her slender neck to keep the wind at bay. The homespun made her look smaller and less of a high-born lady.

When she smiled at him, revealing her deep dimples, he nearly told her it all. But he stopped himself as he thought of the first words and said others instead.

'I will help you to mount.'

When he had her up on her steed he turned away. All he could think about was the taste of her and the softness for it had been a very long time since he had touched someone in such a way.

He refused the offer of dinner with the family that evening and went straight to the stables, to his bed in the loft above the horses, where the warmth of the animals seeped upwards. He liked hearing their movements, liked the smell of them and the sound.

The housekeeper had given him a package of fresh baked bread and cheese and a tankard of ale to wash it down with and when he had finished the meal he took out the harmonica from his haversack and began to play.

Father I stretch my hands to thee,
No other help I know;
If thou withdraw thyself from me,
Ah! Whither shall I go?

He'd always loved the gospel songs with their themes of faith, repentance and salvation. He'd told Christine that he did not believe in anything today, but even that was not quite true.

He did believe in the hope of it and the deliverance. He wanted such himself and it seemed especially important now with Christmas coming and with Advent's religious messages and coloured candles. He wanted the peace, joy, love and purity that Christine had spoken of.

And most of all he wanted her.

He needed to be back in London. He needed to visit the Meltons in order to make sense of what had happened to him and his parents and he needed to make sure that Christine was safe from the threats of Rodney Warrington.

He would take up Lucien Howard's offer of an appointment for it was a way into the Melton town house that did not require any greater explanation, then he would come back to Christine Howard and tell her all of his past.

The sliding notes of the harmonica filled the air about him and the relief of making a decision as to what came next had him leaning back against the hay to begin another song.

There is a fountain filled with blood
Drawn from Immanuel's veins;
And sinners, plunged beneath that flood,
Lose all their guilty stains.

The hope of it had him shutting his eyes to pray.

Chapter Five

She had not seen William Miller since yesterday for he had taken a horse and gone back to London early on the morning after their kiss.

To run, she thought, or to hide, though Lucien was adamant that it was on his bidding he had left to undertake an important errand for him in the city.

Christine was to return alone in the afternoon, Lucien and Alejandra staying on for a day or two with their two small sons. 'To finish the decorating,' Alejandra had told her, 'so that it will all be done for Christmas when you come back again.'

Two sturdy male servants were to accompany her and her maid on the carriage box for the homeward journey as Lucien was taking no chances with her safety.

'Tell Mr Miller I will see him on Wednesday and make certain that you give him this.' Withdrawing a letter sealed in wax, he gave it over to her. 'I like him, Christine. I think he is a good man. Be kind to him.'

Astonished, she simply nodded. Lucien seldom offered his opinions on such matters and to do so now and like this was unprecedented.

'If you would enjoy for him to come at Christmas, I

am sure he will want a family meal, Christine.' Alejandra squeezed her arm with a sort of cheering joviality, her dark eyes smiling, the two small children around her feet.

Sometimes Christine thought her family caught the gist of things before she was able to. Hugging them both she made her way to the carriage and was glad as the horses were spurred on and she could simply lean back against the leather seat and think.

She would confront William Miller the moment she arrived home. She would demand some answers and find out what he meant by the kiss and also by his absence. Had he developed cold feet? Did he regret their closeness? Was he laughing at her even now, a woman who had divulged her secrets and then shown him directly that she wanted more of him?

Had she no shame? Was he at this moment packing his haversack and heading for the harbour? Her eyes went to the missive Lucien had directed her to give him. What was in that? she wondered. Her brother had impressed on her the importance of staying at home until he returned. He had made her promise that if it was imperative she attend to some business then she was to take Mr Miller with her. At all times.

Mr Miller. All her thoughts invariably came back to him and she was impatient to reach the Ross town house just to make certain that he was still there in the plain downstairs room of the garden wing.

He had gone, she thought five hours later, though his belongings still lay in a neat and tidy pile, the slouchy hat laid across the top of it.

Gone, but not left. She let out a sigh of relief and went in to ask the housekeeper of his movements.

* * *

Will had dressed carefully in his best shirt and a clean neckcloth. He had jammed his small knife down in the soft leather of his boot, though, just in case, his mother's warnings ringing in his ears.

They made him wait for a long time, sitting in a chair at the back of the house just outside the kitchen. A busy house, he determined, with twice the number of servants that the Howards employed and they all looked frantic, tending to this, seeing to that. Closing his eyes for a moment, William simply listened. To the hum of the chatter of the maids and the clanking of the pots. The bellows made a whooshing sound and further afield came the cries of a vending lad and the softer sound of horses' hooves on the road.

The music of the everyday soothed him, made him settle and he was almost surprised when his name was finally called out and he was led down a long corridor to a library of sorts, the few books within muddled and old.

Rodney Warrington sat at a large desk, a Christmas decoration at the front of it and the only one in the room. Such a contrast to the festivity at Linden Park.

'Mr Miller. I have five moments only...'

'Then I shall be quick.'

A smile on his cousin's face made him look ugly. 'Are you by any chance being facetious, Mr Miller? You do know who I am, do you not?'

'I do indeed, Mr Warrington. I know that you are a liar and a bully and I have come to warn you that the Howards will not countenance one more threat from you...*or else.*' He used those last two words deliberately and saw the answering shock on the brow of his cousin.

'The Howards are a cultured family of the *ton*, Mr Warrington, but I am not and so my personal warning shall be a lot more blunt. If I see you or your minions anywhere near Lady Christine Howard and frightening her again, I will make it my duty to personally find you and kill you. Are those words easy enough for you to understand, sir? For when your neck breaks in the skull three things happen. You can't move, you stop breathing and your body looses any ability to control your heart. It is not a quick death when administered correctly and I have had a lot of practice in the art of killing.' Will thought of his hunting expeditions up in the western mountains and smiled. 'So there it is. I would make very sure that your death was a slow and painful exit.'

Rodney Warrington stood at that, a vein on his forehead standing out in a way that looked ominous for good health. 'Get out,' he shouted. 'Leave this house this instant or I'll have you thrown from it.'

'I will leave as soon as you tell me that you understand my stated intentions, Mr Warrington.'

He kept his own voice low though he was as furious as he had ever been. If the man was to even look at Christine again, he would not be held responsible for his actions.

And then everything changed just like that.

The door to the library opened slowly and the old lady he had seen in the carriage came through it, her appearance this close more frail than it had seemed from afar and her brow troubled.

'I heard shouting, Rodney, from my drawing room. Is everything all right?'

Her eyes settled upon William, opaque and watery and her mouth simply dropped open as she stared.

'Rupert? Rupert…is that you?'

Then she fell quietly on to the rug below her in a small and crumpled heap, her skirts folded beneath her body in an impossibly neat pattern.

'Get out.' Rodney Warrington's voice rose high over

FREE Merchandise is 'in the Cards' for you!

Dear Reader,

We're giving away FREE MERCHANDISE!

Seriously, we'd like to reward you for reading this novel by giving you **FREE MERCHANDISE** worth over $20 retail. And no purchase is necessary!

You see the Jack of Hearts sticker above? Paste that sticker in the box on the Free Merchandise Voucher inside. Return the Voucher today... and we'll send you Free Merchandise!

Thanks again for reading one of our novels—and enjoy your Free Merchandise with our compliments!

Pam Powers

Pam Powers

P.S. Look inside to see what Free Merchandise is **"in the cards"** for you!

We'd like to send you two free books like the one you are enjoying now. Your two books have a combined price of over $10 retail, but they are yours to keep absolutely FREE! We'll even send you 2 wonderful surprise gifts. You can't lose!

HARLEQUIN HISTORICAL

USA TODAY BESTSELLING AUTHOR
JEANNIE LIN
Silk, Swords and Surrender

HARLEQUIN HISTORICAL

Georgie Lee
The Cinderella Governess

REMEMBER: Your Free Merchandise, consisting of **2 Free Books** and **2 Free Gifts**, is worth over $20 retail! No purchase is necessary, so please send for your Free Merchandise today.

Get TWO FREE GIFTS!
We'll also send you 2 wonderful FREE GIFTS (worth about $10 retail), in addition to your 2 Free books!

Visit us at:
www.ReaderService.com

Books received may not be as shown.

FREE MERCHANDISE VOUCHER

2 FREE
BOOKS
and
2 FREE
GIFTS

Please send my Free Merchandise, consisting of
2 Free Books and **2 Free Mystery Gifts**.
I understand that I am under no obligation to buy
anything, as explained on the back of this card.

246/349 HDL GLVM

Please Print

FIRST NAME

LAST NAME

ADDRESS

APT.#   CITY

STATE/PROV.   ZIP/POSTAL CODE

NO PURCHASE NECESSARY!

HH-N16-FMC15

the chaos as two women came running to kneel beside the Duchess, maids by the look of them and most upset.

'Find a physician.' His cousin's command was the first sensible thing Will had heard come from his mouth as other servants streamed in.

Looking at the old lady one last time, seeing her age and her infirmity and the nasty red lump appearing on her forehead, he nodded his head and left.

Outside he felt sick. Was she dead? Had he killed her? Her last words came back as a plaintive echo.

'Rupert? Rupert...is that you?'

His father's name had been Rupert. She had recognised her son in his features, a family resemblance that had been passed down across the generations. He knew this exactly because even in that first glance of a few seconds of really seeing his grandmother it was as if his own eyes had looked back at him.

He had no other true family save her. He had no other direct relative. Both his mother and his father had called Elizabeth Maythorne conniving and scheming, but she had not seemed it. She had only looked astonished and joyous as if in his unexpected coming she had found the way again. As if salvation lay in his very soul.

Will waited for a few moments on the other side of the street just to make certain that a physician did arrive and that she would be tended to properly. Then he left the square to wind across the busy streets of the city for home and the small bedroom in the garden wing of the Howard town house.

Christine would return later this afternoon and he was pleased for it but he needed a drink first to calm his nerves and the pub on the corner of the nearby street was not far.

An hour later Will knew he had underestimated the gall of Rodney Warrington. Five men had cornered him on his walk home and each held bars of steel in one hand and knives in the other.

He bent to take the blade from his boot and retracted himself into a smaller target just as his father had taught him. The men opposite were made from English softness with panic in their eyes and fear on their breath. He could smell them from here.

They had not been hewn hard like him from traversing the rock of high mountains or swimming rivers deep and wide and fast. They had not borne winters so cold a man could freeze by staying outside too long or summers that burned the very skin off your bones. They had not lived under canvas and hauled timber by river a hundred miles to the nearest civilisation or hunted in the forests for food when the trading had been poor and there was nothing left in the home larder save starvation. The toughness of Virginia had not seeped into their soul.

He came at them fast with his blade raised and took the first man in the shoulder and the second in the arm. The howls of them put the third man off though he had got in some sort of a thrust before William could parry and the pain of it made him take in breath.

'He's bleeding.' This came from the man who had circled behind, distracting him, and the sharp smash of heavy iron landed on his head. Crouching, he cut at him from below and the man lay still. Two more left, though it was getting harder. The blood from the last injury ran into his eyes, giving the world a look of red, and he could hear ringing in his ears.

The fourth man made a mistake in his eagerness after seeing the blood and Will had him upended and quiet before he had taken another breath. The last man simply ran, the sound of feet and shouting and then silence.

No, not quite silence. His own breathing sounded wrong,

shallow and shaky. He put a hand up to his face and felt bubbles coming from his mouth. Blood from his head, he thought in a strange detached way, and then the pain came in.

He needed to get home. He needed to get to Christine. He needed to tell her things he hadn't before the world turned black and still. He needed to say that she was his salvation and his joy. He needed to hold her pale small hand in his and feel the hope of her there.

He began to walk, the dizziness receding with the movement though he had to stop to be sick a few yards down the way.

That done, he began again, one foot in front of the other, a yard and then two more until the Howards' town house stood before him and he began to climb the steps.

The door was opened before he got to the top and she was there, her tears falling across his face as she knelt to him, his blood staining the baby pink of her gown.

'Sorry.' That was the only word he could get out in any coherent form before a blackness gathering in the corner of his eyes moved across his vision and all he felt was the falling.

William would die. She knew he would. No person could survive the loss of all that blood and all those wounds. The fingers on one hand were broken, too, she thought, but she could not dwell upon that. She had to get him breathing again and properly.

He would die on the first week of Advent when everyone else was celebrating the coming of a king and when all she would be thinking of was the going of a prince. Her prince. For ever.

An anger that had laid dormant for all of the years since Joseph's death resurfaced. She could not let this happen again, not with William, not with a man whose face she would never forget in a hundred years or in a thousand.

Sitting him up, she pulled back his head so that his throat straightened and the whistling noise eased.

'Bring warm wet cloths,' she shouted to the servants who had gathered, 'and send for the doctor. Tell him if he is here under ten minutes I will make it well worth his while. Andrew, come here and press down on the wound across his side and don't let up on the pressure. Mary, find ice for his head to stop the swelling and ask the housekeeper to bring me three warm woollen blankets and a hot bedpan because he is freezing.'

When this had been done and he was wrapped in warmth, she lowered her voice and sat with him, willing the calm that she had mustered only by a great force of strength to seep into him as she waited for the physician.

He came awake in a place that was so hot he could not breathe. The heat prickled across his face and his body, down his legs and even under the soles of his feet.

'Water?'

It came, small sips and cool. He needed to concentrate to swallow, close his eyes and find the movements. Then he only felt sick.

'Have another.'

Her voice. She was here with him through the darkness somewhere. He could not quite focus.

'You have had a head injury and there is a wound on your side. From a knife, the doctor thinks. You have also broken a finger on your right hand.'

He tried to make sense of the inventory and the words strung together, long complex phrases that he forgot as soon as she said them.

'You were lucky.'

Lucky. He understood that word.

'Stay with…me?'

'I will.' Now he heard a smile in her voice and he slept.

The fever racked him and had him trembling, almost sitting up with the force of the shakes when he could barely move otherwise.

How on earth had this happened? she wondered There was drink on his breath when he had returned home. Had he been in a fight in a public bar, brawling like the sailors when they came into port after long durations at sea?

She knew so very little about him, that was the trouble, but the worries mounted and she wished Lucien would come back from Kent to help her.

She didn't want others involved in case something truly terrible had transpired and the law was even at this moment looking for him. Could he have killed someone? She had found a bloodied knife tucked down the side of his boot and it was wickedly sharp.

'Please, God, let him be safe,' she whispered. 'Please let me hold him safe.'

Reaching over, she took his hand in her own, winding her fingers around his, liking the contact.

She had removed his shirt and jacket and boots, but had left on his trousers, reasoning that he would want her to do that and there did not seem any blood visible beneath his waist. His chest was well defined, his arms thick with corded muscle. A fit man who had been outdoors a lot. She could see the lines of faded sunlight where his waist met the paler skin beneath. There were scars there, too, both large and small, everywhere, old scars crossing his shoulder and his back and more running down his left arm.

This was why he had not wanted to remove his shirt at her shop in London when she had tried to have him measured for a new jacket. He had known other fights, other battles and many of them. She closed her eyes in worry. He read widely and he spoke well. He owned a farm in the mountains of Virginia and he played the harmonica. Yet life had not been easy on him or kind. Her brother Lucien had his own scars from war, but they were nowhere near as numerous as those of William Miller and she had thought them bad.

Every new fact she found out about him pointed to further questions.

She'd sent the staff to bed save for her maid Anne, who sat outside in the corridor as a sop to morality and the rudimentary observation of manners.

Her mother had taken to her bed again because she did not enjoy the Christmas season and had for years spent most of the month of December in repose. One less worry. Alice would have fretted to find her only unmarried daughter here alone in a room with an injured and half-dressed stranger.

For the first time that night Christine smiled. Perhaps her mother would have reason to be upset, but there seemed no other avenue open to her save leaving the American and finding her own bed and she knew that she could not do that.

She would never rest knowing he lay here lost in fever and sickness.

He stirred an hour later and when she opened her eyes he was watching her, sweat on his brow where the fever had broken.

'How…late…is it?'

Her eyes went to the clock on the mantel, the heavy ticktock of time heard in the room.

'Half past four.'

He then looked down. 'Who undressed me?'

'I did. Not completely, though. I left your trousers on because…'

He smiled and for the first time in hours she thought he might yet live.

'Did you…find my…knife?'

'Yes. It is here.' Opening the small drawer in the bedside table, she took it out.

'Can you put it beside…my left hand…in case…?'

He left the rest unsaid as she did as he asked, though horror washed across her. 'You think the man you fought would come here, to the house?'

He closed his eyes, but she could see them moving behind his eyelids rapidly in thought. 'I don't…want…you hurt.'

Standing, she looked around, at the ornate pulled-thread cover on the bed and the ruffled curtains at the window, at the vase of pink roses on the table and the specially scented French soap by the Sèvres washbasin.

Her life. A good life. A life of luxury and wonder and safety.

And here he was, imagining evil to be broaching such a fortress, to be coming for him or for her she knew not which, even at the dead of night with all the doors double-locked and a watchman stationed in the hallway downstairs awake. Here in one of the best streets in London.

His life was marked and marred and distrusting. So very different from her own.

'You have been hurt before?'

'Yes.'

'By whom?'

He shifted and groaned with the pain, his eyes bloodshot and weary, the growth of new stubble darkening his chin.

'Virginia was not an easy land…to grow in. There were times…'

'Who marked your back?'

'Fire. I got caught in the summer of 1806 in the bush and it came on quick…'

'And your arms?'

'Shifting timber down the James one autumn. By myself that time, for they were already dead.'

'Your parents?'

He didn't answer, but raised his right hand to look at, it frowning deeply. 'My finger isn't broken, I think. It's happened before and it hurt a lot more than it does now.'

'Who did this to you, William?'

'A man without conscience or honesty.'

'Why?'

'For so many reasons I do not even know where to begin. The start of it was all just so very long ago.'

He had shut his eyes and she knew he did not wish to speak longer, though he surprised her by asking one last question.

'When is your brother home?'

'Tomorrow.'

'Stay inside, then. Promise me you will do that, Christine, that you will not go outside. Promise me.'

He lifted his hand then, trying to find hers and she came back to him and they sat there in the light of a candle and the glow of the fire, just being quiet and alone. And Christine could not remember ever being so thankful for such a recovery. She felt peaceful and joyous and in love.

The last thought made her sit straighter than she had been.

It was true. She did love him.

He was mysterious, dangerous, scarred and strong. He was also watching over her and she had not felt that safe for such a long, long time; before her father and brother had died, before the river had taken them, before her mother had fallen into the blackness of depression and never escaped it.

William Miller brought her the light. Like a candle at Advent, the first candle, the purple one that signified a coming.

She sat as still as she could and felt the frost leave her, unfurling piece by piece from the frozen waste of her heart. She sat and watched over him until the morning came and bathed his face in beauty.

Lucien arrived before lunchtime and he had come to London alone. He found her asleep next to William's bed and he did not look at all pleased. She was glad he did not demand her answers there and then, but gestured that he would see her outside.

They left the patient entwined in the arms of sleep, his knife within hand's reach and all the implications of danger that such an action involved.

'Go to bed, Christine. You look exhausted. I will speak with you this evening.'

'You won't hurt him, though. William. You won't send him away?'

'No.' He touched her cheek then, the old marks of tears no doubt upon them. 'You did well looking after him, but I am here now.'

'I love him, Lucien.'

'I know.'

'I don't care what he has done or who he is…a murderer, a pauper, a man without much…'

'He is none of those things. I promise.'

Shock ran through her. 'How do you know this?'

'Go to bed. I will sit with him until you wake again.'

Lucien was there now, watching him, eyes as pale as his sister's, but much more scheming.

'It was that bastard, Warrington, wasn't it? He did this to you?'

'Not personally. But, yes, he probably set them on me.'

'How many?'

'Five.'

Lucien swore. 'I sent you into the lion's den myself. This is my fault. If it is any consolation Rodney Warrington is reported to have left England. Some scandal, it is said. He is escaping with his name intact to foreign shores. Rumour has it he has taken a large part of the Melton finances with him. There should be no more trouble with the shops, at least, for it sounds as if you did a good job of frightening him off. I couldn't imagine what you said to have him running like that...unless it was something you did not say at all.'

'Lucien?'

'Yes.'

'I am on my sickbed. I don't want to answer more of your questions.'

'You have a knock to your head, a badly sprained finger and a knife wound that has passed through no major organ on your side. I think you will be up by tomorrow now that the fever has passed.'

'Did you hear anything of the health of the old Duchess as you delved into your murky channels of intelligence?'

'No, why?'

'Where is your sister?' He wanted her there beside him, Christine with her quiet cleverness and her beautiful smile.

'In her bed. She looked exhausted. I promised her I would watch over you.'

'Like a hungry hawk would watch a wheat field full of mice,' William countered and heard Lucien Howard laugh.

'Or like one lord would watch another in his hour of need, William?'

Will felt a strange pull of friendship that had been so foreign in his life thus far.

'Will,' he returned. 'No one has ever called me William.'

'And was it Miller in the Americas?'

He shook his head. 'No. It was always Melton.'

Will dreamed of the past when he slept. He dreamed of his mother, born in Boston and lost in the back blocks of Virginia. He dreamed of Rupert, too, his father, his anger never truly settling until he had reached a land of wilderness and wasteland, a place that called to his wild untamed nature as England never had. A place he would not leave even in death, his remains buried under a tall red cedar high on the Appalachian slopes and far from any settlement or other humanity.

Just as he had liked it in life. People disappointed him, and he them. In the forest with the trees, breaking in land that had been virgin for all the years of the earth's existence, Rupert had found a solace he had not known before, a place that was his. His mother had tried to like it, but she had died bitter.

'If anything ever happens to us, Will, go back to England, but tread carefully. The Melton family wield much power from what I have heard, enough to see you dead if they feel you to be a nuisance.'

She had said that to him many times, once after the grass fire and again after the winter where they had nearly starved. She had said it when she lost a baby as he turned seven and another when he was nine. She had screamed it when his father had taken to him with a heavy stick after drinking too much, the homemade whisky strong and pure and a sop to his bottomless disappointment. She had sobbed it when she had bound his broken arm with the last of her petticoats and a splint made from hardwood branches that he himself had found on the edge of the forest.

He was a child of violence and of beauty. He was a child of regret and disappointment as well as the hard honest labour of breaking in fields, planting seed, hunting until the moon came up and the quarry came out and the morning brought him home.

For everything he didn't believe in, Rupert had faith in the spiritual and applied it with more gusto than was expected. Every kill had been prayed over, each soul of the dead given their proper rights to see them into the afterlife.

Will had never forgotten that lesson. Even yesterday before coming forward with his knife the words had been there, recited and honest.

For man is a creature of chance and the beasts are creatures of chance, and one mischance awaits them all.

Another of the Bible passages his mother had read and taken up by his father as a learning. Ecclesiastes, if he remembered rightly, and he usually did.

A life of two halves. Of here and there. Could he be enough for her, for Christine? Would she want what was left of him, what he'd cobbled together in the years of aloneness out there on the lower slopes of the high Appalachians?

He wished he could ask Lucien to bring him his haversack for he would have liked to have held his Flowing Hair lucky silver dollar and his golden-crested Melton ring. His whole life in two objects.

But he did not want the nuisance of asking so he turned over and went to sleep.

* * *

He was up when she came to the room that evening, his day clothes upon him and his hair tied back. She saw her brother's letter on the table, the wax seal broken. When she looked closer she saw the name of Melton in the writing, though he pushed the missive into a drawer before she had the chance to look at it further.

'You seem a lot better. Lucien said you had even eaten a substantial meal.'

'You have spoken with your brother about me?'

She frowned, not quite understanding the wariness in his tone. She felt uncertain somehow, with him, with the kiss between them, with the heartfelt confession she had made to her brother, with the sickness gone and the beauty of him returned.

'Lucien has had your things brought up from the garden room. He wants you to stay in the house from now on. With us.'

The haversack lay on the floor near the desk by the window, his hat tucked into one of the leather belts. The bag looked almost empty.

'You travel light, Mr Miller.'

'I always have.'

Christine felt a sense of trepidation creeping across her.

'Lucien told me you had been to see Warrington. I hope that your injuries are not a direct result of your attempt to warn him away from me, for Lucien said he had some hand in writing that note and I wouldn't want you hurt on my account.'

He stood and walked across to her. She was always surprised by how tall he was and how big because men were more usually her height or smaller. His right eye had blackened overnight and there was a graze on his forehead that looked worse than it had.

'You were lucky...' she began and gestured to the wounds, but he shook his head.

'I am sorry if I frightened you.'

She began to say he had not, but then stopped. She had been frightened and he had been drinking and here in the town house in London the kiss from the other day seemed a long time ago and a long way away. She wished they could have been back on the hills above Linden Park, alone and free.

'I wasn't drunk.' It was as if he could see the accusation in her eyes and she looked up at him.

'Then why?' Her brother was no angel, but he had never come home half-dead from public brawling and smelling of the liquor.

'I am not quite the man you think I am. I have family here in London, but...'

'But?'

'They do not know who I am and I am not sure if I want them to.'

Now he was talking in riddles, but as she was about to ask what he meant exactly there was a knock at the door and one of the servants came in.

'There is a visitor downstairs, my lady, that the Earl would like you both to meet.'

Christine frowned. Who would come uninvited this late and why would her brother want William to come down with her?

Ever since meeting the American she had felt off centre and she had barely sat down for a moment to her sewing. Suddenly she wished she could just for the quiet of it and the peace.

With a nod to the maid they followed her out, down the stairs and into the side salon with its wide French doors opening to the garden.

* * *

Will's grandmother, the Duchess of Melton, sat there, on the sofa, her dark blue gown making the white of her hair most remarkable and the red around her eyes more visible.

She stood as she saw him, a handkerchief turned in her fingers and a look in her eyes that Will had seen on his father's face so very many times. Dislocation and anger finely balanced across hope.

'You are Rupert's boy, aren't you? My grandson?' Her voice wavered across the last words and he heard Christine take in a breath. 'You got my letter and came?'

He stayed silent.

'I looked for your father so many times and I prayed...' She could not go on.

And he could not answer either. There was too much in the way of history between them and Rupert had made certain that forgiveness would never be an easy thing.

My own mother chose her husband over me and tossed her only son out. Told me if I did not go she would have me carried off, shanghaied if needs be. That's the tainted blood of betrayal that runs through your veins, Will. Never forget it. Never forgive.

Elizabeth Maythorne was tall and thin and very pale. Like a ghost of what he had imagined for all of those years because she only looked human now with her wrinkled hands spotted with age and the pink of her scalp showing through.

He'd lost his parents when he was just seventeen, left alone in the mountains, miles from anywhere and anyone, and if he'd cried for them he barely remembered it for there was timber to be taken down the river and sold and he was the only one to do it.

'Poor Will Melton with his angry father and his bitter mother.' He'd heard that once in a trading station when he was just thirteen. A woman had said it with a muffled voice behind her hands as he'd passed her by. 'Poor Will Melton.'

And here standing in front of him was the one who had made it such, the only correspondence she had ever sent arriving ten months ago.

I looked for you so many times. Another lie.

'My father hated you.' The words came softly even though the message in them was harsh. 'He never forgave you even as he died.'

He did not look at Christine or at Lucien as he said this because it was not his way to be so mean. He only looked at her...his grandmother, and saw the single tear that fell down one pale cheek at his news. And he swallowed.

'My husband was an angry man, too. Together they were like...poison.'

She said the last word beneath her breath and he believed her.

'I wanted my son safe and if safety was far away then that was my penance. My punishment. I just wanted him alive. They tried to kill each other, you see, more than once, and I could think of no other choice. Love forces your hand sometimes and I have regretted it ever since.'

She was crying now, the words tumbling across sobs, no pretence or defence, nothing hidden even in front of strangers. Without knowing it he moved towards her, taking her into his arms and against his chest, cradling her age and her sadness against his own; like a treasure that had been given when he least expected it. Half-warm.

She held on to him as if she might never let him go. He could feel her frail fingers around him, digging in. *Mine*, they seemed to say, and he closed his eyes and felt it, too. *My grandmother. My blood. My name. My history.* It was so much sweeter for having never had a true idea of family.

'They called me William, but I answer to Will,' he said

when she finally seemed to calm and could listen. 'William Lynton Melton.'

'My father's name,' she said. 'Lynton was my father's name. Perhaps…'

He nodded because even the hope of forgiveness was sweet and he wanted there to be an end to all the bitterness that he had lived with.

Christine went from the room with Lucien and left them there in each other's arms, the tears of the past running down both their cheeks and the promise of an uncertain future.

He was no longer just a groom. He was no longer homeless. He was no longer Mr William Miller either, but William Maythorne, the heir to the Dukedom of Melton and all the property and fanfare that accompanied it.

He would be introduced to society and fêted and claimed. By everyone. He was no longer just hers.

'You knew, Luce. You knew who he was?'

'I guessed and then he told me. The letter I sent with you outlined my summation of his history.'

'It's why Warrington wanted to kill him, then. Because he was a threat to everything he'd worked so very long for, the property and the titles. How would he have known, though?'

'Elizabeth Maythorne saw him when he went to Portman Square to visit at my request. She recognised him as her grandson, for by all accounts the family likeness is most acute.'

'She has his eyes.'

'Or he has hers.' He looked at her then and she saw sadness.

'I can't keep him now. He will be lost to me.' She had not meant to say as much, but she couldn't help it.

'Give him time, Christine, to find out who he is. Allow him the space to find you.'

'There are so many others who will want him now, his title will see to that.' She felt shattered and empty.

'He is a man who has not had a family in years. Would you not want the same chance of knowing the last relative you had if you were in his position?'

'Yes.' She had to give her brother the truth for without honesty there would be nothing left.

Will came upstairs an hour later to retrieve his haversack and she was waiting for him on the landing.

'You are leaving?'

'My grandmother wants me to stay with her and she looks so exhausted I have agreed. I will be back tomorrow to talk to you.' He put out his hand, but she did not take it. Now was not the time for pleas or tears, for Lucien was right. William Lynton Melton needed to find out exactly who he was.

'She looks like a lovely woman, the Duchess. I think when you know her better you will understand her choices, too.'

He smiled at her words and the golden chips in his eyes were as noticeable as they had ever been, burning at the edge of green.

'Tomorrow then?'

And he was gone, across the landing and down the stairs. He did not look back as he reached the bottom, but went straight to his grandmother.

He did not come the next day, nor the next, and not the one after that. She had not seen him for three whole days, though each morning and afternoon he sent a note to her explaining his difficulties, his busy meetings with lawyers and banks and those who held the knowledge of an estate as large as Melton and needed him to know it, too.

She did not send correspondence back because if he had truly wanted to come to her he could have and because she still had her pride even given the kiss at Linden Park with her words of for ever standing in the wind.

She dreamt of him, though, every night for all that time until finally Lucien and Alejandra had had enough of her moping about and insisted that she accompany them to the McFarlane ball that evening in Chelsea.

She had no heart for it, but still she did have a love for beautiful fashion and she chose her very favourite gown tonight. One she needed to give her strength and to bolster her courage.

Her maid curled her hair but did not pin it in the usual way. Tonight she left some ringlets down so that they swung about her shoulders and down her back in long waves of pale spun gold.

She wore no jewellery save for a tiny pin of rubies her grandmother had left her. It seemed fitting somehow.

And when she walked down the stairwell towards her brother and his wife she could see the surprise in their eyes, but also the admiration.

Lady Christine Howard wore a bright silk scarlet gown and he saw her the moment she came into the ballroom of the McFarlanes.

Already the room had hushed on his entrance with his grandmother half an hour earlier and it did so again as the Ross party stood at the top of the stairs and were introduced.

She barely looked real, her hair pale and her gown a frothy red, her height giving her that slender elfin look of a woman who knew her worth. And she smiled at the numerous men who came forward to take her hand and speak, though she did not linger with any one of them.

The Frozen One was how she had named herself. Tonight she looked exactly the opposite, a living flame caught under candlelight, impossibly beautiful and regal. Lady Christine Howard, an earl's daughter, and unmatched.

She had not replied once to the many letters he had sent her. He had seen her brother in town yesterday and asked after her. Busy, Lucien had said, with her whirlwind of a life.

Too busy for him?

His grandmother beside him saw her, too, and she threaded her hand through his arm.

'Ask her to dance, Will. Wait for the waltz to begin and ask her to dance.'

She'd been teaching him the steps after lunch each day, the only dance she thought he might manage with such a short tuition, and they had counted the beat together as she allowed him to partner her. Her renewed energy had surprised him, but she'd been adamant she had waited a long time to meet him and was not going to waste another second of it.

Ten minutes later when the first strains of the waltz sounded he crossed to where Christine stood and asked for her hand in the dance.

There were numerous others there, but when she caught his glance he saw the shock in it and was pleased.

He was here right in front of her, dressed in fine evening clothes that made him look different, sterner, unapproachable. She had never danced the waltz, not once in all her years of being in society, never pencilled any name on her card when it was played, never allowed another to hold her close and still because it reminded her too forcibly of all she would never have.

But tonight she took William Maythorne's hand and allowed him to lead her to the floor and the crowd parted as they went, the whispers of gossip all around them, behind the fans and the hands and the watching eyes.

She could not care. She did not look at anyone save for him, the dark blue of a new jacket stretched across arms that had seen toil and endurance and hardship. The cut of his beige breeches was the height of fashion and the leather was shiny in his silver buckled shoes. He was the new Duke of Melton, a high title commanding much respect. His place here was cemented into the very centre of manners and convention.

When they were in place on the dance floor he simply turned and took her into his arms as though she was meant to be there, as though she fitted.

'You look different,' he said quietly as they stepped into the waltz.

'So do you,' she returned as she followed him. 'And for the life of me I cannot see you learning to dance like this in the wilds of Virginia.'

He laughed then and the ice broke and it was as if they were back on the hill above Linden Park, the wind in their faces and all of the world before them.

'My grandmother taught me each day for an hour. She said I should only manage it with a woman who cared. For me, I think she meant, someone who might forgive my mistakes and see instead the endeavour.'

'You did not come and I waited.' She bared her soul to him in such a truth.

'I love you, Christine,' he returned, just like that. She could barely believe he had said the words here so unexpectedly in the middle of a crowded ballroom, but then he went on. 'I have loved you since the first moment I saw you in Hyde Park.'

Her fingers tightened about his own, holding on to the impossibility, to the wonder. Speechless.

'I could not come because the estate is a large one and every moment of my time had been accounted for. I also thought, perhaps...' He stopped.

'What? What did you think?' She'd found her voice again, the shock in it easily recognisable.

'That you might not wish for all of this. The title. The responsibility. The sheer hard work of it.'

She could not quite understand what he meant and frowned.

'As my wife. As my duchess. I want to marry you, Lady Christine Howard, and if there was room on this floor to get down on my knees and properly ask you then I would.'

She stopped then, simply ceased to move in the middle of the dance in the middle of the floor in the scrambled melee of others and under the light of the numerous chandeliers.

'Yes,' she said and then repeated it just to make sure that he had heard. 'Yes, I will marry you, Lord William Lynton Maythorne, Duke of Melton, and as soon as you can make it happen.'

Around them people whirled, but it was as if they were the only ones in the room. She saw him breathe out in relief, she thought, and look across at his grandmother.

'She knows about us?'

'I told her that I would marry you. She was more than pleased.'

Christine felt a flash of relief. 'Can we leave, Will? Can we go somewhere to talk?'

'Or to kiss?'

'Or that.'

His smile was beautiful, bound up in the knowledge of understanding someone truly. Her soulmate and her friend.

'I can take you home to Melton House. My grandmother will act as chaperon. We could have some privacy there.'

She liked the way his arm came around her waist as they walked from the floor, the engraved gold ring twinkling on his finger.

The Melton crest. Her first clue and then so many others following it. Lucien came and joined them as he saw their wanting to leave.

'You said you would never hurt her, Melton. Make certain that you don't. I expect you home by one, Christine. I'll be waiting up.'

Will spoke then. 'I plan on seeing you tomorrow, Lucien. I need your blessing on a union.'

Her brother tipped his head. 'At eleven, then. I'll open a bottle of my best brandy.'

In the carriage the Duchess looked as though she would fall asleep the moment they got home, her eyes closing for long moments and then opening as a street light impinged on the darkness or a noise came close.

Once inside the house she simply excused herself, but not before kissing Christine's cheek.

'My grandson will have the most beautiful Duchess of the *ton* beside him.'

When she was gone he poured them each a drink and blew out half the candles on the mantel in a large salon off the main front hallway.

'Scarlet suits you, Christine. A lady of secrets.'

He was not laughing at her, rather he was asking a question. She knew all of his secrets and now she must tell him hers.

'I am not a virgin.'

'Well, neither am I.'

She smiled. Sometimes she forgot he was from a world so far from her own.

'Here things like that matter…to men…I mean…to husbands.'

'Why? You were engaged to Burnley. In Virginia a promise is a promise. How were you to know he would die before he could honour it?'

It was all so easy suddenly. For years and years she had worried about something he had given only a fleeting moment's worth of notice to and the relief of it was exhilarating.

When he sat on the sofa she came on to his knee and his arms came around her, holding her close.

'My first bedding was with a prostitute in a brothel in Hampton. It's a sea port on the Atlantic just outside Chesapeake Bay. I'd gone there when I was seventeen to meet a man who had promised to buy my timber at a good rate so I was feeling…successful, I suppose.' He smiled. 'I went with the arrogance of a young lad, the taste of independence heady.

'She asked me into her room and… Well, the back county wasn't a place where you'd find a young lady easily, you understand, and while this one wasn't exactly young she was…generous to me. At least I thought she was.'

'And after that…' Christine could scarcely believe he would bare his soul to her and she liked it. His honesty and his ease, all the stumbling truths of a youthful initiation gone wrong. Like her own.

'I left with my mother's Bible passages ringing in my ears and went back to the mountains.'

With care she placed her arms about his neck and kissed him, liking how he opened his mouth and found hers with a stealthy and undeniable push.

No quiet token here, but the full-blown ardour of a man

who wanted something back from her and was not going to settle for otherwise.

'You even taste scarlet,' he said a few moments later, his finger tracing a pattern on her neck above the silk. 'I could drink you in for ever, but if I am going to make an honest woman of you I want it to be soon. I can apply for a special licence, a way of quickening things up. If you agree to it we could be married on Friday.'

Two days away. When she was a young girl she had imagined her wedding to be complete with a cast of hundreds. She had imagined the most intricate wedding gown in the land with a long trail of cream lace and a veil of silk that fell to her ankles. She had conjured up the flowers and the jewellery, the chapel and the food, all unmatched, all expensive, all in such very good taste.

And now instead of that grandeur she would be happy to be giving her vows in her scarlet gown and her hair undressed if needs be, with barely another accoutrement.

It was love that was important, the love between them, the absolute ease of it. For the first time in her life she did not want to be elsewhere and rushing. She only wanted to be here with him.

'I love you, Will. You have made me whole again.'

They were married on a Friday morning in the second week of December in a tiny chapel in Knightsbridge.

Amethyst and Daniel Wylde were there as well as Adelaide and Gabriel Hughes.

On Will's side his grandmother sat with Alejandra and Alice, her mother's insistence in having a place in the hurried wedding gratifying.

It was a small celebration, but just as she wanted it, and Will smiled at her as she came down the aisle on Lucien's arm.

She had made her own gown of cream satin and decorated the bodice in Brussels lace. A simple design. Her hair was dressed in a loose chignon because she knew her husband-to-be liked it that way best. Around her head was a garland of the smallest winter-white peonies laced in sage ivy.

And when their glances met Christine felt happiness burst into warmth and life around her heart.

Much later in the ducal bedroom at Melton House her new husband placed the garland of flowers away on an oaken desk and used his fingers to spread her hair across her shoulders, the curls softer now and falling longer.

'You have hair of spun gold,' he said, 'and your eyes are like the shade of blue only seen in a mountain stream running shallow.'

She smiled. Her ardent admirers in the *ton* had not thus far found such images to liken her to. Their compliments were of a far more mundane variety. 'I'd like to see Virginia one day. I'd like to see the place that raised you.'

'Then I will take you there, my beautiful wife.'

'You think I am? Beautiful?'

'I know it and so did every other man in the McFarlanes' ballroom.'

'It was the scarlet gown, I expect.'

'I like this one as much.'

His hands slipped the straps of satin off her shoulders so that her skin was seen pearled in the light, almost see through, he thought, as he kissed the expanse beneath the curve of her neck. He had wanted to do this from the very first moment of meeting her, there in the park against the light and the grey of the Serpentine.

Perfect skin without marks or marring.

His mouth dipped lower and he cupped the flesh of one

breast, the size fitting into the palm of his hand. The nipple had hardened and was sweet when his tongue swept across it and sweeter still as he began to suck.

He was not as inexperienced as he had let on, his forays down from the mountains to the various trading posts filled with the promises of many willing women, but after the first one he had been selective and careful and he had never seen another so fine and long limbed as Christine Howard. No, Melton, he amended. The Duchess of Melton now. His wife.

She smelt like rain, fresh and distinct, with hints of meadow and flowers. And sunshine, too, the heat of her against him melting away caution as he brought the rest of the satin across her stomach and her hips and then it fell, pooled at her feet in a quiet whoosh of fabric.

Beneath the gown was a gossamer-thin petticoat, each edge trimmed in soft lace and then it was gone, too, until she stood finally in white stockings and blue garters with velvet ribbons to hold them up.

Every fantasy at night he had ever dreamed up in the ridge on his rough bed did not equate even nearly to this reality. She was slender and shapely and fragile. She was nothing at all like the women he had slept with before, those draped in homespun cloth with their bodies shaped by work and by the elements and by hardship which was as much a part of life on the mountains as breath.

He was suddenly shy of his own body, with its scars and its history. The broken arm that had never quite straightened after his father had belted him, the nail missing from the third finger on his left hand when he had caught it splitting wood. A knife wound in the thigh when he had gone down to the seaport of Hampton after receiving his grandmother's letter to arrange a passage to England.

Even their wedding rings underlined the difference between them. Hers a single diamond flanked by rare blue garnets, his a wide band of white gold. Plainer. Larger. More utilitarian.

'Love me, Christine, and let me love you.'

Her fingers came into his hair, cradling him like a mother might her child and pressing him closer.

'I do and I will, my love. It's for ever.'

She felt him move against her in a way that was no longer quiet and measured. It was as if her words had unleashed something in him far more primal and desperate. He was breathing faster and his heartbeat raced against her own, until the rhythm of both synchronised and matched.

'Let me have you, sweetheart. Let me make you mine.'

His hand slid lower into the very warmth of her, in between her legs and then up into the wet centre that throbbed at his touch, his finger inside her now, thick and hard.

And she wanted him to take away her choice, to plunder and seed and own, to lie there and know the sheer beauty of possession and passion, to understand that in giving there is also a taking, and a price.

The price of love.

The waves began small at first and then they raged against the barriers of her flesh.

'What is happening, Will, here with me?' Alarm warred with ecstasy, but still she needed to know. Those first and fumbled promises with Joseph Burnley had been nothing like these ones primed in fire and shock. She suddenly could not breathe properly, could not take in enough air to fill her lungs, all logic gone with the feel of him inside her stroking and seeking.

'You are so wet.' His words now. Was that good or bad or something else entirely? She cried out as the release took her, feeding off one wave until the next one built, until her body lay stretched with the want of it, the silken mysteries of the flesh.

He was magic and unknown, the throb of her lifted now on to hardness, on to him and a new belonging, a thickness that filled her completely and made her press in to gain closeness.

'Shh.' He gentled her now, as he might have comforted his horses, his hand at her neck stilling her and then his mouth holding her to the passion as he pushed in further, into the very centre of her where she could feel only pleasure and a welcomed core of loss.

Loss of herself. Loss of her body as it joined deep with his, slick and wet and hot. No little loss either, but a growing burning need that dissolved into an ache of release until she cried out and her nails dug into his hard-hewn muscle, clinging to hold him there, to know the magic of for ever, to mark him as he had her.

He pushed harder now and faster and then he too stilled, his head thrown back so that the corded muscle and veins of his throat were blue with tension.

She felt his seed, spreading, hot, deep in the fertility of her womanhood, easing the swollen bruising, branding her with himself.

And finally he collapsed on top of her, though he rolled even as she felt the weight, joined together, his eyes meeting hers.

'Thank you.' His words, husky and raw, the accent softer tonight, almost lost.

'I love you,' she gave him back, and saw the spark of it in his eyes, too, green and gold and smiling.

Much later she sat with him in the moonlight spilling in through undrawn curtains, both sated from their lovemaking as he played her a tune in the darkness, close and quiet.

The harmonica rose against the night and fell with the melody, a gospel song, she thought, a song of redemption and salvation and love.

Like the Advent promised. She smiled and cuddled in, the Christmas spirit with its hope and joy so close.

The tune had changed now and the first drifts of 'Silent Night' filled the room. All was calm and bright and beautiful in her world, and it felt as if it was only them in the entire universe, a small pocket of warmth and love and truth.

'I think I was always waiting for you, Will,' she said as he took a drink from his glass on the side table. Whisky, she thought, from the wedding luncheon and fine. 'But I was waiting on the other side of the earth until you came for me.'

'Perhaps then it was all meant to be, my love. My grandmother's letter that brought me here, Warrington's greed that helped me meet you, even Rupert's anger that he could never quite control. It's like a story winding down to a happy ending.'

'Just us,' she answered and he put the glass down and she settled beneath him, the heat on his breath promising exactly that.

Linden Park was alight with the colour of the season as the last candle of Advent was lit with all of them present. The Dowager Duchess of Melton had come to stay as had her mother and her two brothers so that this year it was an occasion for the complete family, much to the delight of Alejandra Howard.

On the floor behind them in the dining room bursting with decoration and pine boughs and sweet treats of all different natures, her two small nephews played with crinkled paper and a special ball of *papier-mâché* that Alejandra called a *piñata* and swore it was filled with delicacies.

Above them on the walls the portraits of her father and

her lost brother watched them, too, each frame bedecked with colourful ribbon and a part of this family whether in life or in death. Remembered and celebrated.

No one is ever lost, Christine thought. *No one falls into obscurity if they are still in the hearts of those alive who love them.*

She took Will's hand under the table and felt his fingers come around her own.

Family had its ups and its downs, its good and its bad. But in the end it was what Christmas was about.

A time to make peace, a time to restore love, a time of redemption and new beginnings.

Like hers and Will's. Like Elizabeth Maythorne, who had taken the smallest of Lucien's children on her lap now and was singing to him a song from her past, years and years old and still beautiful.

The white candle, the final offering of Advent caught, flickered and flared amidst the wreath of greenery, its light cast across the table.

Purity.

Breathing in, she leaned across to her husband and wished him a very happy Christmas.

* * * * *

Cinderella's
Perfect Christmas

Annie Burrows

Since Christmas (for me) is all about family,
I'd like to welcome Tommy into ours.

Chapter One

'I'm entitled to Christmas Day off,' said Mrs Hughes, planting her hands on her hips. 'And nothing nor nobody is going to stop me.'

'I wouldn't dream of it,' said Alice, taken aback. 'Nor do I quite see how I could.' She had no authority over anyone at Blackthorne Hall. Never had, and never would.

'I know you bin ill,' went on Mrs Hughes, wagging her head. 'But you ain't as ill as what you been making out. Not this last couple of days, at any rate.'

Suddenly Alice couldn't meet the housekeeper's eyes. Mrs Hughes had been the only one to come up here to her room, regularly. Only she had known exactly how sick Alice had been. Neither Aunt Minnie nor Uncle Walter had come near. Her cousins had only hovered on the threshold once or twice and that had been to let her know how angry they were.

'It's just typical of you to contract the influenza at the most inconvenient moment,' Naomi had said. 'We're bound to catch it if we have to be cooped up in the coach with you all the way to Caldicott Abbey.'

'And end up sneezing all over the Earl of Lowton,' had

put in Ruth for good measure. 'Which will put paid to our chances of getting him to fall for either of us.'

Alice had kept the reflection that he wasn't likely to fall for either of them anyway to herself. The widowed Earl was bound to have the pick of society's beauties, if he ever decided to marry again—and her cousins were no beauties.

Not that it was going to stop them from doing their utmost to entrap the poor man. It wasn't every day that girls like them received invitations to the same house party where such a high-ranking man was the guest of honour.

She'd shivered. Half from the chills running up and down her spine and half at the prospect of having to watch her cousins carry out the plans they'd been hatching ever since they'd heard that an earl had agreed to spend part of the season with the old friend from his schooldays who now owned Caldicott Abbey. Hadn't the poor man suffered enough already? According to the gossip, there had been some sort of scandal surrounding his first marriage, which had meant he'd been obliged to live abroad in a state of penury. Even after his wife had died, the rift with her aristocratic family hadn't been healed. So that when he had succeeded to a title of his own, and could have returned and taken up his rightful place in society, he'd been in no hurry to do so. And now he was about to spend his first Christmas back in England under attack from two of the most avaricious and determined husband-hunters in the county.

'I just hope you don't transmit your horrid complaint to the servants,' Ruth had scolded from the doorway, on seeing that shiver. 'They'll be sure to pass it on to us. And I shall end up with a nose as red as yours, which will put paid to any hope of getting the Earl to fall for me over Christmas,' she'd said bitterly.

'It would be just like her,' put in Naomi, 'to develop

an inflammation of the lung, or something. Just when we need her most.'

Needed her to fetch and carry. To tend to their clothes and help them change, and do their hair and generally be at their beck and call. As well as suffering all the other slights and indignities that were the lot of poor relations when visiting grand houses. Neither guest nor servant, she wouldn't really belong anywhere.

Just once, she'd like to have the liberty to celebrate Christmas herself. Paid servants like Mrs Hughes got a day off, or a gift, or a bonus of some sort. And their masters attended parties and balls and feasts.

Why not poor relations? Was it really too much to ask?

And that was when Naomi had uttered the fatal words. 'You had better hurry up and get well, Alice Waverly, or we won't be taking you with us.'

They'd really leave her behind? There was actually a chance she could escape the relentless drudgery—and at Christmas to boot?

It had sounded too good to be true. Nevertheless, she hadn't been able to resist the temptation to fake a dry, hacking cough if she heard anyone walking along the landing, and speaking to Mrs Hughes only in a faint, croaky voice. And, miraculously, no order had come for her to get up and pack her things. Just to be on the safe side, she'd stayed in bed until she'd heard the carriage bearing her aunt, uncle and cousins go rattling down the drive.

'Not that I'm blaming you, mind,' Mrs Hughes added, rather less severely. 'I can see exactly why you'd want to be spared *that* sort of Christmas. Only you are up to looking after yourself now. Aren't you?'

Guiltily, Alice nodded her head.

'Just as I thought. But look at that sky.' The housekeeper waved one arm in the direction of Alice's bedroom window.

Alice could see thick, brownish clouds roiling over the moors.

'Jem says it's going to snow real bad before the day's out. He come over just now special, to warn me that if I wanted to get over to my sister's place I'd better go quick smart, or I won't be getting there at all. Not on foot.'

'Well, then of course you must go,' said Alice, suddenly understanding Mrs Hughes's disquiet. Jem was Uncle Walter's shepherd. And something of a weather prophet. If he said it was going to snow so much that nobody would be able to travel anywhere on foot for the next few days, then that was exactly what would happen.

'I *am* going,' said the housekeeper. 'Only, well, I won't be able to bake those pies as I promised you before I go. Nor even start mixing of the cake.'

'It doesn't matter, Mrs H.,' Alice assured her. And she almost meant it, because she'd never really been able to believe in the cake and pies in the first place. She could still hardly believe her luck at being left to her own devices for more than a whole week while the family went off to celebrate Christmas elsewhere as it was. One miracle at Christmas was more than anyone could ask for.

'Susan can cook, a bit. And Billy can do any fetching and carrying as wants doing. You will be fine,' said Mrs Hughes, as if to reassure herself as much as Alice.

'I am sure I will,' said Alice. 'You get off and enjoy your visit to your family.'

Not five minutes later, Alice heard the kitchen door slam. She went to look out of the window, but the frost was too thick for her to see out. She pulled her sleeve down over her wrist and rubbed a tiny square through which she could peer down to the back lane. Sure enough, there went the crown of Mrs Hughes's bonnet, distorted by the shawl she'd tied over it, bobbing along on the other side of the hedge. And not a moment too soon by the looks of things. Tiny flakes of snow were already starting to swirl past her window.

She gave a little laugh of sheer delight. She was alone in the house, apart from the scullery maid and boot boy. And therefore free to celebrate Christmas however she chose.

She wondered what Susan could cook. She couldn't wait to find out. She shucked the eiderdown she'd wrapped round her shoulders, draped it neatly over the foot of her bed, and made her way down to the kitchen.

Susan was leaning with her back against the sink at which she spent the majority of her day, her arms folded. Several strands of lank, greasy hair had escaped her mob-cap and straggled across her sullen face.

'Mrs H. told me that Jem warned her of a blizzard, so she had to leave before we're cut off,' said Alice. 'And she told me that you would do the cooking while she's away.'

Susan's eyes took on a wary look.

'I ain't allowed to do no more 'n stir soup and gravy. Or chop things.'

'But wouldn't you *like* to have a go at making something?'

Was there a flicker of interest in the girl's eyes?

'After all,' Alice pointed out, 'Mrs H. is supposed to be training you up as a kitchen maid.' It was the condition on which the orphanage had sent her to Blackthorne Hall.

'It will be good practice for you,' she said, as a further inducement. Susan was the third scullery maid her aunt and uncle had acquired this way since Alice had been brought here. According to Mrs Hughes, they always ran off once she'd taught them enough for them to find work elsewhere.

'Mrs H. won't let me help meself to things out of the larder.'

'You won't be helping yourself,' Alice said. 'You will be fetching out ingredients to make meals for me and Billy.'

Susan's eyes flicked in the direction of the boot boy, who was gazing out of the window at the whirling snowflakes.

'Billy would be very impressed if he could see you presiding over the stove,' said Alice, hoping that the scullery maid's infatuation with the boot boy might, for once, come in handy.

Susan slouched over to the larder, leaned up against the open door and folded her arms across her stomach again.

Alice followed, to see what provisions the cook-housekeeper had left. The shelves looked depressingly bare. She couldn't help looking at the empty space on the lower shelf, where, if it hadn't been for the threat of a blizzard, there might have been a couple of pies and a cake.

Though it wasn't as if she'd ever had a pie baked especially for her, before. So how could she complain about the lack of one now? She was well used to existing on everyone else's leftovers. At least she wasn't going to have to do *that* this Christmas. For the first time since she'd come to live at Blackthorne Hall, she could choose exactly what she ate.

Provided that Susan knew how to cook it, that was.

'I dunno,' said Susan hesitantly. 'I could…only…Miss Alice…' She shifted from one foot to the other. 'You won't tell Mrs H. it was me as took things out of the larder? Only I don't want to be accused of being light-fingered and lose me place.'

Conditions might not be all that comfortable for a scullery maid in Blackthorne Hall, but Susan had nowhere else to go. 'I tell you what,' she told the anxious girl. 'You need only point to what you want to make our meals and *I* will bring it out of the larder. Then we can both truthfully say that I was responsible.'

Susan shot her a sly grin. 'That'd work.' She scanned the

shelves. 'I could make us all a suet pudding. Suet's easy. Just mix it and boil it.'

It wasn't a pie, but a suet pudding would at least fill them up. 'That sounds wonderful, Susan.'

The girl brightened up a bit more. 'I'll need some flour.' She pointed to the bin. 'And suet,' she added, as Alice went to fetch the brass scoop with which to measure out the ingredients. 'Raisins,' she added daringly. 'And spices…'

Alice hesitated. It was starting to sound as though Susan intended to do more than mix and boil a simple pudding.

But then why shouldn't they take what they could to feed themselves? Nobody was going to give them anything, not even though it was so close to Christmas.

There might be hell to pay when her Cartwright cousins returned, and they discovered she'd been helping herself to expensive ingredients from the larder.

But in the meantime, they might as well enjoy themselves.

'Susan, that was delicious,' said Alice some time later as she pushed her empty plate away. After putting the pudding on to steam, Susan had taken the ingredients that should have gone into the pies and made them into a sort of hash. Meanwhile the wind picked up, turning the snow into the blizzard Jem had forecast. Before very long they couldn't see much more than a foot from the kitchen window. It was just as well Mrs Hughes had set out when she did. With the way the wind was blowing, the snow would be settling in drifts, so that it would be hard to distinguish hedge from ditch, never mind make out the road to her sister's farm.

Inside the kitchen, though, it was warm and cosy. And Alice was indulging in a rebellious fantasy of carrying a bucket of coal up to her bedroom and lighting a fire, while there was nobody here to forbid it. Oh, how lovely it would be to sit before it, basking in solitude. How luxurious to air her clothes before putting them on.

Billy's face looked as if he was imagining something equally pleasant, as he sat watching the snowflakes whirling madly beyond the window.

'That pudding what's boiling now,' said Susan, proving that she, too, had been busy with her own plots and plans, 'will serve for dinner, won't it?'

'It certainly will,' said Alice. She was looking forward to sampling the experiment she'd helped create and which was releasing delicious aromas into the kitchen.

'With custard,' said Susan defiantly. 'I'd like to have a go at making custard.'

'We ain't gonna live on pudding till Mrs H. comes back, are we?' said Billy.

'I'd like to see you make any kind of pudding,' said Susan. Face flushed, she started clearing the empty plates from the table. 'You can't do nothing, you can't.'

'I make the fires and clean the boots,' said Billy truculently.

'And today,' Alice said to him firmly, 'you will be washing the pots.'

'That's *'er* job,' he protested, jerking his head at Susan.

'Not today,' said Alice. She sympathised with Billy, but it wasn't fair to expect her and Susan to do all the work. 'Today, Susan is the cook. Have you ever seen a cook do the dishes?'

Just as Billy opened his mouth to protest, there came the sound of someone pounding on the front door.

Susan screamed and dropped the plates. Fortunately they landed on the table, so there were no breakages.

'Whatever are you screaming for?' asked Alice, puzzled.

'Burglars,' she cried.

'Don't be silly,' said Billy scornfully. 'Burglars don't

knock on the front door. They climb in at night, through the winders.'

That turned out not to have been a very sensible thing to say, since Susan screamed again and looked wildly round at the windows.

'Come to murder us in our beds!'

'That's even sillier than your last remark,' snapped Alice. 'Since we are none of us *in* our beds.' And to be completely truthful, Billy didn't even have a bed. At night, he spread a rug under the kitchen table and slept there.

'Nobody up to any good would be out in this weather though, would they?' said Billy, casting an anxious glance out of the window.

'I don't know where you two get your horrid ideas from,' said Alice. 'Billy, just go and open the door, will you please?'

'I ain't allowed to show meself to visitors,' he retorted.

'I thought you agreed with Susan that they must be burglars,' she couldn't resist pointing out. 'Not visitors.'

Billy stuck his hands in his pockets and thrust out his lower lip. 'Burglars or visitors, it's all the same. I ain't allowed to show meself to nobody what comes in at the front.'

'Oh, good grief.' She was about to explain that surely the rules could be relaxed while Mrs Hughes and the family were away when the pounding on the front door started up again.

'I suppose I'd better go,' she said. She probably was the only one qualified to deal with whoever was out there. Neither Susan nor Billy had the training to greet a genuine visitor to the house. Nor would either of them dare stand up to anyone who really was up to no good.

She got to her feet, pausing only to take up a shawl from the hook by the door that led into the front hall. Not only was the kitchen the only room in which there was a fire now, but the direction from which the wind was blowing would mean that the moment she opened the front door, a good deal of snow was likely to swirl inside.

The thick iron bolts which fastened the front door shut were heavy and cold to the touch. She wrapped the shawl round her fingers after a bit, but it still took her a further minute or two to work them through the tight-fitting loops.

But the moment she lifted the latch, the door burst inwards, thrusting her backwards and to one side as a cloud of snow and two large men carrying muskets barged inside.

Chapter Two

For a moment Alice was so shocked all she could do was gape at the intruders. She'd told Billy that burglars couldn't possibly knock on the front door, but what kind of men would burst in like this, carrying weapons?

'We saw your light,' said the taller of the two, taking another stride into the hall.

Behind the men were two enormous horses which could have been of any colour, they were so densely covered in snow. As the men advanced, the horses too inched forward, as though intending to follow the humans into the house.

She couldn't help retreating a step, wishing she'd paused to pick up a poker as well as a shawl before she'd left the kitchen. Though what good one poker would be against two burglars armed with muskets she couldn't think. Especially the dark, dangerous-looking one who appeared to be the leader. His face was hard. His eyes were cold as steel. His mouth an uncompromising slash chiselled into a firm jaw.

'There's nothing worth stealing here,' she said.

'Stealing?' Captain Jack Grayling frowned at the girl in the drab brown dress and shawl. 'Why should you think we have come to steal anything? We just need shelter. For the children and the horses.'

'Children?' Now it was the housemaid's turn to look confused. Which perhaps wasn't that surprising, considering he was carrying Harry inside his greatcoat, while Sergeant Hopkins had Isabella tucked snugly inside his.

He supposed he couldn't blame her for being a bit scared. She was only a little slip of a thing, who'd struggled to even get the door unbolted. He'd listened impatiently from the doorstep, wondering if she'd ever get the squeakily protesting bolts undone.

She'd probably be less wary of him if she could see that he was telling the truth about the children. So he unbuttoned his greatcoat and motioned to Hopkins to do likewise.

Her dark eyes widened at the sight of Harry, who was clinging to his neck like a monkey. Then flashed with what looked like outrage.

'You took children outside in this weather?'

He flinched. He'd half hoped that the moment she saw his son, she'd apologise for ever thinking he could be a criminal. Instead, she'd hit on the very thing he'd been berating himself for these past several hours.

'It wasn't snowing when we set out,' he said to soothe his own guilty conscience more than through any need to explain his actions to her.

'Not much, leastways,' added Hopkins.

One good thing had come from her flash of anger. It had completely demolished her fear of him.

'You'd better bring the children into the kitchen,' she said. And then, at last with a hint of apology, 'It's the warmest room in the house.'

Not exactly the apology he'd hoped for. But at least she was no longer treating him as an intruder, but a guest.

'If you wouldn't mind taking your little girl now, Captain,' said Hopkins, 'I'll see to getting the horses into shelter. If you can point me to the stables, miss,' he addressed the little housemaid.

'Go round to your right,' she said, 'and follow the path until it goes under a gated arch. The stable and coach house are just across that yard. Only—' she frowned '—I'm sorry, there's nobody to help you with the horses. Mr Bayliss— that's the coachman—is away, you see. He's taken the family to a house party. Nobody will be back until after Twelfth Night.'

She then sucked her lower lip into her mouth, briefly chewing on it in agitation. As though she wished she hadn't blurted out the fact that the owners of the house were away. While he was still trying to think of the best way to reassure her, Hopkins continued.

'We tried that way before, but the gate was locked.'

'What?' She looked confused, briefly. And then her face cleared. 'The back gate isn't locked. It just tends to stick a bit in damp weather. You need to give it a hefty shove.'

'Had we really been ruffians,' Jack hastened to point out, 'we would have kicked the gate down in the first place, rather than coming all the way round to the front of the house and knocking on the door.'

She reared back as though he'd struck her. Then she lowered her head so that a hank of her dark brown hair slid forward, obscuring her face.

Dammit, he hadn't meant the remark as a rebuke. He'd just been trying to reassure her that they meant no harm.

'And it doesn't matter about the lack of a coachman,' he continued, deliberately gentling his voice. Because, according to his in-laws, the way he delivered every remark as though it was an order barked out across a parade ground could be intimidating. 'Sergeant Hopkins is well able to see to the horses. Provided there is fodder and straw for them?'

'Well, I suppose there must be,' she said, raising her head and tucking her hair behind her ear again. 'That is, I don't really know.'

'If the coachman is worth his salt he'll have provender for his own livestock ready against his return,' put in Hopkins. Then he adjusted his hold on Isabella and held her out to the Captain.

'No!' All trace of wariness vanished from the housemaid as she sprang forward. 'His coat is covered in snow. If he takes the little girl she'll get soaked. Let me take her.' She held out her arms. Even though she was such a slight woman, he didn't think she'd have any difficulty carrying his daughter, since Isabella herself was little more than a bundle of clothing and a mass of golden curls. Provided Isabella would permit it, that was. She didn't take to strangers easily. But the maid was right about his coat, so he nodded. 'That's very sensible of you. My thanks.'

'It's nothing,' she murmured.

Nothing? It wasn't nothing. She'd stood up to a man of whom she'd been terrified not two minutes ago, in order to protect a child. Not many servants would have the nerve.

Isabella barely reacted as Hopkins handed her over to the maid. And even though she opened her eyes, they looked alarmingly vague.

'Please hurry and close the door, Sergeant Hopkins,' the maid said, rather sternly. 'We need to get the little ones warmed up as quickly as possible.'

Hopkins snapped to attention, looking as though he barely refrained from saluting before striding out and shutting the door carefully behind him.

'Come on,' said the little housemaid. 'It's this way to the kitchen.' She turned and set off along a short passage that led deeper into the house. The place wasn't as big as it had looked on their way up here. It was its position at the top of the hill that had made it look so imposing. It was certainly built to withstand whatever the elements threw at it, rather than for beauty, with its tiny windows and thick walls of grey stone. And therefore, to his soldier's eye, it had looked the perfect place to shelter from the snowstorm.

'It's the only room with a fire, I'm afraid,' she admitted. 'What with the family all being away, we had no reason to light one in any of the better rooms.'

'That's fine,' he said. 'So long as I can get my children out of the storm.'

She glanced over her shoulder, frowning down at the musket he clutched in his free hand.

'We didn't mean to frighten you,' he said. 'We were just so desperate to get in out of the snow, I never thought what effect our muskets might have. I have been on active duty until very recently, you see, and therefore in the habit of carrying a weapon to hand when travelling through unknown terrain.'

She raised one eyebrow in disbelief, as though regarding his decision to travel armed through Yorkshire as the height of absurdity.

But then she'd never walked into an ambush. Seen men mown down because of the carelessness of their commanding officer. And, yes, this might be England, but who was to say the roads nowadays were free from armed robbers? Better to be prepared, than risk the safety of those in his care.

'If you saw the light from our kitchen window,' she said thoughtfully, 'you must have been travelling along the road that winds through the valley to Tadburne.'

'Tadburne?' He frowned. 'Never heard of the place. We were on our way to stay with some friends for Christmas. They live just outside a place called Mexworth.'

'Oh, Mexworth. Yes, we aren't all that far from Mexworth.'

'So I wasn't wrong to think I could reach my destination in an easy day's ride.' He sighed with relief. 'We *would* have made it if not for the snow. It blew up so suddenly, and fell so thickly that within half an hour we couldn't tell what was road and what was moorland.'

'It does tend to blow up suddenly in these parts,' she said kindly.

'And blows over just as quickly?'

'Um, no, sorry. According to Jem—he is our local weather prophet and he's rarely wrong—it is likely to keep on snowing for a couple of days. I don't think it will be safe for you to continue your journey. Not with the children, anyway.'

'No matter.'

'Well, you might change your mind when you hear that the only servants who haven't gone away to visit relatives for Christmas are the scullery maid and the boot boy, who cannot do so, since they came here from the orphan wing of the workhouse in Mexworth and therefore have no family to visit. And that the larder is almost empty. I'm afraid you are going to find conditions here a bit, um, Spartan.'

They reached the end of the passage and the maid gestured with her shoulder for him to open the door, since she had her hands full of Isabella. There was an awkward moment when they shuffled round each other in the narrow space. He couldn't help breathing in her scent, which was slightly floral. And very appealing.

He stepped past her swiftly, banishing the rogue thought about her feminine appeal in self-disgust. He had no business reacting to females at a time like this. He needed to check if conditions really were as bad as she had implied. Focus on his children's needs.

He examined the room, noting the closed stove which was pouring out heat and the delicious scent of something simmering in a pan on its top. A young girl was cowering behind an even younger boy, who was puffing out his chest in an attempt to look as though he wasn't scared. Both were dressed in clean, if simple clothing.

'This isn't my idea of Spartan,' he said, at least it wasn't compared to some of the hovels in which he'd taken shelter in the past. 'I've been a serving soldier all my adult life, so this looks to me like a most commodious billet.'

'Susan, Billy,' said the housemaid, stepping into the kitchen behind him, and shutting the hall door. 'This is Captain…er…'

'Grayling,' he said. Because until very recently that *had* been who he was. And it had been his identity for so long that he wasn't ready to let it go. Not until he absolutely had to. Which was why he'd told Hopkins not to 'my lord' him when the lawyers had given him the news that, through a series of unfortunate accidents to men who hadn't had the foresight to marry and beget heirs, he'd inherited a title and a fortune.

And because he just didn't feel like an earl.

And because he shuddered at the thought of these people bowing and scraping and calling him 'my lord'. It would be far more comfortable for everyone if he remained Captain Grayling for however long he had to stay here.

'And his children,' she was saying, while he was still justifying his decision to be a touch economical with the truth. 'They were out in the storm and saw our light. They need shelter.'

Susan and Billy looked at his children, and their faces, too, went from trepidation to disapproval.

'This would happen, the first day I have complete charge of them,' he muttered, as he propped his musket by the door and removed his hat.

The maid, who should have known better than to question a guest in her employer's home, said, 'Your first day in charge of your own children? How can that be?'

'I left their mother in England, after Corunna, so that she'd never have to suffer the hardships of life on the march again,' he found himself saying, though it was none of her business. He banged his hat against his knee in irritation, as much as to dislodge the snow. 'Since then they have been with her parents…'

What the devil was he doing, blurting all this out to a complete stranger? The snow must have got into his brain, or something. And was melting his common sense, the way the snow that he'd just knocked to the floor was oozing into the cracks between the stone flags.

'You have been serving abroad?'

He nodded, absurdly relieved that all she showed on her face was sympathy. 'I only sold out very recently. Not so much need for me now that Wellington is pushing up through France. And besides…' He glanced down at the little boy clinging to his neck. 'Other priorities,' he finished shortly.

She nodded, as though coming to a decision about him. A favourable one, if he was any judge.

'Susan,' she said, turning to the other maid. 'Why don't you fetch some cushions from the front parlour and put them on the floor in front of the stove? Then the children can warm themselves in comfort.'

'Mrs H. will have my hide,' said Susan.

'Mrs H. would ask you to do the exact same if she was here,' said his little housemaid firmly.

His little housemaid? Since when?

'Billy, pull a chair up to the stove in the meantime, would you? So that Captain Grayling can sit and warm himself.'

As Susan flounced from the room, Billy grudgingly pushed a kitchen chair closer to the stove. Captain Grayling knew that he ought to offer the chair to the housemaid, since Isabella was like a dead weight in her slender arms. And yet exhaustion, or something he couldn't define, had him meekly walking to the chair she indicated and sinking down on to it in gratitude. The maid came to stand next to him, so that Isabella was as close to the fire as Harry.

There was a moment's tense silence, during which Billy stood staring suspiciously at him, while his children, poor mites, must have been wondering what new horror their long-absent father was about to inflict upon them.

'You haven't told me your name,' said the maid presently to Isabella, who was lying limp in her arms.

'It's Isabella,' he said, since he hadn't yet heard Isabella say a single word and wasn't at all sure she could speak. 'And my son's name is Harry.'

At this point Harry struggled from his father's lap and made a stiff little bow.

The maid smiled and complimented him on his manners, but they didn't please Captain Grayling. At least, not the way they would have done if he'd seen any spark of real life in his son up to now. He was like a little marionette, drilled into saying and doing the correct thing at all costs. By God, if he'd known that leaving him with his grandparents would have resulted in having his spirit crushed like this…

The greasy-haired maid, Susan, came back then, with a couple of cushions and a knitted blanket. She eyed the fist he'd clenched in his lap as his mind had returned to what he'd found at Meerings and tossed the cushions to the floor in front of the stove from a safe distance.

''Ere,' she said. 'Now the bairns can sit down comfy and toast their toes.'

Harry held out his hand for the blanket. 'I shall take that, thank you, miss,' he said stiffly. Then he knelt on the cushions and turned to look up at the sweet-smelling housemaid. 'I can take care of my sister now,' he said firmly. 'If you would just place her on my lap.'

The moment Harry spoke, Isabella started to squirm out of the maid's hold. She very sensibly didn't attempt to restrain her, but rather sank down to her knees so Isabella could toddle over to her big brother. Harry enfolded his sister in the shawl as she clambered into his lap. She laid her head on his shoulder, then gave a little sigh, as if in relief that she'd come to a safe and familiar place.

'What a good little boy, to take such care of his sister,' said the maid who'd been holding Isabella, in evident surprise. He knew how she felt. Most boys of Harry's age would regard girls of any age as targets for pranks and teasing. Not defenceless creatures in need of protection.

Not that he intended to let his son think he disapproved. It was about time the lad heard some words of praise and encouragement for a change.

'He knows it is his duty to look after those smaller and weaker than himself,' he therefore said. 'That is what the man of the house does.'

And then Harry glanced up at him in surprise. And disbelief.

Which smote him to the core.

Chapter Three

Alice only wished someone had taught Uncle Walter that a man's primary function in life was to *protect* those weaker than himself. Then he might not have ended up the way he was.

'Susan,' she said, determinedly bringing her mind back to the task in hand. 'Everyone will warm up faster if you could make them hot drinks.'

Predictably, Susan pouted. 'We got some milk we could heat up for the littl'uns, what I were going to use to make the custard. But what can we give the men?'

She had a point.

'I'm sorry, but I don't have the key to the tea caddy,' Alice explained to the Captain. It was on Mrs Hughes's belt, with all the other keys to the house.

The corner of his harsh mouth lifted just a fraction. Of course, he was remembering her assumption that he'd come here to burgle the place. If he was really a burglar, then the lock on a tea caddy wouldn't keep him out. He'd pry it open with…with a bayonet, or something. Or simply smash the flimsy lid with the butt of his musket.

She felt her face flush under his sardonic gaze.

But then, fortunately, Billy spoke up.

'Mulled ale,' he said.

Alice broke free from the look in the Captain's eyes that had made her feel as though they were holding a silent conversation, and turned to Billy in surprise.

'I seen Mr Bayliss make it when he's come in from driving Sir Walter home from market in cold weather,' Billy explained. 'He heats a poker and sticks it in his tankard.'

Alice wasn't at all sure it was a good idea to break out the ale and serve it to two strange men.

But the Captain looked decidedly heartened.

'If you could fetch me two tankards of ale, and set a poker heating in the fire, I can do the rest. And,' he said as Billy made for the larder, where Mrs Hughes stored the ale, 'perhaps you wouldn't mind taking my coat and hanging it up to dry somewhere?'

'O' course, sir,' said Billy with what looked like—but, no, it couldn't be, could it? Not willingness?

She'd never seen him obey an order with anything but sullen resentment before. But then, he'd scarcely taken his eyes off the Captain's musket since he'd come into the kitchen. And once the Captain stood up and threw off his heavy greatcoat, those eyes went positively round in awe at the sight of all the gold braid and shiny brass buttons glittering on the man's scarlet jacket.

Though she could hardly blame him. The Captain was an impressive sight.

She'd never been this close to a man in uniform before. She'd occasionally glimpsed officers from the militia who'd been training nearby swaggering along the high street. With boys like Billy scampering along behind them like a pack of slavish hounds. She'd thought them all very silly.

And yet she couldn't help thinking that Captain Grayling's jacket did look rather splendid. Those buttons, marching down the front in double ranks, made his shoulders look broader, and his waist look more slender, too.

And she'd already noted the way his light brown hair was cut in a style that was remarkably flattering, the moment he'd removed his hat.

As Billy backed away, the coat held reverently over his forearms, Alice took herself to task. The Captain might have a certain sort of attractiveness, but only a fool would start admiring a perfect stranger just because his jacket fitted exceptionally well and he had a good haircut. And, she reminded herself, he was by no means perfect. He'd made his children undertake a journey in appalling weather. Children who didn't appear to trust him. They were huddled together on the cushions, taking comfort from each other, rather than looking to him. Which made her wonder if, in spite of one or two signs to the contrary, he was the kind of man who expected others to obey his orders without question. Like her Uncle Walter.

But then she noticed that his jacket was wet. As were his white cord breeches.

'You are soaked through,' she observed. 'And covered in mud.'

'I beg your pardon,' he said stiffly. 'My main concern was keeping the weather off Harry. And the snow was drifting. We lost our footing once or twice, ending up in ditches instead of finding the road.'

And yet he'd managed to keep both the children dry, if not completely warm. He'd also expressed remorse about accidentally exposing them to a blizzard. Which told her that whatever mistakes he'd made with his children were not due to any hardness of heart.

'Nevertheless, I apologise for dirtying your floor, and your furniture.'

'That isn't what I meant,' she retorted, appalled that

he'd thought she was making a complaint. 'I meant that you must be cold. If you don't get out of your wet things, you might take a chill.'

His expression thawed, just a little. 'I am unlikely to take a chill,' he said. 'If the winters in the Peninsula failed to harm me, a couple of hours in an English snowstorm are unlikely to do so. I have a strong constitution,' he said with a wry twist to his lips. 'However, I do have a change of clothing in my saddlebags and would be grateful to get into them when Sergeant Hopkins brings them in. If you would not mind showing me to my room?'

'Oh, um…' said Alice, clasping her hands together at the waist. 'I'm afraid that won't be possible. I mean, showing you to your room, that is.'

Captain Grayling turned to look at her, raising one rather imperious eyebrow.

'I told you that we are the only ones left in the house. That we are only keeping this one room warm, since there's nobody to haul coal or logs up and down the stairs.'

The eyebrow went down. Actually, both of them did.

'I don't expect you to wait on us. Hopkins and I are both able to do any heavy work required.'

'Oh, it isn't that. Not entirely. It's just…well, I really daren't offer any of the family rooms for your use while the family is absent. And there is no guest room.' Uncle Walter hated having strangers in his house and did all he could to discourage them. 'If people come to visit, they have to put up at the Blue Boar in Tadburne. And dine there, too, as often as not. But I was thinking that perhaps you could make use of the front parlour. It backs on to the kitchen, so it will not be as chilled as any of the other rooms, anyway. It will heat up far quicker than any of the bedrooms.'

His eyebrows lowered still further. Into a veritable scowl.

'You had better let me see it,' he said, tersely.

'You had better remove your boots first,' she insisted. Even though she felt terrible about not being able to offer him and his family proper hospitality, she still didn't dare let him march over the best carpet in damp and muddy footwear.

His eyebrows shot up again. But then he looked down at his dirty boots and gave a brisk nod. 'Is there a boot jack somewhere?'

'Outside the back porch.' She pointed.

He went across to the kitchen door, then through it to the porch. Harry followed his movements with narrowed eyes. The little girl just carried on sucking her thumb, drowsily.

Captain Grayling soon returned, minus his boots. And socks. At least, they weren't on his feet, but in his hand.

'Is there somewhere I can hang these up to dry?' he asked, holding the much-darned items aloft.

Her stomach gave a funny little lurch upon seeing his bare feet. It proved very difficult to tear her gaze from them, in order to walk to the kitchen window, where the handle to the drying rack was located.

'My thanks,' he said as she cranked the handle to lower the rack.

As soon as he'd draped his sodden socks on it, she raised it back up, swiftly, hoping he'd put her glowing cheeks down to exertion.

'I feel as if I'm raising my standard,' he said as he watched his socks mount jerkily towards the ceiling. 'It's making me start to feel quite at home, since that's always among the first things a soldier does when setting up camp.' Since he addressed the remark to his children, she assumed he was trying to help them get used to their predicament.

'Harry, you won't mind looking after your little sister while I go and get into some dry clothing, will you?'

The little boy lifted his chin and met his father's questioning eyes with a look that was all steel.

'I know,' said the Captain. 'It is what you have been doing all along, isn't it?' He bent and ruffled the boy's short flaxen hair. Then bent closer and murmured, 'Things will be better now that I'm home, my boy. That is my solemn promise.'

Since she was fairly certain he hadn't wanted anyone but his son to hear that last remark, Alice kept her face as blank as she could, though his vow melted away the last of her doubts about him. Of course the children acted as though they didn't know him. He'd been away, fighting for his country. By the sound of it, for most of their young lives. He was trying to do his best for them now, even if so far he had been making a bit of a hash of things.

'Lead on,' he said to her, a rather bleak expression on his face. 'I am now ready to reconnoitre.'

By which she assumed he meant he was ready to take a look at the front parlour to see how it would suit. So she took him there.

He came to a halt in the doorway, his eyes flicking over the sofa, the high wing-back armchairs grouped round the hearth, the writing desk under one of the windows and the rather dreary pictures on the walls.

'I know it looks a bit gloomy,' she said apologetically, 'but the fact that the windows are too small to let in much light means they don't let in many draughts, either. And it will look much cosier once Billy gets the fire going. And once we draw the curtains. Honestly, when the family are at home, this is where they spend most of their time during the day, because it is the easiest to heat. I think it's because it's on the more sheltered side of the house.'

She petered out in the face of his stern expression. But then, to her immense relief, he gave a brief nod. 'This will certainly do as a place to change my clothing, but you are also suggesting we all sleep in here, is that correct?'

She nodded, too ashamed of the way Blackthorne Hall was run to admit it aloud.

'Well,' he said, taking a step into the room, 'I have slept in worse places. Do you at least have spare linen? Pillows?'

'Yes,' she said on a rush of relief. 'And I can probably find a couple of mattresses, too.'

He grunted. 'I think, given the circumstances, that it would actually be better for us all to sleep close together tonight anyway. The children are…' His face stiffened, as though regretting expressing so much.

'I know. They must be frightened, after having such a horrid day,' she said. 'They are bound to be much happier if you all stay together, while they are being obliged to stay with strangers.'

Something flickered across his face, before he turned from her, went across to the fireplace, and bent to examine the kindling in the grate.

'Oh, Billy can see to that,' she said.

He looked at her over one shoulder. 'I'm perfectly capable of lighting a campfire myself,' he said gruffly.

'I'm not disputing that. But you are, after all, guests in this house and…'

'Guests who are not permitted above stairs,' he said, reaching for the tinderbox. 'Guests you mistook for brigands,' he added wryly.

'Yes, well, I'm sorry, but if you will go banging on people's doors with muskets…'

'Yet you took us in,' he said, striking a spark. 'For which I am so grateful that I hope you will no longer regard us as guests, but as…' he leaned forward to blow the smouldering kindling to life '…an extra pair of hands about the place. Or two.'

Flames leapt and crackled through the twists of paper and one or two of the smaller chips of wood began to smoke.

'You are certainly very handy,' she admitted. And not at all like most men she knew. Instead of demanding everyone drop everything in order to serve him and make him comfortable, he'd accepted their limitations without complaint and set to work with a will.

He leaned forward and blew again, drawing her eyes to the way his breeches strained over a very neat posterior.

At which moment a noise from behind her alerted her to the approach of Sergeant Hopkins. He had a saddlebag slung over each shoulder and a rather mocking expression on his face. She flushed guiltily. What on earth had come over her? She didn't ogle men. Especially not their behinds. No matter how trim they were.

But how dare Sergeant Hopkins mock her?

'Don't come in here with those muddy boots on,' she snapped, furious with him for catching her behaving so badly.

'We have fallen into the hands of a regular termagant,' said the Captain, looking over his shoulder at her with a grin, so that she knew he didn't really mean it. 'No muddy boots permitted in her front parlour. Not even mine,' he said, wiggling his toes. 'You'd better go and remove your offending footwear, Hopkins. Leave the packs in the doorway and I'll fetch them in and start getting our clothes aired,' he said, getting to his feet and striding towards them.

With a huff, Sergeant Hopkins dropped the saddlebags on the floor and stomped in the direction of the kitchen.

'You will need something to drape your clothes over, to dry when you get your wet things off,' said Alice as he came to a halt right beside her.

'And there I was planning to throw them over the good furniture,' he said with a teasing glint in his eyes.

My, but he was tall. And broad.

And she was all alone with him. And his feet were bare. Which suddenly seemed highly improper. She didn't know why. Perhaps it was the playful look in his eye when he'd wiggled his toes.

Or the look in the Sergeant's, when he'd caught her looking at his Captain's behind.

Whichever it was, she was starting to feel very…very… *wrong*. The Captain's children were in the kitchen. Which meant he must be a married man. So she had no business admiring the fit of his breeches, or the shape of his behind, or the arch of his feet, or to respond to the teasing note in his voice, or the glint in his eye, or his nearness. Besides, it wasn't the kind of thing she ever did. She had never been interested in men, not even if they were in uniform, and seemed very capable, and didn't shout and bark orders and make her feel as though she was an infernal nuisance every time she drew breath.

Good grief, had she been infected by Naomi and Ruth's husband-hunting fever? She'd had to listen to endless prattle about their idea of the perfect husband during the past few weeks. She'd disagreed with them, in her head, about the need for a title, or wealth, or position, thinking it would be far more comfortable to live with a man who was kind and generous. Perhaps that had been her mistake. She shouldn't have argued with them, even privately to herself. She should have let all the talk wash over her. Kept herself clear of it, the way they'd stayed clear of her the moment she'd started sneezing.

Which reflection brought her back down to earth. She might be mooning over the Captain, but he would certainly never do more than tease her. Her fist closed over the handkerchief in her apron pocket as she tore herself away from him and made her way back to the kitchen. It reminded her that though it was no longer running, after two weeks of constant sneezing and coughing, her nose was red and raw.

Besides which it was utterly ridiculous to think of the Captain as a prospective husband. Even if he wasn't already married. She'd long ago accepted the fact that with or without a red nose, she had nothing to attract a man. No money, no beauty and no charm. She shrank into the background like a little mouse whenever she went into company. And it wasn't only because Aunt Minnie had warned her there would be dire consequences if she tried to push herself forward. She hadn't specified what the dire consequences would be, but anyway, Alice hadn't ever really been tempted to 'push herself forward'. Because she'd known what the outcome would be. If she'd ever started fluttering her eyelashes, or twirling her hair round her fingers, or simpering whenever an eligible male came near, they would think she was desperate and rather ridiculous and they'd either pity her or sneer. The one thing they wouldn't do would be to propose. Not to a girl without a dowry.

She paused with her hand on the kitchen door-latch, unwilling to enter the kitchen and face the others until she'd calmed down. She might have no dowry, but she did know how she should behave. She took a deep breath and let it out slowly.

Despite propriety, how could she help admiring the Captain's physique? She had eyes, didn't she? And they told her that he was a magnificent specimen of manhood.

He was also the most decent man she'd ever met, as far as she could tell in the half-hour she'd known him. And she didn't meet many men. So it wasn't surprising he set her heart fluttering a little, was it? There was nothing wrong with that, as long as she didn't start getting silly ideas.

Having delivered that little lecture, she opened the kitchen door and marched in.

'Susan,' she said, 'would you please take a couple of clothes maidens into the parlour, so the Captain can air his fresh clothes, then dry out his wet ones when he takes them off? I need to go upstairs and raid the linen closet.'

'I'm doing the custard,' Susan retorted. 'Can't stir custard and go fetching and carrying.'

'Oh, of course, well, get on with that then. Where's Billy?'

'Sergeant Hopkins told him to clean the muck off his and the Captain's boots, and stuff them with paper to get them drying,' said Susan with a tight smile. 'And to hop to it. So Billy hopped to it.'

'Goodness. Billy hopped?'

'Like a little rabbit. All shiny eyes and twitching whiskers. Just coz the Sergeant has a musket and a fancy uniform. Men,' she finished on a sniff.

'Well, I'll just…' She waved her hands in the direction of the scullery, where the maidens were kept, along with all sorts of other items of cleaning equipment.

As Alice struggled to disentangle one maiden from another, she realised that spending all that time in bed, eating only the few meals Mrs Hughes had the time to bring her, had seriously depleted her strength. It didn't help that the contraption she managed to wrestle into the hall kept on unfolding itself as she dragged it to the parlour.

She paused to push a strand of hair from her sticky forehead. If carrying one wooden clothes maiden had made her break into a sweat, how on earth was she going to fare hauling mattresses down the stairs?

She'd have to ask the Captain if either he or Sergeant Hopkins would help her. Even though it went against the grain to treat guests like beasts of burden, he had said she should regard them as an extra pair of hands. And she could certainly do with them.

Having come to that decision, she started the tricky job of manoeuvring the maiden into the parlour whilst holding open the door. She ended up propping the door open with one hip and swivelling backwards into the room.

Sergeant Hopkins said a rather rude word, which naturally made her look in his direction. Just in time to see him dart behind one of the wing-backed chairs, from where he scowled at her.

She clucked her tongue. He must have heard her coming along the hallway. She'd been half dragging the maiden, to the accompaniment of a lot of clattering and banging. He'd had plenty of time to get behind cover.

And so had the Captain.

Yet he was standing on the hearthrug, glaring at her.

Totally naked.

Chapter Four

Alice gasped.

Good Lord, but if he'd been easy on the eye in his uniform, then without it he was simply stunning. All rippling muscles and long lean limbs.

'Like what you see, do you?'

Her eyes flicked up to his face. He was still glaring at her. And no wonder. She was still standing there, transfixed, when by rights she should have lowered her gaze and scurried away, blushing.

She couldn't understand why she hadn't done just that. What on earth had come over her?

'Clearly, you are not repulsed by my scars,' he said drily. 'I suppose I should be flattered.'

'Sc…scars?' She only just about managed to squeak the word. Heavens, but she was going to remember this moment for the rest of her life. Her first, and probably only, sight of a naked man. And what a man. She sighed. And kept on looking. Because this was something, she suddenly realised, she *wanted* to be able to remember throughout the long lonely years of spinsterhood that doubtless awaited her.

He had his hands over his private parts, thankfully, or she really would have had to scuttle away. It was one thing to indulge in a few moments of virginal curiosity, but there were limits.

'Or my goose flesh,' he added.

Lord, he must be freezing!

'I beg your pardon,' she said, coming to herself with a jerk. And dropping the maiden on the floor. 'I will just...' She bent to pick it up and recommenced wrestling with the contraption, which became more determined to unfold itself the more earnestly she attempted to set it up.

'For the love of God,' said the Captain, 'just leave the thing and get out.'

'I'm sorry, I'm sorry, I just...' She gave the maiden one last kick, which at least moved it far enough away from the door that she could close it behind her as she darted out.

To the sound of the Captain's laughter ringing in her ears.

'Looks like you're in luck with the little brunette, Captain,' observed Hopkins, as he emerged from behind his cover.

'Hmmph,' he said, reaching for a clean shirt.

'Truly. You should have seen the way she was ogling yer backside, before, when you was lighting the fire. Hot for you, she is, and no mistake.'

It said something about his state of mind that the remark, coupled with the hungry way her eyes had just been devouring him, made him feel less of a failure, less of a wreck and less unlovable than he'd done for a very long time. She'd known he would be stripping off, that he couldn't possibly have had time to get fully dressed again, yet she hadn't sent the boot boy here with the clothes rack.

As he pulled the shirt over his head, his thoughts turned to the moment, in the kitchen, when she'd taken note of his wet clothing, and appeared to care about his well-being.

Had he ever come across a female who both desired him and wanted to care for him? Nurture him? He frowned as he slid his arms into the sleeves. No. The women in his life had invariably wanted something from him. Had made demands he hadn't been able to meet, either financially or emotionally.

Nevertheless, he wasn't so desperate for a female that he would take advantage of some lonely little housemaid, no matter how pretty she was.

'Hot she may be,' he growled, 'but I have the children with me. I'm not about to do anything that will give them a worse impression of their father than they already have.'

'Just needs time, that's all, Capt'n,' said Hopkins as he pulled on his own clean shirt. 'They'll soon see you ain't the ogre yer wife's family have made you out to be.'

Would they? Harry looked at him with distrust and suspicion. And Isabella with fear. And why should she not? To all intents and purposes, he was a stranger. What little girl wouldn't be frightened by a stranger coming along, ripping her from the only home she'd ever known and carrying her off—into a snowstorm, for God's sake?

The only reason she wasn't completely terrified was because of Harry. Every time something went awry in her world, she held out her arms to him. And he went to her, as though he was used to doing so.

As soon as Jack was fully dressed, he returned to the kitchen to find Harry still sitting on the floor before the stove, with Isabella fast asleep on his lap.

While Harry's unnatural protectiveness made him uneasy, he couldn't deny that he was glad, for her sake, that she had somebody.

He frowned. A little girl of that age shouldn't look to her brother for comfort, though. She should have had a nurse, or even a doll to cuddle, or something.

He went over to feel his daughter's flushed face and little white hands. She was much warmer now.

He looked Harry over, too, but surreptitiously. The boy always seemed to flinch and close up if he thought an adult was examining him. As though he expected punishment. Had they beaten him? He hadn't seen any bruises. But the lad gave every sign of having been whipped into submission at some stage.

'Good lad,' he said, patting him lightly on the shoulder. 'Your little sister is nice and warm now.'

Harry said nothing, just gave him a steady, steely stare.

'I know, you don't need to tell me, I shouldn't have brought you out and exposed you to such weather.'

Harry's eyes widened, fractionally, before he hid his reaction. Clearly the boy had never heard an adult apologising before. Though plenty had let him down.

And speaking of down, perhaps it was time to get down to his son's level. Hang his dignity—he hated standing over his own children in what probably looked like a threatening manner.

'This may not be the most luxurious of places,' he said as he knelt down on the floor next to Harry, 'but it is warm and dry, and we have food to eat. Isabella will be safe here, lad.'

Harry didn't appear to know how to react to having an adult kneel beside him and talk to him, rather than taking a vacant chair nearby. His little eyes darted round the kitchen in confusion.

'These people may be poor,' said Jack, leaning close so that only Harry could hear his words and not the girl stirring something at the stove, or the boy stuffing paper into his boots, 'but they are willing to share what little they have. We should be grateful.'

Something flared in his son's eyes.

'What is it?'

Harry lowered his head, his little shoulders hunching.

'Tell me,' said Jack, as gently as he could, mindful of his mother-in-law's remarks about his parade ground voice scaring the children.

As if they hadn't been timid enough already.

'If something is troubling you, you need to tell me, so that I can put it right.'

Harry glanced up in disbelief. Then looked down at Isabella's golden curls, before he took a deep breath, as though daring himself to leap off a cliff.

'I just wondered,' said the boy, 'where we were going to sleep tonight. That lady said we aren't allowed upstairs.'

Jack's jaw tightened. The fact that Harry was worried by that remark showed that he almost expected harsh treatment.

Nevertheless, he was glad Harry had plucked up the courage to share his fears. It meant he was beginning to see that his father was not cut from the same cloth as his grandparents. He was beginning to trust him. Or at least, to want to trust him.

'The lady, as you call her,' he explained, 'is in fact only a servant. And she told me that she daren't offer us her employer's beds.'

Harry nodded, solemnly. As though he already knew that a servant would not dare flout her employers, not even to shield a child.

'Besides which, there aren't enough servants here to keep fires lit in the bedrooms. However,' he said, when Harry started to look troubled again, 'I have done some reconnoitring, and found the front parlour to be a good place for us to bivouac for the night.'

'Bivouac?' For the first time since he'd come back into his son's life, his little face showed open interest. 'Like you did in the army?'

In the few letters his wife had written to him, during the final months of her pregnancy with Isabella, she'd told him that although her family had taken her back, they had forbidden her to speak of the time she'd spent following the drum. From what he could tell, the ban on mentioning the army or the brief part Elizabeth had played in it as an officer's wife had extended to his children.

Which appeared to have given his son the kind of curiosity that all small boys—and most men, too—felt towards the forbidden.

'*Just* like when I was in the army,' he therefore said without a trace of shame. 'Would you like to come and see? I think it should be warm enough in there by now for your sister to finish her nap in peace. And you will both be more comfortable in there on the sofa than on this hard stone floor. Here, let me take her,' he said firmly.

Harry didn't appear as reluctant to hand over his sister as he would have done earlier in the day. Which was a step in the right direction.

When they reached the parlour, it was to see Hopkins propping a couple of feather mattresses against the fireside chairs.

'Miss Alice found these up in an attic,' he said. 'She reckons they just need airing, but I don't think we'll get the smell of mice out in a hurry.'

Alice? That must be the pretty housemaid's name. She never had introduced herself properly. *Alice*, he mused. The name suited her somehow, with her contrasting mixture of caring attitude and tart tongue, her warm heart and her hot eyes.

'Just the two mattresses?' He pulled his mind back to the task in hand.

Hopkins nodded. Captain Grayling scanned the room again. And had an idea. 'When they are as free from damp as you can get them, put one under that desk, there, for the children. And then we can turn it into a den.'

Harry's eyes widened in what looked like interest, rather than suspicion, as his father gently put Isabella down on the sofa, then tucked the blanket round her.

'We will need sheets to spread over the desk, and something heavy to keep them in place. Harry, fetch me some books from the shelves over there, would you?'

As he began to drape sheets over the desk, Harry darted across the room and selected the heaviest books he could carry.

It took them a few attempts to pin the sheets exactly as they wanted them. At first Harry flinched every time something went wrong, especially when both sheets slithered to the floor and they had to start constructing the den all over again.

'Somebody's been doing a lot of polishing, I think,' said Jack with a grin. 'We'll have to be extra quick with placing the books down, so the sheets don't make a bid for freedom, won't we?'

Harry firmed his jaw.

'I won't let the sheets get away this time, Papa,' he said.

He didn't. But Jack almost did. Because hearing his son call him Papa, for the very first time, made him want to get down on his knees and crush the boy to his chest.

He cleared his throat. 'Good lad,' was all he managed to say. But it seemed to be the right thing. Because Harry began to look positively cheerful as they painstakingly constructed their makeshift tent.

'That's secure enough now,' said Jack, when Harry began to show signs that lifting the heavy books was tiring him. 'We just need one last thing.'

He went to the linen pile and fetched a blanket, which

he arranged so that it hung down over the gap at the front of the 'tent', making a door flap.

'There,' he said. 'You will be snug as anything in there, tonight.'

Harry was so keen to try out his den that he darted inside without asking permission.

'This is the best tent ever,' he said, poking his head back out through the door flap.

And then a troubled look flickered across his face.

'Where will you sleep, Papa? There isn't enough room in here for you and Sergeant Hopkins.'

'Why, we will be on guard, naturally,' he said, waving his hand towards the mattress by the fireplace. 'Hopkins will have the mattress by the fire, and I will do my guarding from the sofa, with my feet up,' he admitted.

'And Izzy will be safe,' said Harry.

'You will both be safe now,' he vowed. 'I am never going to leave you behind ever again.'

Chapter Five

When they returned to the kitchen, Captain Grayling saw that Alice was setting only six places at the table.

'Your daughter isn't big enough to reach the table from her own chair, is she?' she said at once, as though she'd heard his unspoken question about the missing place setting. 'I thought you might want to have her on your lap.' And then she looked down and blushed. As though she was remembering the earlier incident and picturing him naked.

Fortunately, nobody noticed his instant reaction to the way she'd looked at him in all the bustle of getting to table. He gritted his teeth and got himself under control.

Taking a seat beside Harry, Jack concentrated on his daughter's needs. It was just as well Alice had arranged for Izzy to sit on his lap—she would not have been able to reach the table and needed help with her spoon. Which Harry provided with an expertise an eight-year-old boy should not have.

And clearly, Alice thought so, too, from the troubled glances she sent the lad's way from time to time. She must think he was a terrible father. Though she couldn't think any worse of him than he did of himself.

* * *

He'd made so many mistakes. And that night, counting them kept him awake. It was no use blaming the proportions of the sofa, it was his guilty conscience that made him too uncomfortable to fall asleep.

Every good intention he'd had, in regard to his children, had ended up being a bad choice. Even removing them from their cold, tyrannical grandparents had meant exposing them to a blizzard.

Though at least getting stranded here was giving them all time to get to know each other in an informal setting. He'd been so worried about his son, before they'd started making camp in this parlour, earlier. Until then, Harry hadn't spoken unless asked a direct question. Though boys of his age usually asked dozens of them. And spent their days climbing trees and shooting birds, and generally getting into mischief.

Yes, he'd been able to see his way forward with his son, because he'd been a little boy once and had loved making dens. But what of his daughter? How was he to break through to her, when the only person to whom she responded in a positive manner was Harry? What did he know of little girls?

What did he know about anything, but war?

He tossed his blankets aside, deciding he might as well take a walk to stretch his cramped legs and get the lie of the land. Sometimes, on campaign, it had helped to walk the perimeter upon setting up a new base in strange terrain, to check all was secure. It was certainly better than lying here twitching and fuming and listening to Hopkins snoring.

He stole, barefoot, across the room and gently lifted the latch. Thank goodness, he could see light spilling from round the edges of the kitchen door. He hadn't wanted to go stumbling around in the dark and waking anyone else.

But when he opened that door, he came to an abrupt halt at the sight of the housemaid—Alice—sitting in a chair by the stove, with a pile of what looked like mending on her lap.

'Oh,' she said, looking up at him. 'Is there something you need?'

You, he wanted to say. Having a woman would help him get to sleep even quicker and a whole lot more pleasurably, than going for a walk. Especially when it was a woman who had no ulterior motive, no hidden agenda. Who wanted him just because she liked what she saw.

As if she could guess what he was thinking, a flush spread across her cheeks.

'I couldn't sleep,' he said, turning to shut the kitchen door quietly behind him. 'So I thought I might as well go for a walk.'

'A walk?' She darted a glance at the window. 'I don't think you ought to go outside just now. It's still snowing.'

'Ah. And it was enough trouble getting me dried the last time, wasn't it?'

Her blush intensified. She was picturing him naked, he was sure of it. And so was he. At least, he was picturing the rapt expression on her face, and the way it had made him feel while he'd been standing there letting her look her fill. And just like earlier, that memory sent a rush of blood to his loins.

'Do you mind if I join you?'

She gave a little shake of her head, which he took for assent. So he went to the table and snagged a chair, which he carried over to the stove and set down as close to her as he could.

Her eyes darted about all over the place, looking anywhere but at him. And when he sat down beside her she lowered her head and, instead of shooting him a coy glance from under her long lashes, stared very intently at the pile of stuff in her lap.

'Do you normally stay up this late?' he couldn't resist asking her. It was just possible she'd been hoping for a chance to be alone with him, even if she didn't have a clue how to flirt.

She shook her head. Bit down on her lower lip.

His heart sped up.

'I made a very silly mistake. I suggested Susan share with me tonight. I thought we could light just the one fire, you see, and it would keep us fairly warm until morning. But...' she darted an anxious look in the direction of the table '...she snores.'

Ah. So it was as simple as that.

'So does Hopkins,' he admitted ruefully.

But then she did smile up at him. Though it wasn't in the slightest bit coy. On the contrary, she looked as though she was sharing a joke with him.

'And then,' she continued, dragging her gaze from him with what looked like an effort, 'my mind started to whirl. It occurred to me that it will be Christmas the day after tomorrow and you will all still be stranded here, and the children ought to have presents. So I thought I might make a rag doll for Isabella.'

'A doll?' He glanced down at the pile of stuff in her lap. 'That is what you are sitting here doing, at midnight?'

Her hands fluttered over her sewing as if to conceal it. 'It isn't anything very much. Just a bit of sheeting stuffed with wool and a scrap of fabric remaining from the last ball-gown we made for Naomi for a dress, and a bit of ribbon to make a waist, then I'm going to sew a couple of buttons on for eyes. I don't know what I will do for hair, though,' she finished ruefully.

He felt something tighten in his chest. He'd felt so alone,

lying awake worrying about his children. But in another part of the house, she'd been lying awake thinking about them, too. And she'd answered his concern about what to do for his daughter, in a very practical manner. By making her a doll. Out of whatever scraps she could find.

Only a few hours since, he'd been thinking that Isabella ought to have a doll. And now this woman, this lovely woman, was making her one, when she clearly had so little of her own. Because it was Christmas.

While he, wretch that he was, had been permitting carnal thoughts about Alice to take centre stage.

'It will be a perfect gift for her,' he managed to say through the lump in his throat. 'May I see?'

Shyly, Alice uncovered the scraps of fabric which were already taking shape.

'She will love the feel of the material,' he said, reaching out to stroke his thumb over the scrap of puce satin that was going to be its dress. 'And I have an idea about how to give her hair. One of the men in my regiment once wove little plaits from hair he cadged from the manes and tails of horses. He had his…er…wife stitch it on to a rag doll she made for their own daughter. She loved it.'

'Why, yes, that would be the very thing!' She looked at him as if he was a genius.

But her smile faded abruptly. 'If only it were as easy to think of something I could give Harry.'

'Harry.' He sat back and speared his fingers through his hair. What was he to do about Harry? 'I only wish *I* knew what I could give him. The boy deserves something really splendid. But the sad fact of the matter is, I was so impatient to get them both away from their grandparents, I never stopped to pack their toys, or to ask if anyone had bought them anything for Christmas. I've made a mull of it.'

'Oh, I'm sure you haven't.'

He gave a bitter laugh. 'You don't know the half of it, or you wouldn't say that.'

And then, he didn't know why, but he found himself wanting to tell her everything. Perhaps it was just that he needed to tell someone and she was there, her warm brown eyes gazing at him so trustingly, so admiringly.

'I've been a terrible father. Right from the start. If there was a wrong way to go about things, I took that way.' Just like now. He'd been lusting after this pretty housemaid instead of concentrating on what his children needed.

'But you were trying to do your best for them, weren't you? That is all any parent can do.'

He squeezed his eyes shut and lowered his head in gratitude. For she'd said the very thing he'd needed to hear. The very thing he'd been trying to persuade himself was the case, when he'd been unable to sleep.

He opened his eyes and gazed down at her. Would it help to tell her the worst and let her judge?

Though once she knew it all, would she still look at him the same way?

'It was the retreat to Corunna that made me send them away,' he confessed. Because didn't they say confession was good for the soul? 'I don't know how much you know about it?'

Alice shook her head. 'I have never followed the course of the war in the Peninsula closely. It all seems so far away,' she explained as though apologising.

'Most people would agree with you,' he said. Poor Lizzie hadn't had the faintest notion of what it would mean to be an officer's wife. Once the thrill of running away with a soldier had worn off, the grim realities of the life had proved too much for her.

'Well, when Harry was about the age Isabella is now,' he said, 'the entire British army had to retreat across northern Spain during the winter. Soult's forces harried us all the way. And when we got to Corunna, it was to find the ships which were supposed to be taking us to safety hadn't arrived. It was a shambles. So many women and children died.' He stopped short of telling her some of the terrible things that had happened on that retreat. It was bad enough that they were seared into his own memory.

'Elizabeth, my wife, was carrying Isabella at the time. I couldn't bear the thought of exposing her to such danger ever again. Or of her having to suffer the rigours of child-birth for the second time in a foreign country. So I left them behind in England the next time my regiment was posted abroad. Where I thought they'd be safe. Safe,' he scoffed.

'Well, they have been safe, haven't they? I mean, they are both well.'

'My children both live, yes. But their poor mother died anyway. Leaving Harry and Isabella at the mercy of the most flinty-hearted, miserly pair of people you can imagine. When I got to Meerings last week, I...' He shook his head again, words failing him.

'You mounted a rescue,' she finished for him.

'Yes. But the devil of it is, in doing so, I exposed them to the very dangers I'd meant to spare them in the first place. It is why I couldn't sleep,' he found himself confessing. 'Every time I shut my eyes I kept seeing those children, lying frozen in the snow, and thinking how close I'd brought Harry and Izzy to the same fate.'

She leaned forward and placed her hand over his. 'No, you didn't. You kept them warm and dry, and found shelter for them. They are sleeping safely in the front parlour. And in a day you are going to give them the best Christmas they've ever had.'

She wasn't just saying it. She really believed it. He could see sincerity blazing from her eyes. 'Thank you for believing in me, even though we've only just met,' he said, lifting her hand and pressing his lips to it. She gasped and snatched it away.

'You are a good father,' she said, burying the hand he'd kissed in the bundle of scraps on her lap. 'Anyone can see that.'

'Hah. When I went to visit them last week, my son behaved like a little automaton and my daughter didn't even dare look at me. Children of their age, the ones I've been used to seeing running about camp, are always full of high spirits. They get into everything. They may be barefoot, or close to starvation, or prone to all sorts of illness, but while they are alive, they are *really* alive.'

'Well,' she said thoughtfully. 'I had noticed that they seem unusually well behaved. I did wonder at first if you'd done something to frighten them. But I soon changed my mind. It is more as though they are so used to being punished they daren't put a foot wrong.'

'Yes, that's exactly what I think. Which is why I brought them away with me.'

'Then, as long as you mean to be kind to them, they will soon recover their spirits.'

'Of course I mean to be kind to them!'

She smiled up at him from her needlework. 'There you are. That is what makes you a good father. Not what you have done wrong in the past, but what you mean to do right in the future.'

He could have kissed her. But just as he was thinking of leaning forward and brushing his lips against the soft curve of her cheek, there came a grating noise from the direction of the table which made him nearly leap out of his seat. Especially as it was followed by a disembodied voice, saying, 'A sword.'

He instinctively reached for the one that should have

been hanging at his side. Though Alice hadn't reacted at all. Hadn't she heard the voice?

'Or a gun,' said the same voice. 'That's what you should give Harry for Christmas.'

'Who the devil,' he asked, 'is that?'

'Billy,' said Alice on a little giggle.

Billy? Of course it was Billy. Now that she'd pointed it out, he recognised the lad's voice. And he also understood why she'd glanced at the table when mentioning the fact that Susan snored. She'd known the lad was there and hadn't wanted him to overhear.

'What the deuce is he doing under the table?'

'It's where he sleeps,' said Alice.

'Good God, why?'

'Coz I'm an orphin,' came Billy's voice. 'And orphins don't get their own rooms when the master takes them off the parish out of the goodness of his 'eart,' said Billy with heavy sarcasm. 'Nor the right to an unbroken night's sleep, neither,' he finished pointedly.

'I'm sorry Billy,' said Alice. 'Did we wake you up with our chatter? I thought we were speaking very quietly.'

'Wasn't asleep anyhow,' said the boot boy. 'I was thinking. Captain, do you think they'd have me in the army?'

'How old are you?'

'Don't know exactly. Prob'ly about twelve.'

'Then, no,' he said mendaciously. 'You are a bit young yet. Why do you want to join up, anyway? It's a very hard life, you know.'

'It'd be more exciting than cleaning boots and emptying chamber pots though, wouldn't it? And I'd get paid 'n' all.'

He didn't get paid? And was forced to sleep under the table?

It crossed his mind that his own children were doing

the exact same thing and regarding it as an adventure. But then it was not their lot all the time.

No wonder the boot boy thought the army sounded more appealing.

But he couldn't encourage him to join up. Boys of that age thought all the travelling sounded exciting. They didn't take into account the fact that they'd be shot at and probably starved into the bargain.

'If it's decent pay you are after, perhaps you'd consider working for me?'

'What as?'

'Well, why don't we see what you can do over the next few days while I'm staying here and then we can discuss it?'

Alice narrowed her eyes and glared at him. When he quirked an eyebrow at her, she made very stern shooing motions in the direction of the door. It felt like being ordered about by an infuriated kitten. Nevertheless, he got to his feet and left the kitchen, with her stalking behind him.

'Don't,' she hissed, the moment they reached the hallway, 'get his hopes up.'

'Why not?'

'Because he'll be crushed when you leave, that's why.'

'Not if I take him with me and give him a decent job.'

'And you mean to do that, do you? Really?'

'Why not?' He shrugged. And stepped closer so that he could speak without there being any risk of Billy overhearing. 'I've recently inherited a property from a distant cousin. That is one of the reasons I sold out and returned to England. I don't know how many staff I have there, but I should think I could find employ for one small, miserable boy, don't you?'

'Oh.' She slumped back against the wall, as though all

the fight had gone out of her. 'Well, as long as you really mean it, then I suppose…'

'What do you suppose?' He searched her face, which was turned up to him. They were standing so close he'd only have to bend, just a fraction, and he'd be able to kiss her.

And suddenly it was all he could think about. He'd been wanting to kiss her almost from the first moment he'd seen her. So he took her chin in one hand, lowered his head to hers and brushed his lips across her mouth.

She gasped. Went rigid.

For a moment he feared she was going to slap his face.

But then she melted against him. And her mouth blossomed under his. So he put his free arm round her waist and pulled her closer. It was like reaching a crystal-clear spring after trudging through a parched and barren land.

So he drank, and drank, and drank.

When she slid her arms round his neck need went raging through him. The need to lift her skirts and seek the release he'd find between her soft thighs.

He jerked away from her with a curse. What was he doing? She wasn't the kind of girl he could take up against a wall. She deserved better than that. The way she spoke to him—almost as an equal, the way she cared about his children…

She was the kind of girl, he realised, that he should have married in the first place. A girl who would have been a help to him on campaign, rather than an extra burden.

He speared his fingers through his hair in self-disgust at the disloyal thoughts about poor Lizzie. If she'd only survived, she would be coming into her own now. She'd been born to be a countess. She'd have excelled in the role. Instead she was lying cold in her grave…and he was betraying her memory by wishing he'd met someone like Alice instead.

Cursing himself, the blizzard that had stranded him here and fate for bringing the wrong woman into his life, at the worst possible moment, yet again, he stalked back to the parlour and shut the door firmly on temptation.

Chapter Six

Alice sagged back against the wall, her fingers to her lips.

He'd kissed her.

And on a wave of relief on discovering he wasn't married, that she hadn't been having inappropriate responses to someone's husband, she'd kissed him back.

And would have kept on kissing him if he hadn't broken away, with an oath, and stalked off, shoulders hunched, as though burdened with regret.

But she had no regrets. Not one. It was Christmas, after all. Lots of people kissed under the mistletoe at this time of year. Not that there was any mistletoe in Blackthorne Hall, but still.

Her first kiss. Probably her only kiss. For where was she ever likely to meet anyone who'd want to kiss her, ever again? Even Captain Grayling had regretted whatever impulse had driven him to do it almost at once.

Nevertheless, he *had* kissed her. And it had been the most wonderful, perfectly blissful experience of her life.

She drifted upstairs, her whole body thrumming to the echo of his touch.

Alice bounced out of bed the next morning, though she had scarcely slept a wink all night. Through the window she could see snow lying crisp and bright over the whole countryside, sparkling in the pale sunshine. Had there ever dawned a more magical Christmas Eve? If so, she couldn't recall it.

It wasn't until she stepped into the kitchen and ran up against a cold reception from Captain Grayling that she had to face the way they'd parted. From the forbidding expression on his face it was clear that he hadn't spent the night going over and over every second of that kiss with delight.

Naturally, the moment she registered the pall of regret hanging over him was the very moment she got the job of spooning porridge into Isabella's mouth. It didn't help that the little girl was perched on the Captain's knee, so that his face and hers were almost as close as they'd been the night before.

Not that she could actually look him in the face. Not knowing how differently they viewed that…episode.

Nor could she think of anything to say.

And he didn't make any effort to make conversation.

Which meant they all sat in awkward silence, until Hopkins, who'd been outside seeing to the horses, came into the kitchen, stamping his feet and rubbing his hands.

'Could do with clearing a path to the stables now it's stopped snowing,' he said. 'Can you point me in the direction of a shovel?'

Billy thrust his empty bowl aside and leaped to his feet. 'I'll fetch some shovels and help you,' he said, darting a look over his shoulder to make sure Captain Grayling had seen what a keen and willing worker he could be, before scuttling out through the door. Soon they could all hear the sound of shovelling above the noise of spoons scooping up porridge, as Billy and Hopkins set to work.

'May I get down from the table?' Harry had waited until

Alice finished feeding Isabella, though he'd finished his own breakfast some time before.

'Of course,' said Captain Grayling.

Alice dipped her head as Harry went across to the window overlooking the stable yard and pressed his nose to the pane. Once Isabella wriggled out of Captain Grayling's hold and toddled after her big brother, she and the Captain were alone at table. And still unable to speak to each other. Both of them watched as Harry lifted Isabella up beside him so she could see out, rather than looking at each other. Though she was excruciatingly aware of him.

After a bit, it didn't seem right to keep sitting there, hoping for...well, she wasn't sure what. For him to look at her and smile, perhaps? In short, another miracle. She'd already had more than she'd ever expected this Christmas. Respite from her cousins and her first kiss. She'd be greedy to hope for more.

So she got up and cleared the bowls from the table. Though she couldn't prevent heaving just one sigh of regret as she made her way to the scullery. Which brought her up short. She'd better put that kiss right out of her mind. Or at least, think of it with fondness and finality, since he'd made his position clear without having to say a single word. He regretted kissing her. And she knew from experience that hankering for the impossible only made her thoroughly miserable.

Having come to that decision, she promptly went to the door and peeped through a crack to see what he was doing. He'd left the table, too, and was standing stiffly behind Harry and Isabella, who had their noses pressed to the glass as though they longed to get outside and romp in the snow.

She didn't think she'd ever seen a more awkward family group. What was he doing, standing there, when they clearly wanted to go outside and play? He must know they were too timid to ask an adult for anything. Couldn't he see that there would be no better way to get to know his children, and for them to come to trust him, than for them all to play together in the snow?

Evidently not. Someone was going to have to show him. And since she was the only one to have noticed his predicament, it looked as if it was going to have to be her. Abandoning the dishes for Billy to see to later, she wiped her hands on her apron and left the scullery.

'Harry,' she said, 'would you like to build a snowman?'

Harry looked at her with hope in his eyes and squirmed in his seat as though straining at an invisible leash. But then said, 'Won't it be a bit too cold for Isabella out there? The snow is so deep. And she is so little.'

'Billy and Sergeant Hopkins have already made a good start on clearing a pathway through it,' said Alice. 'And we can wrap her up well and bring her straight back inside the moment she starts to look unhappy.'

'Isabella has never built a snowman,' said the serious little boy, as though he didn't dare admit to wanting anything for himself. 'I think she would enjoy it.'

'I think so, too,' said Captain Grayling and the matter was settled.

It seemed natural to help him bundle both children up in an assortment of coats, gloves, scarves and hats, and to reach for her own coat as he put on his.

'Do you wish to build a snowman, too, Alice?'

She almost jumped out of her skin as Captain Grayling spoke the first words he'd addressed directly to her since that kiss.

'Yes,' she said, tilting her chin in defiance lest he think it a very childish pursuit. 'And that mound of snow, there, the one that Billy and Sergeant Hopkins have shovelled aside, looks like a good base for the body.'

He looked as though he wanted to laugh. But instead of doing so, he turned to his children and pointed them to the very mound of snow she'd suggested.

Harry set to with a will, but Isabella was too intent on crouching down, examining the white squishy stuff and poking at it with her gloved fingers, to make much of a contribution. Eventually she looked round for Harry and, when she saw what he was doing, began to copy, by gathering tiny scoops of snow to add to their sculpture.

Alice was just bending down to show the little girl how to make her contribution stick by patting it several times, when a freezing dollop of snow hit her right in the back of the neck.

She whirled round. 'Who threw that?'

Billy was bending over his shovel with a frown of concentration, Hopkins was leaning on his, looking extremely innocent, the Captain was busily moulding snow into the shape of a human head and Harry was looking shocked.

The boy had obviously seen who'd thrown the snowball at her. But she didn't have the heart to alarm him further by demanding he tell her who'd done it.

Instead, she bent down, scooped up as much snow as she could, patted it into a ball and threw it at Billy.

'Oi!' He whirled round, looking aggrieved. 'What was that for?'

'Someone,' she declared, planting her hands on her hips, 'threw a snowball at me.'

'Well, there was no call to go throwing one at me,' he said.

'Oh, yes, there was, because you—' She was prevented from accusing him of the crime when another snowball, thrown by Hopkins, hit her full in the face.

'Can't let anyone get away with attacking one of my team,' he declared.

'Not fair,' said Captain Grayling. 'That's two against one.' He ran to her side, as though to defend her, and all four adults started flinging missiles at each other. Harry swooped on Isabella and carried her out of the line of fire, behind the beginnings of the snowman. It wasn't long before Alice joined them, laughing and breathless. Swiftly followed by Captain Grayling.

'Harry,' he said, as a hail of snowballs rained down upon them, 'don't just sit there. We need to defend our womenfolk against the dastardly foe.'

After only a moment's hesitation, the boy saluted, said 'Yes, sir!' and eagerly joined in the fray.

For a moment, Isabella looked a bit bewildered. But as she saw that everyone around her was laughing and whooping—even Harry—she began to copy them, hurling her own inexpertly formed little missiles in the general direction of their attackers.

Just then the back door burst open, and Susan, a shawl wrapped over her head and knotted at her waist, came barrelling out.

'I'll help you, Miss Alice,' she cried, joining them behind their flimsy barricade.

'This ain't fair,' cried Billy as several snowballs splattered the front of his coat. 'Not five against two!'

'He's right,' said Captain Grayling. Then he stood, holding up his hand. 'Ceasefire,' he yelled. Amazingly, everyone did cease firing. With a grin for his son, he explained, 'I will leave you in charge of defence here, Harry, while I join the men to make it a fairer contest.'

He hadn't quite made it to Billy's side before Susan got him on the back of his shoulder with a well-aimed snowball. With a roar, Hopkins launched the missile he'd been holding at the ready and a battle royal broke out.

Before long Alice became caked in so much snow her

clothing could no longer keep it out. Her gloves were sodden and moisture seeped down the inside of her boots.

'We're going to have to surrender,' she panted.

'Never!' Susan's face was ruddy with cold and exertion, but she'd never looked so animated.

'Oh, do we have to?' Harry looked really disappointed.

'I'm afraid so,' she said. 'It has been fun, but we are all rather wet and Isabella will be getting a chill if we don't get her inside and dry.'

He sobered at once.

Alice scooped Isabella up to carry her indoors. She'd thought the men would have let her go, but, no, they kept on pelting her with snowballs all the way, with Harry and Susan fighting a rearguard action and Isabella giggling her head off.

'That was such fun,' panted Susan when they reached the safety of the back porch. 'We gave a good account of ourselves, didn't we, Miss Alice?'

'We did,' Alice agreed, hurrying through to the kitchen and warmth. 'But, oh, good heavens, Harry, look at the state of you.' He'd put up a good fight to get indoors, but in the process he'd become so smothered in snow he looked almost like a little walking snowman. As she bent to put Isabella down, a chunk of slush fell from his sleeve and landed with a plop on the kitchen floor.

He froze. Looked up at Alice as though expecting a scold for making a mess. Alice's heart turned over. Poor little mite. She hadn't meant to reprimand him, but her words must have sounded as though she was annoyed, because all the fun of the morning had melted from him even faster than the snow dripping from his clothing.

Captain Grayling froze, too. If she scolded his son now, it would undo all the progress Harry, nay, *both* his children, had made this morning. And yet he had no right to expect anything from her today. Some women, he knew, would even take this opportunity to have their revenge on him, through his children. Especially after the way he'd leaped on her like a ravening beast last night. Then flung her aside without explanation as guilt swamped him.

'Hurry and get out of your wet clothes, Harry, while I see to Isabella,' she said, fumbling her hands out of her sodden gloves. 'We need to all get warmed up as quickly as we can,' she explained with a smile. 'I don't want *either* of you catching a chill.'

He let out the breath he hadn't realised he'd been holding. With little smiles and encouraging gestures, Alice was letting Harry know her concern was for him, not the state of the floor. He should have known Alice wouldn't punish a child for a sin the father had committed. She wasn't that sort of person.

'Take Isabella over to the stove,' said Alice, while Harry unbuttoned his coat with the jerky movements of someone who'd just been let off the hook, 'and get yourselves warmed up while I take your coats back to the porch, where they can drip without making any more mess.'

When she drew near, to pass him, the urge to haul her into his arms and kiss her lovely mouth was so strong it was all he could do to resist. But he couldn't do that to her. Not in front of the others.

Not at all, dammit!

They'd think he'd started up a dalliance with her if he kissed her in public. Though a dalliance was all he could have with her since he'd become an earl. He'd been on the verge of asking her if she'd be his mistress a dozen times that morning. Only to draw back on a wave of shame. She wasn't that sort of girl. Oh, the way she'd looked at him, the way she'd kissed him, might lead some men to think she'd be willing to oblige. But she hadn't given him any flirtatious glances or coy smiles to remind him of their scorching kiss. On the contrary, she'd been awkward around him. She hadn't even been able to look him in the face at breakfast. And then the way she'd played in the snow with his children had opened his eyes to how very young and innocent she was.

He shoved his hands in his pockets, to keep from reaching for her trim little waist as she hung up his children's damp clothes. It would be the act of a monster to debauch her, for his own selfish pleasure.

She turned, then, and looked from him to his children and back, as though willing him to go and reassure them that all was well. The trouble was, all was not well with him. He wanted Alice so badly that he was almost shaking with it.

He gritted his teeth.

Last time he'd met a woman he felt this strongly about, he'd persuaded her to marry him. And it had been the worst thing he could have done to her. Since he was no fool, he wasn't going to make the same mistake twice. Alice didn't belong in the world he was going to have to move in now, any more than Lizzie had belonged in the army. Society would never accept a housemaid into their midst. People would snub her and slight her, and make her miserable.

This time, he wasn't going to be selfish. This time, he was going to do the right thing. He was going to stay away from Alice, and focus on his children's needs. To that end, he took himself off to the stables, to gather some horse-hair for Izzy's doll.

'Captain?'

Jack looked up, some time later, from the hank of horse-hair in his hand, to see Billy standing before him, with a few bits of wood in his hand.

'I thought these would do to make a sword for Harry,' he said. 'And I got some twine to lash the bits together.'

Straight away, his mind went back to the night before, when they'd first discussed Christmas presents for his children. Presents that Alice had thought of.

She'd make a wonderful mother for his children...

But no. Marrying a woman not of his class would cause no end of problems. Not only for her, but his children, too. They'd suffered enough upheaval in their lives already. They needed stability, tranquillity, not a stepmother who'd be awkward and unhappy because she wouldn't fit in with his new role.

'And I just wondered if you'd like a capon or a goose for yer Christmas dinner.'

'What?' He'd been so deep in thought that he'd forgotten Billy was standing there. 'A capon, you say?'

Billy's face brightened. 'You could get to the village on 'orseback, I reckon. I'll show you the way.'

Just what he needed. To go on a fool's errand and end up buried in a snowdrift, no doubt.

Still, it would get him away from Alice for an hour or so. And maybe getting buried in a snowdrift would cool him down.

Nothing else seemed to be working.

Before he set out, he went back to the kitchen, to let them know where he was going and why. The last thing he wanted was for Harry to think he'd disappeared, just as the lad was starting to trust him.

Jack found the children seated on a pile of cushions by the stove, clutching mugs of hot chocolate and singing the Sussex carol.

His heart clenched, almost squeezing a drop of moisture from his eye. It had only taken one day for his children to start behaving like real children. He'd made a start with Harry, but most of it was down to Alice. She'd broken through all the awkwardness and got them romping together in the snow, and now they were sprawled on either side of her, relaxed and happy. Singing. Even Isabella was trying to join in, warbling, *news, news,* whenever it came to the chorus.

He stood still, silently watching, loath to interrupt in case he shattered the moment. When they came to the end of the last verse, Harry raised his cup to his mouth and drained the last of his drink, leaving a little chocolate moustache on his upper lip. For once he'd forgotten he was supposed to be immaculately turned out, his behaviour rigidly controlled.

Until he saw his father standing, watching. And then he straightened up and adopted a guilty expression, which wrung Captain Grayling's heart. And helped him come to a decision.

A decision which would atone for all the ways he'd let his children down thus far in their young lives.

He would relinquish all thoughts of having any sort of relationship with Alice and hire her to look after them instead.

What was more, his trip to the village would be the perfect way to find out if it was the right decision.

'Billy says he thinks we should be able to get into the village, on horseback,' he said. 'So we will be going to fetch provisions.' Only yesterday, he'd never have dreamed of letting his children out of his sight for as much as five minutes. But now it was essential he saw their reaction. And it was just as he'd expected. Harry went stony-faced, then gathered Izzy on to his lap. But then, tellingly, he inched closer to Alice. Because he trusted her. 'Is there anything,' he said through the choked-up feeling in his throat, 'in particular you would like us to get, if we are able?'

Susan told him a dozen or more things she'd like. But

Alice wouldn't even look at him, let alone ask him for a favour. Had he ruined everything by giving in to his need to kiss her last night? Fortunately, he'd managed to rein back and retreat in good form, before taking things too far, though it had been the hardest thing he'd ever done. She'd tasted so sweet. Like hope.

But he had no right to hope for anything from that quarter. Even if he hadn't decided it would be wrong, her behaviour today had been easy enough to interpret. It was as if she'd retreated behind invisible ramparts.

Surprisingly, Billy's prediction that a horse could get through to the village proved correct. They managed to purchase a capon, plus a few extras which would make the Christmas Day meal something special. Although, from the smells emanating from the kitchen when they returned, some special baking had already been taking place.

'That's a lovely treat to come home to, after an afternoon spent foraging,' said Captain Grayling, sniffing the air appreciatively. 'Is that gingerbread?' He went over to the plates set out on the kitchen table, piled with a variety of creations that had clearly been made by his children. Many of them were just blobs which looked as though they'd oozed across the baking tray. On another plate was a pile of star-shaped biscuits that were charred round the edges. He took one item from each plate and devoured them with relish, while his children beamed up at him with delight. 'Thank you, Harry,' he said, ruffling the boy's hair, which had streaks of flour in it. 'Thank you, Izzy,' he said, dropping a kiss on the crown of her head.

'And thank you, Alice,' he said, turning to her with an intense look, 'for making this Christmas such a happy one for my children.'

'It isn't Christmas yet,' she protested.

'In this kitchen it is,' he said firmly. 'There is more of Christmas here than anywhere I've ever been. And it's down to you.'

Chapter Seven

He'd never forget the look on Harry's face when he crawled out of his tent on Christmas morning.

'Presents, Izzy,' he'd gasped. 'We've got Christmas presents!'

Jack watched Izzy fall instantly in love with her black-haired doll and its gaudy satin dress. And Harry didn't care that the sword lying there was a crude thing, lashed together with old bits of twine. He just wanted to take it to the breakfast table so he could show it to Billy.

The moment breakfast was done, Billy armed himself with a rolled-up newspaper and challenged Harry to a duel. When the two boys dashed outside, Izzy squirmed in the Captain's lap, wanting to follow them.

'Shall we join the boys outside,' he asked Alice, 'and carry on working on the snowman we started yesterday?'

She shook her head. 'It isn't fair to leave all the work to Susan,' she said primly, gesturing to the sink where the girl was preparing vegetables.

Which answer convinced him he'd made the right decision. She was a hard-working girl with strong ethics, who'd never consent to becoming any man's mistress.

* * *

She reinforced her position throughout the day by busying herself with a variety of chores which effectively kept him at bay.

Even when he volunteered to help with clearing up after the Christmas dinner, hoping he could get her alone in the scullery, she enlisted the others, too.

'If we all do a little, the work will be done faster, then we can *all* go out sledging,' she said firmly.

Even with them all doing their part, the sun was getting low in the sky by the time they reached a suitable slope beyond the stable yard, armed with a variety of serving trays.

'You are going to be in trouble with the family when they return,' he observed, as Harry trudged back up the hill with the badly dented tin tray on which he'd just slid down it, tucked under his arm.

She shrugged. 'I'm going to be in trouble anyway, for a lot of things, so one more misdeed doesn't seem to matter all that much. Not when you count it against the fun your children are having.'

'You may as well be hung for a sheep, as a lamb?'

She smiled. 'Something like that.'

For the first time that day she seemed to have forgotten about the dangerously fierce attraction sparking between them. Or perhaps she regarded the presence of the children, sliding down the hillside beneath them, as sufficient chaperonage. It was true that kissing was out of the question, in full view of so many other people. But there was nothing to stop him from speaking to her. He wasn't likely to get a better chance to put his proposition to her. Not given the fact she was so determined to avoid being alone with him again. So he cleared his throat.

'What if I could offer you a way to escape censure altogether? To escape…everything?'

She frowned. 'What do you mean?'

'I mean…' He drew in a deep breath and took the plunge. 'I would like you to come with me when I leave.'

'Do you really mean that?' She could hardly believe it.

'Yes. You are so good for my children. I have never seen them so happy. So…normal. When I went to visit the home of my late wife's family, I planned only to inform everyone that I was back in England, and that I was on my way to visit my new property, to ensure it was habitable, before returning for my children with a nurse in tow. For what do I know of caring for children? I'm a soldier. Have been on active service all my adult life. But when I saw how… crushed they were, I simply couldn't leave them there. I snatched them up and took them out into that snowstorm.' His face twisted with guilt. 'Exposed them to danger.'

'You didn't mean to.'

'Nevertheless, it just goes to prove that I need help in caring for them. When I reach my new house I'm not going to have much time to devote to them. I will have so much to learn about my new duties. Estate management and so forth. But I don't want to leave them in the care of yet more strangers. I want you.'

So she hadn't been mistaken in comparing the way he'd been looking at her, to the way Uncle Walter sometimes looked at the collection plate as it passed through his hands in church. A sort of frustrated covetousness.

As though he wanted her, but was fighting it.

Well, he wasn't fighting it any longer. He reached out and lightly touched her hands, which she had clasped over her waist. 'You are so good for them,' he said. 'You have a way with them. You seem to know instinctively what they need. And they trust you.'

Her cheeks heated with pleasure at the compliment. 'Thank you.'

'So will you come with us? And look after them for me?'

What a strange way to propose. Though, since he was so determined to be a good father, she supposed it was natural for him to stress how important it was to him that she would be a good mother.

'You can even hire another nursery maid if you like,' he rushed on, while the shock of his proposal kept her speechless. 'I wouldn't want them to be too much of a burden.'

'What?' *Another* nursery maid? A cold sensation gnawed at the pit of her stomach. He wasn't proposing marriage at all. All he wanted was staff for his new home. He was trying to recruit her, the way he'd recruited Billy. Why hadn't she seen this coming? It was the way everyone saw her. Even Aunt Minnie had only become reconciled to her presence about the house when Uncle Walter had pointed out that she would save them the expense of hiring a lady's maid for Ruth and Naomi.

'I know it will be hard for you to up and leave your home—' he said, while she was still gasping for breath at the hurt lodged under her breastbone, wondering how she could have been such an idiot. For why would a man as handsome and experienced as Captain Grayling ask a plain, dowdy girl like her to marry him? '—with someone you have only known a matter of days, but your wages would reflect that.'

'My...my wages?' So it was true, then. He wanted only to employ her as a nursery maid.

'Yes.' He frowned at her, as though baffled by her lack of enthusiasm. 'I am prepared to be generous. I will double whatever you are paid for your services here.'

A slightly hysterical laugh burst from her lips. All he could double would be the amount of humiliation she experienced every day, serving other people while never quite being one of the family.

'Triple it, then!' He looked downright annoyed with her now.

'Oh, for goodness' sake,' she snapped. 'You cannot triple nothing.'

'What?'

'Nothing. Which is what I am paid here. I am fed and clothed and housed, for which I am expected to be grateful.'

'Like Billy?'

'No!' She retreated a pace, removing her hands from his touch. 'Thank you very much for your offer of employment as a nursery maid,' she said, lifting her chin. 'But I am afraid I must decline.'

'What? But...they need you. I thought you cared about them.'

'I do.' She would have loved them as if they were her own if he'd given her the chance. But he only saw her as a nurse, not their mother. Never his wife.

'But...not enough, as it turns out.' She wouldn't be able to bear seeing him every day, remembering the way he'd made her feel when he'd kissed her and wondering why he hadn't wanted to do it again. She briefly raised her hand to her mouth, which was quivering with pain. 'Not nearly enough.'

Christmas lost its magic for Alice after that. As if to mirror her mood, it started to rain, so they all had to return to the house and stay indoors.

As they walked back inside, she decided that the kiss must have been more her doing than his. She'd probably made him think she was a bit fast, that first day, the way she'd ogled him. Twice. And once while he'd been naked and shivering, at that. Of course he'd thought she was amenable to…dalliance. At least he'd been a gentleman about it. At least he'd drawn back and not started pestering her in an unseemly manner when he realised she wasn't that kind of girl after all.

And at least he'd explained exactly what he'd been proposing before she'd done anything rash like flinging herself into his arms and saying that, yes, of course she'd marry him. At least she'd escaped with some shreds of dignity intact.

Even so, the way he kept on scowling at her made her feel as though she'd let him down.

In his opinion, she probably had.

All he'd been trying to do was provide for his children. And she couldn't fault him for that.

Nevertheless, she had to draw on every ounce of pride she possessed to prevent anyone from noticing that he'd just casually crushed her, by forcing her to face the fact that he wasn't interested her in a romantic way. She made herself carry out her duties around the house as though nothing was amiss. She sang along with Christmas carols which no longer had the power to lift her spirits. And organised silly games for the children to make them laugh, when it felt as though her insides were scraped raw. And finally, she sat at the kitchen table with them all and tried to eat a supper for which she had no appetite.

And then, to crown it all, after Captain Grayling had put his children to bed, then stalked through the kitchen on his way to the stables without deigning to look at her at all, Susan and Billy began to fight over who was going to do the dishes.

'I need to help with the horses,' he said, making for the back door.

'No, you don't. There's two of them out there already. And you're the scullion while Mrs H. is away and I'm the cook!'

'Well, that's where you're wrong,' said Billy defiantly, slapping his cap on his head. 'When they leave, I'm going with them. Captain Grayling is going to give me a job in his stables. For wages. So there!'

Susan gaped at the door after he'd gone through it. Then tears started streaming down her cheeks.

'He's leaving,' she gasped. 'I'll be all on me own.'

Since Alice knew exactly how she felt, she broke with tradition by going to her and putting her arm about her shoulders.

'You could come, too,' said Captain Grayling's voice, from the back door. He was standing there, hat in hand, regarding them coldly. 'I will have need of someone to help me care for the children on the road. And when we arrive. And Alice doesn't want the job.'

His words stabbed her to the heart. Not only did he not care for her in a romantic way, but now it seemed she was replaceable as a nurse to his children, too.

'You've asked *her* to go with you to care for your children?' Susan's shock at hearing this piece of news was so great she stopped crying at once.

'Yes,' Alice confirmed bitterly. 'For the most generous wages, too.'

'But, but...' Susan's eyes flicked from one to the other in what looked like desperation. 'If I go, then *you* will be here all on your own.'

'Until the family return,' Alice agreed. And then, because she could see how desperately Susan wanted to follow Billy, she added, 'If you want the job, you should take it. You are never likely to receive another offer as good. You mustn't worry about me. It's not as if you will be leaving until the weather clears, is it? And by then, Mrs H. might be on her way back, even though the house party at Caldicott Abbey might not have broken up.'

'Caldicott Abbey?' Captain Grayling gave her a strange look. 'Are the family that own this house attending a house party at Caldicott Abbey?'

'Yes. Why do you ask?'

'Because that was where I was headed. To spend Christmas with my friends there. Not that it matters now, I don't suppose.'

'No,' said Alice coolly.

'What does matter,' he continued, 'is that your local weather prophet, Jem, just dropped into the stables, with the prediction that the weather will be propitious for travelling tomorrow. So, Miss Susan, you will need to make your mind up swiftly. If you wish to help me get my children to their new home and have a job with me looking after them, you will need to be ready to leave in the morning.'

With one last scathing look at Alice, he turned and left the kitchen.

It rained all night. By morning most of the snow round the house had turned into ugly grey slush.

Christmas was well and truly over.

Just like her brief interlude with Captain Grayling and his children.

The Captain couldn't wait to leave. He had the children up before the sun rose, and ordered Hopkins to get the horses saddled before they'd even finished breakfast.

'Be ready to leave in ten minutes,' he snapped at Susan, as he put on his coat.

'Ten minutes! But what about the dishes?' Susan cried, gesturing to the wreckage of the breakfast table.

'I will see to them,' said Alice.

Harry paused in the act of buttoning up his own coat. 'Aren't you coming with us?'

She shook her head, unable to speak for the tears clogging her throat. To make matters worse, Harry rushed over to give her a brief, but fierce hug.

'I wish you were coming with us,' he said.

'So do I,' Alice managed to say, before kissing his forehead.

Captain Grayling gave her a look loaded with scorn before gathering up his party and marching them out of the back door.

Leaving Alice alone.

And broken.

Chapter Eight

Captain Grayling hoisted Harry on to the front of the horse on which Billy was already mounted, trying to ignore the look on his face. As though he'd caught him drowning a sack full of kittens. As though it was *his* fault they were leaving Alice behind. As though *he'd* made her look as if someone had just dealt her a mortal blow. Well, it wasn't his fault! He'd asked her to come with them and she'd refused. And that was that.

Hopkins, meanwhile, was trying to persuade a protesting Izzy on to the second horse and into Susan's arms. But since Susan was sobbing, Izzy kept right on reaching for Harry. When Susan eventually gripped her hard enough to prevent her getting her way, Izzy began to wail.

'Some nursemaid you are,' said Billy scornfully. 'We haven't even got out of the yard and you've made your charge cry.'

'It ain't my fault,' Susan protested.

Jack was inclined to agree. He blamed Alice. Her absence was casting a pall over the entire party. If she'd only agreed to come as well, they'd all be chatting and laughing, instead of sobbing and bickering.

By the time they reached the bottom of the hill down

which his children had been sledging the day before, he'd had enough. He brought the miserable cavalcade to a halt.

'If you don't stop this at once,' he said to his newest servants, 'you can get down and walk.'

They fell silent at once. Neither of them had stout boots and the ground was thick with muddy slush.

He tugged on the rein of the lead horse and they all set off again. In silence. But though none of them said a word, he could feel Harry's disappointment, and Izzy's confusion, and Susan's guilt peppering his back like buckshot.

But what could he do about it? It wasn't as if he could have forced Alice to come with them.

Though why on earth the dratted woman would rather remain alone in that ugly monstrosity of a house, in a post where she wasn't fully appreciated, than take up a position where she'd have generous wages and far better conditions, he couldn't comprehend.

He should have demanded an explanation when she turned him down flat, that's what he should have done. But he'd been so sickened by the way she'd started haggling over her wages. He'd never have expected it of her. Not when the welfare of children was at stake. The discovery that she was as mercenary as every other woman he'd ever met had been such a blow he'd just turned and walked away, pretending he didn't care. When the truth was it had hurt more than he would have believed.

Especially since he could have sworn she was going to accept his offer. She'd looked so eager to begin with, that was what was so confusing. When he'd said, *'I would like you to come with me when I leave'*, she'd looked as though he'd just offered her the sun, moon and stars.

He stumbled on a frozen rut and cursed himself for an idiot. He'd meant to say, come away with *us*, he recalled, but when it came to it, he'd asked the question from his heart.

Had that slip made her think he was proposing something of a personal nature? It wouldn't have been surprising, given the way he'd kissed her, he supposed. Even when he'd decided it would be selfish to attempt to take things any further with her, since his children needed her far more, he hadn't actually spelled it out to her. On the contrary, knowing she was forbidden fruit, he'd started watching her the way a starving man looked at a five-course banquet. Then he'd asked her to come away with him. With *him*.

And she'd wanted to. If he'd admitted how he felt about her, she'd have flung herself into his arms and…

Hold hard, though. He was pretty sure she wouldn't have agreed to accept the only kind of relationship he could offer her. In fact…oh, hell. Perhaps that was why she'd recoiled as if he'd insulted her when he'd started talking about wages. Especially since she hadn't relented, no matter how much he'd offered.

But if that was so, then her initial enthusiasm must have meant that in her innocence, and inexperience, she'd thought he was trying to make an honest, if rather clumsy, proposal.

Of marriage.

No wonder she'd been so upset when she realised he was only offering her a position as a nursery maid. Why she'd spent the rest of the day avoiding him. Why she'd looked on the verge of tears so many times.

He came to a dead standstill as everything fell into place.

She'd fallen for him. And had hoped he'd fallen for her, too.

His offer of paid employment must have been the cruellest form of insult to a girl who'd thought she was about to become a true mother to his children.

And now she was sitting there, amidst the dirty dishes, feeling abandoned, and foolish, and humiliated.

After giving his family the best Christmas they'd had for years. The first Christmas when they'd actually felt anything like a family.

And this was how he'd repaid her. By leading her on and abandoning her. At least, that was what she was probably thinking. And that was how she'd remember him. As a man who toyed with a woman's affections, then told her she was only good enough to be his servant.

When the truth was he'd always wanted her to be so much more than that. He wanted the right to kiss her without shame or regret. He wanted to wake up to her smile every morning and to be the last thing he saw every night.

Which was impossible. Even if not for the disparity in their rank which had made him discount marriage in the first place, she must hate him now. She'd never agree to marry him after the way he'd treated her.

And yet...

What did he have to lose by going back and telling her the truth? All of it? If she still hated him, well, he would be no worse off than he was now.

At least he would have done his best.

Alice sat frozen at the table, torn between the need to weep and a bewildering urge to break out into hysterical laughter. Because a few days ago, this was exactly what she'd thought she wanted. Freedom. Freedom to do as she pleased and eat what she pleased. Freedom from drudgery and criticism.

She'd thought it would be blissful.

But it wasn't. It was cold. And rather terrible.

She was never going to be able to stop thinking of those children. Wondering if Susan was looking after them properly. And wishing she hadn't been too proud to accept the post herself. Because even though they weren't her own children, she could have loved them as if they were, because they were the children of the man she...

No, she didn't love him. She couldn't have fallen in love overnight.

She rubbed her hands over her chest, where there was a deep, jagged pain. Hearts couldn't break. She was sure they couldn't. Yet it felt just as though something inside was tearing apart. Something that fractured a little bit more every time she reflected how foolish she'd been, to make so much out of one kiss, a few heated glances and a few words of praise from the first handsome man with whom she'd ever been alone.

She didn't know how long she'd been sitting at the table, wrestling with her alternating need to throw back her head and howl, or bury it on her forearms to sob into the dirty breakfast bowls, when the sound of horses approaching brought her up sharp.

This time, even though she was all alone, she couldn't be bothered getting to her feet, let alone arming herself with a poker. What did she care if burglars did break in? They were welcome to take whatever they wished. Besides, it was more likely to be Mrs Hughes returning early. She'd probably rather cut her holiday short than risk facing Uncle Walter's wrath if the weather closed in again and she became stranded at her sister's farm.

She wiped her face on the apron she'd tied round her waist when she'd thought she was going to do the breakfast dishes and blew her nose on the handkerchief she kept in its pocket. And lifted her head and faced the doorway through which she could hear the sound of approaching footsteps.

Her face was probably blotchy and her nose red. But if anyone noticed, they'd just assume it was due to her illness.

Not that they would notice. Or if they did, they wouldn't care enough to ask if she'd been crying.

But then instead of the brisk, light step of a woman, she heard what sounded like a man's boots clumping across the cobbles.

And...was that the sound of children's voices, too?

She started to rise from her chair, her heart lodged somewhere halfway up her throat as the door swung open to reveal Captain Grayling.

Looking grim.

'What is it? Why have you come back? Has something happened to the children?'

But then they tumbled in behind him, all smiles, and her legs gave out, so that she dropped back down on to her chair again.

'We've come back for you,' said Harry.

'She ain't no good for a nurse,' said Billy, nodding his head in Susan's direction as she came into the kitchen.

'That's not true,' said Hopkins, swatting Billy round the back of his head. 'That's not why we've come back and you know it.'

Susan proved him right by taking Izzy straight over to the stove and undoing the strings of her little bonnet.

While Captain Grayling just stood there, glowering at her.

Was he going to repeat his offer? And if he did, would she have the strength to refuse him a second time?

Did she even want to? It might be painful living under his roof and never being anything more to him than a servant, but just now she'd faced the prospect of never seeing him again. And that had felt as though it would have been a far worse fate.

'I need a moment alone with Alice,' declared Captain

Grayling, never taking his brooding gaze off her. 'Would you, all of you, go into the front parlour?'

'It'll be cold in there,' grumbled Billy.

'Not as cold as it was outside and you can soon light a fire,' said Captain Grayling firmly.

The others all trooped out of the kitchen, leaving them alone.

'I haven't been honest with you,' he said, tugging off his gloves and stalking to the table. 'Not entirely. I never really wanted you to be a nurse for the children. Which is why it was so easy to take Susan in your place.'

She shook her head, her bewilderment increasing.

He sat down, reached across the table and seized her hand all in one move, knocking the stack of bowls aside with a clatter.

'Don't refuse me before you've even heard what I've come to say.'

'I…' She couldn't speak. Her heart was beating so fast it felt as if it was going to jump out of her chest. He was holding her hand. Looking at her as though…

But, no. She'd been fooled by that sort of look before. This time, she wasn't going to assume anything.

'Very well,' she managed to get out. 'Say whatever you've come to say.'

He grimaced. 'This isn't going to be easy. It doesn't reflect well on me. I've been guilty of damnable pride, where you are concerned. I…' He paused, squeezing her hand so tightly it felt as though the bones might crack.

'If I had still been just a captain in the army, I *would* have proposed marriage to you, that day on the hill,' he said with what looked like defiance. 'I wouldn't have cared tuppence that you are just a housemaid.'

'Oh, but—'

'Please, don't say anything. Just listen. I need to make a full confession.'

'Very well, but—'

'No. You can say whatever you want when I've finished,' he said sternly. So she closed her mouth, though a rising surge of hope was making her feel a touch giddy. He'd mistakenly thought she was merely a housemaid. Of course! Why hadn't she seen that before? The way they were living, the shabbiness of her clothing, the chores she was performing as though it was perfectly normal...

'You brought light into our lives,' he said, through her daze. 'Made me feel things I thought I was no longer capable of. I couldn't believe you could have come to mean so much to me, within such a short space of time. But when I saw how good you were with the children, I decided I had no right to seek my own happiness when I'd already let them down so badly. I thought that asking you to care for them was the only way I could, legitimately, keep you in my life.

'And when you said no, I was so hurt, so angry, that I stormed away without considering how you must have felt about my proposition, after the way I'd kissed you. You must think I'm a complete scoundrel.'

'No, I—'

He held up his hand to silence her.

'When we left, it was like...turning my back on the first good thing to happen to me for years. And it wasn't just me. We *all* missed you. You have never seen such a miserable troop of people, trailing through the snow. And all of it my fault. But you must understand, Alice...' he squeezed her hand again '...that coming into the title had momentarily thrown me. I thought I had to live up to some sort of damn-fool expectations. But when I thought about it, just now,' he said, shuffling his chair closer, 'I saw what nonsense it was to think that way. I married a titled lady the first time round and it was a disaster. I should never have persuaded her to run away with me when her parents forbade the match. In short, I made such a hash of things that time round, through being hot-headed, that I was afraid I was going to make the same mistake again.' He speared his fingers through his hair, dislodging his hat in the process. 'But this time round I'm no longer ineligible. I can marry whoever I damn well please, and my rank will drop over her like a mantle. Well?'

Alice was reeling from the jumbled series of confessions. She could hardly believe any of it.

'Are you...are you really asking me to marry you this time?'

'Yes, dammit. Haven't I made it clear enough?'

'Even...even if I was merely a housemaid?'

'Yes,' he said staunchly.

'Even though you've recently come into some sort of title?'

'Yes. Didn't I say?' Captain Grayling frowned, as though going back over all he'd said. 'I've become an earl. To be precise, the Earl of Lowton.'

'What?'

'No need to look so horrified. Becoming my countess won't be so bad, will it? I will protect you from any unkind gossip, Alice, I swear it. We can live quietly in the country if you like. And nobody can say anything about the succession, because I have Harry for my heir. Any children we have will be ours, Alice, yours and mine, and we will love them. And I'll make a damn sight better job of being a father to them, with you as their mother, than I've done so far.'

'Oh...' she breathed, as all the misery that had been swamping her rolled away. 'You really want me. Me. No matter what I am.'

'I do,' he assured her, taking her hand and raising it to his lips.

'Oh, that's so sweet of you,' she said, blinking back a fresh wave of tears. Though this time they were from sheer joy. 'But there will be no need to protect me from society in general, because I am not the housemaid here, you see. The family who own this house are distant cousins of my mother's. Which is one of the reasons I wouldn't accept the post as a nursery maid, when you offered it. Women of my class are taught that it is shameful to have to take paid employment. Besides,' she added, determined to make a full confession, 'it would have meant seeing you every day and being nothing to you, and then probably having to watch you look for a suitable mother for your children...'

'Oh, my dear,' he said, gripping her hands harder. 'I hurt you so badly. I never meant it, you know.'

'I know. But never mind that now.' She wasn't going to have to face that particular form of torture after all.

'So you forgive me?'

She nodded.

A slow smile spread across his face. 'So that is why Susan and Billy keep calling you Miss Alice. I thought it was...' He shook his head. 'I don't know what I thought. But it was never, for one moment, that you were one of the family who owns this place.' He burst out laughing. 'Serves me right for getting so high in the instep the moment I inherit a title. That'll teach me.' But then his smile faded abruptly. 'Why didn't they take you with them? Why are you working in the kitchen, dressed like...like that?'

'Well, I'm dressed like this—' she gestured to her drab dress '—because I'm only the poor relation. And I'm working in the kitchen because it wouldn't have been fair to expect Susan and Billy to wait on me when they don't really know how. And I chose to stay behind when the family went off to Caldicott Abbey, because I was sick—' she felt her cheeks heat '—of being at everyone's beck and call. I wanted Christmas off. I didn't think it was too much to ask.'

He gave her hands another squeeze. 'Of course not. And I'm glad you stayed here, or I'd never have met you. But, may I remind you that you haven't yet given me your answer?'

'Oh! Why, it's yes. Of course it's yes, but—'

Captain Grayling didn't let her finish. Just leapt to his feet and swept her into his arms. And kissed her. And then swung her round and round until she was physically giddy, as well as emotionally.

'So, it's decided. We will be married as soon as I can find a vicar to do the deed.' He linked his arms about her waist and smiled down at her. 'There's bound to be one hanging about at Caldicott Abbey. My friends will make us all welcome once I explain why I was delayed. And we will have warm beds and good food, and you will have servants to wait on you for a change. So go and pack your things, and—'

'Caldicott Abbey? No, no I cannot possibly go there. Have you forgotten?'

His smile faded. 'If you are worried it will be a touch awkward because of your family being there already, let me remind you that my rank will act as a deterrent to any nastiness they might formerly have indulged in. Besides,' he said, giving her a squeeze, 'I shan't let them bully you.'

'Oh, it isn't that. It's something worse. Far worse.'

'How can it be worse?'

'Well, for one thing they are going to be furious when they see you've poached Billy and Susan…'

He snorted. 'That is entirely their own fault for treating

them appallingly and not paying them properly. Come on, what is your real objection?'

'Oh, dear. This is so…awkward.' She placed her hands on his chest and gazed up into his eyes, knowing she'd have to prepare him for what awaited him at Caldicott Abbey, no matter how embarrassing it would be to tell him. 'You see, my cousins have been talking of nothing else but the Earl they'd heard had been invited to the same house party as them. That was why it was so easy to induce them to leave me behind. They went on and on about how they were going to get themselves an earl for Christmas and how they'd never do it if they caught my cold, and ended up with red noses…'

Far from seeming annoyed at their presumption, he burst out laughing.

'I've never heard anything so preposterous.' Captain Grayling bent to kiss her nose. Her red, shiny nose. 'It is you I love. The woman you are. It makes no difference to me what you look like.' He winced. 'That is not to say that I don't find you very attractive, obviously. I mean… oh, hang it.' He swooped and kissed her again, more thoroughly this time. To show her, she surmised, how he felt without having to use words, which were subject to misinterpretation.

'I love you, too,' she admitted, when he broke off to draw breath.

'Then, do you think you could possibly start calling me Jack?'

'Is that your name? Your real name?'

He grimaced as though it was flashing through his mind that he hadn't told her who he really was at the outset.

'I'm glad,' she explained, 'that when I met you, you didn't tell me you were the Earl of Lowton, because I'd become sick of hearing that name on Ruth's and Naomi's lips. It left me free to fall in love with Captain Grayling. And now I'm happy to be marrying Jack. Do you see?'

'I see.' He nodded. Then he sighed with contentment.

And then, just to convince her he saw *exactly* what she meant, he kissed her again.

Epilogue

'I now pronounce you man and wife.'

Alice had never been so happy. Not even the sour expressions on Ruth's and Naomi's faces could dim the glow of pure joy that filled her. Because Captain Grayling, the Earl of Lowton—that was Jack—had loved her enough to marry her, even when he'd thought she was a maid. Even though her nose was red. He'd seen something in her that had made him ready to defy convention and return to Blackthorne Hall, and beg her to forgive him for ever wavering.

And they were going to live happily ever after. It was just as Jack had said. Once they heard she was about to become a countess, everyone started treating her differently.

At this very moment, Aunt Minnie was sitting in the front pew with a sickly smile on her face, occasionally digging Ruth or Naomi in the sides with her elbow to remind them they were supposed to be rejoicing in her good fortune. Which could be theirs, too, because, after all, Alice now had the ability to introduce them into echelons of society they could never have aspired to before.

And far from giving her a thundering scold for encouraging Billy and Susan to desert their posts, Uncle Walter had shrugged his shoulders and made a tasteless joke about the inexhaustible supply of orphans to be had from Mex-worth workhouse.

Jack stooped to kiss her, then, and someone began to clap their hands. The applause spread throughout the congregation, formed from all the guests who'd been stranded at Caldicott Abbey since Christmas. Even Ruth and Naomi joined in. What else could they do? They knew which side their bread was buttered.

Not that she cared any longer what made them behave the way they did. Or what they thought of her. For Jack had his arms round her and Harry was grinning, and Izzy was laughing and clapping her chubby little hands, too. Alice had a new family. Made up of people who loved her.

Which was the most perfect gift she could ever have wished for. At Christmas, or any other time.

* * * * *

If you enjoyed this story,
you won't want to miss these great full-length
Historical reads from Annie Burrows:

PORTRAIT OF A SCANDAL
LORD HAVELOCK'S LIST
THE CAPTAIN'S CHRISTMAS BRIDE
IN BED WITH THE DUKE

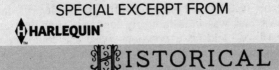
I have come this far… I cannot give up now.

She sucked in a deep breath and reached for the huge
iron knocker. Still she hesitated, her fingers curled around
the cold metal. It felt stiff, as though it was rarely used.
She released it, nerves fluttering.

Before she could gather her courage again, a loud
bark followed by a sudden rush of feet had her spinning
on the spot. A pack of dogs, all colors and sizes, leaped
and woofed and panted around her. Heart in mouth, she
backed against the door, her bag clutched up to her chest
for protection. In desperation, she bent her leg at the knee
and drummed her heel against the door behind her.

After what felt like an hour, she heard the welcome
sound of bolts being drawn and the creak of hinges as the
door was opened.

Grace turned slowly. She looked up…and up. And
swallowed. Hard. A powerfully built man towered over

her, his face averted, only the left side visible. His dark brown hair was unfashionably long, his shoulders and chest broad and his expression—what she could see of it—grim.

"You're late," he growled. "You look too young to be a governess. I expected someone older."

Anticipation spiraled as the implications of the man's words sank in. If Lord Ravenwell was expecting a governess, why should it not be her? She was trained. If his lordship thought her suitable, she could stay. She would see Clara every day and could see for herself that her daughter was happy and loved.

The man's gaze lowered, and lingered. Grace glanced down and saw the muddy streaks upon her gray cloak.

"That was your dogs' fault," she pointed out indignantly.

The man grunted and stood aside, opening the door fully, gesturing to her to come in. Gathering her courage, Grace stepped past him, catching a whiff of fresh air and leather and the tang of shaving soap. She took two steps and froze.

On the left-hand side, a staircase rose to a half landing and then turned to climb across the back wall to a galleried landing that overlooked the hall on three sides. There, halfway up the second flight of stairs, a small face—eyes huge, mouth drooping—peered through the wooden balustrade. Grace's heart lurched.

Clara.

Don't miss
THE GOVERNESS'S SECRET BABY by Janice Preston,
available December 2016 wherever
Harlequin® Historical books and ebooks are sold.

www.Harlequin.com